THE RETURN OF THE MANHATTAN

THE RETURN OF THE MANHATTAN

LEE ECKER

iUniverse LLC
Bloomington

The Return of the Manhattan

iUniverse books may be ordered through booksellers or by contacting:

iUniverse LLC
1663 Liberty Drive
Bloomington, IN 47403
www.iuniverse.com
1-800-Authors (1-800-288-4677)

ISBN: 978-1-4917-0277-2 (sc)
ISBN: 978-1-4917-0279-6 (hc)
ISBN: 978-1-4917-0278-9 (ebk)

Library of Congress Control Number: 2013914678

Printed in the United States of America

iUniverse rev. date: 09/03/2013

CHAPTER 1

Lieutenant Commander David Ashton was dimly aware of the beauty of the bright spring day as he leisurely strolled toward the White House gate along Pennsylvania Avenue. He arrived a couple hours earlier and spent his time in solitude wandering aimlessly, blissfully unaware of bystanders and tourists alike who stopped and stared, gawking at his tall, slim, handsome appearance in the immaculate dress blue uniform of the Space Command. Half of his mind was mentally alert keeping himself on track, ever watching for something out of place, but the other half was miles away. He thrived on excitement, and this was definitely different and could well be a new adventure. His life was far from normal, always in the midst of dramatic adventure even on what he now considered a routine voyage in space, but that was the reason he joined the Space Command several years earlier. He hadn't had a decent night's sleep thinking about those unusual orders since his arrival back on Earth. As he and his family stepped off the shuttle craft taking him from his ship, the Centaur II which was now in orbit, to his home port at the Norfolk Naval Air Station, he had been handed a sealed envelope by a military courier. The young ensign checked his identification and got his signature on the transferal receipt and left. Inside, he found brief orders:

Lieutenant Commander David S. Ashton:

Report to the White House at 0930 hours, May 7, 2572. Speak to no one concerning these orders.

Present sealed envelope to guard at the gate.

Signed: President Hugh Gardiner

David was the youngest executive officer in Space Command rising rapidly to serve as third in command aboard the Centaur II on a mission to Mars supporting geologists in search of uranium and other rare minerals. Five years earlier, he met his wife, Marie, an astronaut trainee while aboard another vehicle traveling through and mapping remote planets within the solar system working with NASA preparing astronauts for the rigors of space travel. After three years of marriage, their daughter, Laura, was born while in orbit over Mars.

He couldn't discuss this morning's adventure with Marie, nor tell her where he would be today. Fortunately, Marie was on duty shuttling to and from orbit delivering their precious cargo of uranium, and would remain on duty until the mission was complete. After the cargo was delivered, she would be off with him expecting extended shore leave. She understood and supported him when he often worked on confidential matters involving other crew members, and the tables were turned when he needed to support her with her duties aboard the shuttle. She wanted some time off with her family, but David wasn't certain that was in the cards considering his new orders.

At precisely 0930 hours, he handed the envelope to the guard and presented his Identification. The guard broke the seal, read the instructions and motioned David through the security scanners before he was guided toward the Oval Office. He had never been inside the presidential mansion before, and couldn't help gawking at the historic memorabilia and artwork hung on the walls, nestled in and around nooks and crannies along the corridors as he was escorted toward a small conference room where he found an old friend. Admiral Thomas White was a large man who was military all the way, but made an exception in David's case. Before David could offer a salute, the admiral stretched out his arms and hugged him, "David, it's been a long time. It's good to see you. How's it been going?" Admiral White had been David's first commander, and they had lots of fond memories to share.

"I'm enjoying every minute especially since I met my wife. At the moment, I'm speechless; I hardly know what to say. It's so good to see you sir! What's up?"

"Hold on, have patience." He laughed wholeheartedly, "I'm really not at liberty to say. The President will be with us shortly and explain everything." He changed the subject abruptly, "I heard you and your wife have a baby girl."

"A real doll. She's almost two and has us wrapped around her little finger."

"And how's Gladys? As I recall, she was the most beautiful red headed gal I ever saw."

David hesitated, "She's great! She really bloomed after Laura was born. She goes by her middle name, Marie. I had to stop and think for a minute when you called her Gladys."

"I remember. We'll have to get together one of . . ."

He broke off as one of President Gardiner's aides entered speaking courteously, but without any pleasantries. "Gentlemen, the President is ready. Follow me please?"

They stood at attention as the president walked around his desk and extending his hand in greeting. "At ease gentlemen, Glad to see you. David, congratulations on the birth of your daughter."

"Thanks sir." He held his curiosity, waiting for the president to get down to business.

The president shifted his attention to the Admiral, "How's it going with you Tom?"

"Great! All my affairs are in order."

"Good, because it's a go. Congress has approved. Please sit and get comfortable. David, Tom has been in on this from the get-go. He will command a space expedition that reaches way out beyond the solar system, and he wants you as his executive officer. I'd like to say you would leave tomorrow, as the timing is critical, but we won't be ready to embark for several months. I know you just returned from a voyage, but Tom will allow ample time to relax with your family. Are you interested?"

His eyes glowed and his heart raced with the excitement and anticipation, "Yes Sir! I would be proud to serve with Admiral White. How long will we be gone?"

"I honestly don't know! Experts on my staff say ten to fifteen years or more."

"Sir, I don't know how Marie will take it, but my answer is yes! That's what I've trained for all my life."

"Good. That's what we thought. And if I'm any judge of human nature, Marie will back you one hundred per cent." He opened a file drawer from an unlocked safe behind him and handed each man a thick package. "You can look through these at your leisure, but treat the information as Top Secret. You will need to divulge part of it with volunteers before they accept their assignments, and those parts you can share are clearly indicated. Gentlemen, I'm giving you the authority and Congress has authorized the funds to procure whatever is required to take the largest battle cruiser available, stripped of all unnecessary military hardware, to a small planet we have designated O-2113 and return with her hangar bay and all available decks filled to the gills with crude oil.

We, every nation on Earth, have depleted our oil reserves. The situation is critical and our economy will soon be at a complete standstill unless we find a way to replenish our supply. As you are aware, many plastics and synthetic products we depend on have their roots in oil and other fossil fuels. We substitute other materials for most of those applications, but our transportation industry and other energy dependent industries, are based on the electro-magnetic propulsion units which absolutely will not operate without key ingredients found only in natural crude oil. The world would probably end up in a major depression in which I see no way out.

We sent a group of geologists with drilling equipment in a smaller craft nearly ten years ago. Our hopes rest on the assumption that they have found oil and will have it ready for shipment upon your arrival. Of course we cannot confirm either their arrival or success because of the distance involved. The planet is over one hundred light years away, so any radio signals would take at least that long to reach us. If you fail to find them, or fail in your mission in any other way, we are doomed!"

CHAPTER 2

Gladys Marie Ashton had several scheduled days of work ahead of her and was slightly surprised to see her commanding officer enter the cockpit as she made her final preflight inspections prior to departing the Centaur II. "Marie, I want to say, and please pass this on to David. As far as I'm concerned, both of you are the best. You have made my job so much easier. I would have preferred to throw a party for you, but my orders and yours call for immediate action." He hesitated as Marie tried to assimilate what he was saying. "This will be your last shuttle. You have new orders. There should be a replacement pilot waiting for you when you land. God speed!"

She hugged him, said goodbye and returned to her tasks. It seemed strange and Marie didn't know what to make of it. It didn't matter at the moment; she needed to place her full concentration on her current mission of reentry.

Marie looked more like a beauty contestant than an astronaut except for her uniform of the Space Command. Her flaming, flowing red hair was flamboyant in style, but cut according to Space Command regulations barely reaching her shoulders. In spite of her red hair, her golden complexion had never been pale, and she looked like she just spent the last few days on a beach in the tropics. She was well aware her beauty, but there was no one aboard the shuttle she could impress even if that was what she wanted. She was a bit conceited, but her outlook had changed since her marriage and motherhood, and the competitive edge of her personality was reserved for doing her job with precision and professionalism. The return from orbit had become routine, but remained hazardous. Her craft could become an instant fireball, if she entered the atmosphere improperly at a velocity too high to control with her available engine power. Shuttle aircraft were constructed of newer heat resistant alloys and relied on force field heat shields rather than costly ceramic tiles, but they had to reduce their initial velocity and rely on a slower descent completely controlled by their aircraft engines and onboard computers, which had to operate at peak performance during re-entry.

The shuttle aircraft in use were sleek but utilitarian. Her shuttle was little more than an elaborate cockpit with powerful engines capable of lifting much larger objects into orbit, or re-entry with soft landings at unprepared landing sites on the surface of any planet. The shuttles were highly maneuverable craft capable of carrying a few persons, but much more useful when docked with a variety of passenger or cargo compartments. Each shuttle was equipped with energy shields which deflected space debris and provided a cocoon of safety from hostile missiles or midair collisions. The shields had their limits and could only be used as heat protection during periods of high energy usage such as re-entry, or attaining orbit while lifting heavy loads. Even at best they could not develop enough power to protect against the latest Laser weapons systems of most starfighters. Weight was critical and the last step before departing the starship was always a weight check, which was accurate enough to detect a stowaway or extra unauthorized cargo. If the weight was too high based on the available engine power of the shuttle, someone had made a critical error, and the cargo had to be unloaded and reprocessed.

Her re-entry and landing were uneventful as Marie eased the craft on to the landing pad without a noticeable bump.

Marie worked at every landing as though the cargo was the most precious or she transported the highest level VIP. Today, there was even someone to watch as her replacement pilot stood waiting for her. She turned everything over to him and punched her mother's home address into her pcom (personal communicator) requesting a vehicle to take her from the uranium processing plant in Oak Ridge, Tennessee to her mother's home in Springfield, Virginia. Her mother was pleased to care for Laura while Marie's last minute flight duties were satisfied, as she hadn't even seen Laura prior to one week earlier, and was just becoming acquainted. Laura assumed David would be there as he had been off duty during the last week.

Today, she didn't have long to wait and she had the entire car to herself, which lifted off and was underway as she settled into her seat. David didn't answer nor did she get the busy tone when she used her pcom to call him. "That's odd," she thought, "He never shuts the thing off. I wonder if something's wrong. She wasn't too concerned, but felt a strange sense of foreboding."

She punched in the code for her mother who answered calmly, "Hello Marie!"

"Hi, Mom. I'm on my way home. Is David with you?"

"No . . . He hasn't been here all day. He left early saying he had business or something. What's wrong? Why are you coming home?" Her mother was one of those women who never stopped talking and seldom listened for an answer even when she asked a question. She was always cheerful in an upbeat sort of way.

She would have kept talking but Marie interrupted, "Mom . . . Something's wrong. David is never out of touch. Even when on vacation, he leaves his pcom on. It's not like him."

"Maybe the battery gave out. Mercy sakes, I remember one time when Dad couldn't be reached for hours. He probably . . . ."

"Mom . . . . You know those batteries never give out. They always give lots of warning."

"Well, maybe he's in an important meeting and can't be disturbed. I bet if you give him a few minutes, you'll reach him."

"You're probably right and I was supposed to be on duty all day. How's Laura? Tell her Mommy can't wait to see her and I'll be there soon."

"She's jabbering up a storm pretending she's an astronaut. She thinks of little else. I took her to the park to play today, and all she wanted was a toy airplane. I don't think she knows what a doll is."

"That's all she's ever known. Maybe when we get settled in a house of our own, she will learn what being a girl is all about." Marie giggled, "Although I don't remember ever playing with dolls."

"Well, you did, if only when the boys across the street weren't around. You know what they are up to these days? Remember Tom, the little blond boy; he owns and operates a little hardware store here in town, and Mike. Well, he doesn't do much of anything. If only you would have settled down and married one of them, maybe I would see you more often. But you were never satisfied with normal life; you had to have the perfect career. I think you were selfish. Always gallivanting somewhere round the universe, I swear. I never should have let your father talk me into not having any more babies after your birth. Now with father gone and all, I get so lonesome when you're out on one of your voyages you know."

"Mom, we've been through this before. Make the most of your time with your granddaughter. One of these days, Laura will be grown up and away from home on her own too. You know I was already in Space Command before I married David. Yes that was what I wanted, and if that was being selfish, that's who I am. Anyway, I should be home in about fifteen minutes. I'm going to try and get hold of David again."

"Okay. Even if you don't, he will be back before long I'm sure. He can't stay away from his daughter very long."

CHAPTER 3

Marie no sooner disconnected when the incoming message light on her pcom began blinking. She hadn't changed the mode after landing. While flying, she always left it in the blink only mode to allow for no distractions during a critical flight phase. She pushed the talk button, "Lieutenant Ashton."

"Hi sweetheart. Are you home yet?"

Marie stammered, "What . . . What do you mean? Where are you and what's wrong with your pcom? How did you know I was on my way? I've been trying to reach you."

David chuckled, "I should be at your mother's in twenty minutes. There isn't anything wrong with my pcom; I'm talking to you, aren't I? I turned it off while in conference with President Gardiner. What time will you be home?"

Marie was totally confused, "Don't change the subject! I'll be there in five minutes. What about the president?"

Marie was waiting with Laura outside her mother's home as David's vehicle came to a stop. Laura didn't want to wait any longer before squirming out of her mother's arms taking a few faltering steps until David swept her off her feet. She babbled contentedly as her Daddy whirled her over his head and then held her in one arm while holding her mother close with the other.

After the evening meal, Marie's mother took Laura getting her ready for bed allowing David and Marie a few minutes alone together. Marie's curiosity was getting the best of her and she wanted a blow by blow account of David's experiences at the White House. "How long have you known about this morning's meeting and you never said a word?"

"Well, remember that envelope I was given when we arrived at Norfolk? That was it and my orders were to speak to no one about it, and that included you. However, you must remember that you were the one who has been away from me for most of the week."

"I suppose, but a meeting with the president? Marie sat on his lap while playfully feeding him grapes.

"Yeah, exciting huh?"

"Don't tell me that. I know what that type of exposure means! Tell me all about it."

"Well, he asked me to volunteer for a long space voyage and I said yes."

"Without consulting me!" Marie slid off his lap and moved away, pouting. "We just got back and I want a long time back on Earth before I set foot on a starship again. How could you?" She demanded. "How many are going on this mission?" As the full impact of his statement sunk in, she asked reproachfully, "Can I go?"

"I had about two minutes to decide and I think you would have done the same and you will volunteer. But that's up to you. If you decide not to go, then you will know nothing more, and I must tell you, anything I have already said or even the fact that I'm going somewhere is Top Secret. I assumed you want to go."

"Okay, what can you tell me, and how long before we leave?"

"We? You mean you've decided?"

"If you think I'm going to stay here and raise Laura by myself, you've got another think coming! Of course, I couldn't leave Laura behind!"

"I wouldn't leave her behind either, that is, unless you decide not to go. I have already told President Gardiner we are going."

"All right. Tell me all you can."

"We will be going on a voyage beyond the solar system and it could take up to fifteen years or more. It's a vital mission essential to the survival of the United States and that's about all I can say before you officially volunteer. There will probably be several couples going although I don't know yet who or if there will be any other children. Laura can go, if we decide that would be best for her."

"That's it?

"Yup!"

"Who do I see to volunteer?"

"Just me."

"All right. I'll probably regret it, and Mom's going to kill me, but I'm in." She climbed back onto his lap content with her decision.

"Good!" David pulled her closer and kissed her deeply while his hands roved over her body, keeping her from asking more questions for the moment.

Marie responded hungrily for a couple minutes before pulling back and poking him in the ribs, "Well, where are we going?"

"I don't know exactly. It's a small earthlike planet in a solar system on the southern edge of the Milky Way. All I know is; it's over one hundred light years away."

"Are you sure we can do that? Nobody has ever traveled that far."

"No, we aren't sure if we can do it nor do we know if it's safe. But we do know, we are doomed if we don't accomplish this mission one way or another. President Gardiner probably has other options, but this is our shot. You remember meeting Admiral White? He will be the commander and I will be his Executive Officer. Our mission is very simple, and that is to bring back the largest cargo of crude oil that we can possibly load on a starship. Not too many people are aware of the problem, but the world is running out of oil. President Gardiner says if our supply is not replenished in the next thirty or forty years, we cannot continue to survive economically."

"But, we don't use oil for fuel any more. What's the problem?"

"Most importantly, the propulsion units we use all require raw materials found only in crude oil."

"I see. What chance do we have of finding oil? Isn't this really a wildcat expedition?"

"Maybe, but President Gardiner sent out a geological team a few years ago and they should have already exceeded light speed. They are accelerating and apparently all is going well. If no oil is found on the planet they selected, there are a few other sites near by which show promise. We will be getting reports from the earlier team so it won't be completely unknown territory. If they can do it, we can too."

"What about me?"

"You will be a key member of the crew. The starship will only be capable of orbiting the planet. You, with whatever number of pilots you need, will shuttle to the surface delivering supplies and bringing oil to the ship."

"And what are we supposed to do during the voyage?"

"You will continue to train and remain current with your simulator. If you agree, you will be the flight commander for all the pilots. Admiral White was a starfighter pilot, but I certainly don't have any expertise in that area. The rest of your time will be spent however you choose. Of course, there will be excellent opportunities to get advanced degrees, or to do research in a number of fields. There will be education facilities available for whatever children are aboard. You could teach school. Most of the education for the children will be in virtual reality using the computers, but human teachers will provide that personal touch needed for that age group. Best of all, we will be together as a family."

"Sounds like something I wouldn't want to miss," she said sarcastically, "When do we leave?"

"Don't know yet. Depends on how soon Tom and I can get our plans developed and get the volunteers we need. It'll be months if not longer. President Gardiner wants us to be underway as soon as possible."

"Well, that'll give us a little time with our family and friends. Mom won't be happy, but she'll get over it. That is if she is alive when we get back, or should I say, if we get back?"

CHAPTER 4

"Two weeks on a houseboat?" Marie was never sure what David would spring on her next especially on short notice, but she liked the idea although she wasn't ready to acknowledge that fact to David.

"Yup, that's what it's all about. We were lucky to get reservations. I don't know how, but President Gardiner probably had something to do with it. He suggested a vacation at Lake Powell. I think he grew up in that area. It's one of the few remote areas that has not been developed, and one of the few vacation spots not overrun by hoards of sightseers. But it won't be entirely fun and games, Tom and his wife Elaine will be aboard, and it will be a working vacation. We have a lot of work to do before we start interviewing crewmembers."

"Well, I guess it will be all right."

"It's only two weeks and you can plan another vacation for the two of us if you'd like."

"Maybe I will. I think a romantic cruise through the Greek Islands, or maybe a trip to Acapulco."

"Anything you'd like. We can't waste time though. Every day, we have work to do. We want you to review the list of volunteers from the astronaut corps. You will need to interview all of those you select without divulging much information.

Most of the volunteers will know nothing of the mission until after we depart, and they will have to confirm their volunteer status before they can be accepted. President Gardiner wants a tight lid on this."

"I'd like to spend some time with Mom and my old friends. At least the few I have considering the amount of time I've spent in space."

"You know what they say—space, the final frontier—. Anything worthwhile has a price to pay." David reached over and turned on the entertainment system and requested vacation previews. He found what he was looking for and they settled back to relax. The opposite wall seemed to open up to the expanse of Lake Powell and they were sitting in lounge chairs feeling the warm sun, light breeze and occasion spray of mist over the bow of the boat. The sales pitch wasn't necessary as they experienced part of the thrill of being there without the hassle of travel and packing.

The days and weeks passed quickly and almost every moment was spent in developing plans and selecting personnel for the voyage. Their pool of volunteers was smaller than they had anticipated. Many of them had been weeded out immediately due to psychological profiles or qualifications. Every conceivable effort was made to match qualifications with requirements. Their two weeks on the lake were filled with work constantly in communication with volunteers by video phone and checking references and recommendations.

Occasionally, they took breaks swimming, waterskiing, or relaxing on the water. These moments allowed a time to prepare themselves mentally for the months and years they would spend aboard ship en route to O-2113. David never tired of watching Marie and enjoyed himself immensely taking every opportunity to watch Marie in her bikini cavorting in the water, especially when she had Laura in her arms, thinking how blessed he was to be married to such a gorgeous gal, and fortunate enough to have such a precious, beautiful daughter.

Tom and David chose a newly commissioned military starship, the Excalibur, which had recently returned from her shakedown cruise visiting planets and space stations nearest Earth. The Excalibur was the largest starship ever built and normally carried a complement of over one thousand starfighters, crews, and close to 10,000 in support staff. The Excalibur was designed for deep space travel and could remain in space almost indefinitely. The waste recycling and food producing decks were artificially maintained but capable of supporting the crew and their families for long periods during military missions. The main computers aboard the ship were capable of storing the world's vast data base of knowledge that could be accessed in flight to solve problems or to educate the crew and family members. Tom directed the renovations required to tear out most of the starfighter storage and maintenance facilities along with much of the housing areas, and convert that space to cargo storage.

The Excalibur had been built in space connected to a space station while in Earth orbit. Many of the exotic alloys were processed aboard the space station from minerals mined on other planets within the Solar System. Many smaller electronic and highly technical equipment items had to be lifted into orbit with the Space Shuttle System operated by NASA. This system had grown into a routine operation with shuttle craft operating to and from orbit several times daily.

The Excalibur was over 10 miles long and 2 miles wide, boasting fifteen levels with number six level three hundred feet in height capable of launching and retrieving starfighter and freight shuttle craft. Each craft would be launched into space or retrieved using a powerful invisible power beam that could move the craft easily within short range of the battle cruiser. The Excalibur when stripped of its starfighters could not be considered an offensive weapons system, but its defensive capabilities with powerful force fields and massive laser weapons made it near impregnable.

The first or top level was the command and control deck with officer living quarters. It would also house the conference and education facilities. The second and third levels contained quarters for the rest of the crew, passengers, and recreation facilities. The fourth and fifth levels were devoted to food production and waste recycling. The sixth level was the hangar deck with the seventh and eighth levels providing for aircraft storage and maintenance facilities. The next deck down was the power plant which David and Tom also decided to modify to double the thrust available in cruise. They wanted to insure enough thrust to obtain and maintain light speeds. The remainder of the ship could be used for any purpose, and they intended to fill those areas and the excess aircraft storage decks with crude oil on the return trip. The Excalibur, as modified, would be described as the supertanker of the space age.

There was a vast ground support system to get the bulk of the job done and the ship properly prepared for such a voyage. On normal space missions, the ground control system operated out of the Houston Space Center controlling every aspect of the mission. This mission was different on several levels. Houston Control had a more difficult job since most of the ground support personnel had no idea of the destination and would not be flight following on any portion of the mission after they left the solar system. First, any ground control or contact would be impossible after warp speeds were attained, and the overall shroud of security kept most out of the loop when considering the destination or the mission objective. All the ground support teams needed to know was that deep space computer navigation was required along with sufficient supplies to maintain self-support over an unknown number of years. The ship, the Excalibur, was more than capable of providing that part of the mission objective. Another difference from routine missions was that Tom was the mission director, but would also be part of the crew and when leaving Earth orbit, they would be on their own. After providing their requirements to the ground teams, Tom and David were primarily interested in the personnel makeup of the crew and the technical expertise required while operating within all the flight parameters they expected. There was some training involved, but it would be minimal since they were recruiting from experienced crews with many months of time already served in space.

Their pool of volunteers did not include the expertise level Tom and David wanted and they got President Gardiner's approval to get out and recruit on their own. Marie made the rounds of space pilot squadrons while Tom went after a medical doctor specializing in inflight medicine. David set out to find a physicist who would understand the problems associated with velocities exceeding light speed. After visiting several universities and consulting with the science department heads to find who they considered the best in their fields, only a few names were repeated again and again. At the top of the list, the name Roger Dorn from the Massachusetts Institute of Technology appeared most frequently. David decided to start there.

He arrived outside the physics lecture hall where a student directed him to the classroom where Roger was teaching. He took a vacant seat near the back and listened as Dr. Roger Dorn made his classroom assignment wrapping up his lecture. "Your assignment for tomorrow is to research Dr. Albert Einstein's theory of relativity. What did he have to say about the speed of light?" He paused for effect as he paced across behind the podium. "There is a little ditty that says 'There once was a gal named Miss Bright. She could travel much faster than the speed of light. She left one day in an Einsteinium way and returned on the previous night.' I want you to find out what that riddle is all about and if there is any credence to that view."

Dr. Dorn stopped to chat with a few of his students while David made his way slowly toward the front holding back waiting for the rest of the students to leave. Apparently, Dr. Dorn was a popular professor and all their conversations were not about physics. He started to leave and David had to call out to get his attention, "Dr. Dorn! Please sir, a moment of your time."

He waited curiously, "I'm sorry; I don't think we've met, have we?"

David held out his hand and noticed the firm grip offered, "No, but I talked with your secretary this morning and she said I would be able to catch you after class." He flashed his ID and White House credentials.

Roger arched his brow, "I guess I can spare a few moments, what's on your mind?"

"You've worked with NASA on several projects, and we have another project you might be interested in. Why don't we go get a cup of coffee?"

They chatted about inconsequential matters while settling in a corner booth at a local campus cafe and ordered coffee. Roger cut through the chatter, "All right, you've come all the way up here from Washington. But my time is valuable, please get to the point."

David grinned, setting his coffee on the table, "Admiral Thomas White and I have been given a deep space mission and I'm out recruiting. You come highly recommended and . . ."

Roger cut in, "You're wasting your time and mine. I've wasted too many years on worthless government projects. Nothing they ever do in Washington has ever been worth a hoot!"

"Maybe. I don't know whether you fit the bill anyway. But I'd like your views on our project and if you don't fit, maybe you can recommend someone else for the job. Besides, if you don't hear me out, you will always wonder what we are up to."

Roger sighed, "I suppose. I don't really have anything pressing for the next couple of hours so keep talking."

"Dr. Dorn, what do you consider the most pressing problem facing America today?"

"Anybody except those fools in Washington knows the answer to that. We have squandered our sources of raw materials. We have wasted our natural resources for centuries. Hundreds of years ago, there were warnings, but nobody listened."

David asked for a refill before acknowledging, "I believe you, I just recently returned from Mars with a cargo of uranium.

"Ya, but that isn't the most critical raw material?"

"Oh! And what is?"

"Fossil fuels and oil in particular!"

"Why?"

"Other materials are available within our solar system even if they are expensive, but not oil. We have not found any sign of life in the solar system except on Earth, and without life, there cannot be any fossil fuels."

David changed the subject, "I heard the assignment you gave your students. Do you think it's possible to travel faster than the speed of light?"

"I shouldn't answer since few agree with me, but yes I think so." His gaze centered on some distant object out the window as he paused. "Someday, I'd like to prove it."

"I don't think you will."

"Why not?"

"I must tell you this information is classified, but if you have any interest, we may be able to talk. I can't tell you much more unless you at least make a commitment to advise our group."

Roger was hooked although he didn't want to admit it. "I have my family to think of and a mission of that magnitude would mean considerable time away from home. I'm not that interested."

"I know you're married, but I checked and know you have no other immediate family. Believe me, that's not a problem. I'm married too, and I have a little girl that was born on our last space cruise. Both will be an integral part of this mission."

"Are they going with you?" Roger's interest jumped up another notch.

"Going where? Who said anything about a trip? You're jumping to conclusions which I can't and will not deny or confirm."

"How can I make a decision if I don't know any details?"

"All I have to know is, are you interested and will you consider my offer? That's all."

"All right, you have me hooked and you know it."

"I thought so. I was particularly looking for someone like you interested in the Theory of Relativity and the speed of light. We are talking of a voyage of over one hundred light years and we expect the round trip to be less than fifteen years. As a minimum, we need a man of your expertise to check our theories and plans."

"All right I will be your man!"

"Good, now I can tell you that an advance expedition left a few years ago and radio reports are beginning to come in; they have exceeded the speed of light!"

CHAPTER 5

Thomas White returned from an equally profitable recruiting venture getting a renowned medical doctor for the voyage. Doctor Warren Baker had been a flight surgeon assigned to NASA for several years. He made two voyages within the solar system and was eager for another. Marie was immersed in her quest for pilots, but was having little trouble getting enough qualified applicants.

Dr. Baker's specialty involved placing human subjects in deep sleep close to coma states which had been successfully achieved for short durations. Warren was anxious to pursue his research under the operational conditions in deep space. Most of the crew had no required duties during the high speed portion of the voyage and would be given the option of deep sleep where they could remain young or at least not age physically. For those choosing the opposite, time could be utilized to attain university level degrees, or to branch out with on the job training in many specific fields where systems were in use aboard ship. Spaceships like the Excalibur were proven to be ideal laboratories with the sterile environment and low gravity conditions, and individual research avenues were available to match one's interest and abilities. As with major universities with a few quality professors who made cameo appearances in many classes, Dr. Baker and Dr. Dorn would both teach classes during the voyage. David and Marie both intended to pursue advance degrees in their respective fields, but would also take courses in medicine and physics taking advantage of the celebrated members of the crew.

The months passed as the preparations and final plans were completed concurrently with crewmember procurement and training. The only remaining tasks were the final modifications to the propulsion units and the outfitting of the cargo bays with the tanks capable of holding the crude oil. Most of the supplies they would deliver to O-2113 were stowed onboard. They carried a huge supply of farming equipment and the equipment to set up industrial factories on the planet, as well as the latest fashionable clothing.

Their skeleton crew was small compared to those operating similar ships, but they were scheduled to pick up a load of passengers at a small space station on the fringe of the Solar System who would settle on the remote planet to establish a colony and a maintenance base for further exploration of that solar system. The planet was believed to be rich in natural resources with earthlike climate and atmosphere. Up to this time, it was believed to be uninhabited, based on limited data received from a deep space probe launched centuries earlier.

David's previous experience had been aboard heavily armed ships where the hangar bay left home port with over 100 starship fighters with a typical mission of maintaining a semblance of order within the solar system. Only once had he seen any significant action against a far inferior force of a rebel army with 20 or 30 state of the art fighters. After a show of force, the rebels broke off and scattered. The starships of the United States were seldom challenged, but smaller isolated single ships without star fighter escort occasionally were intercepted, hijacked, or destroyed. The Excalibur's success, on this mission, depended on secrecy and deception. They would carry a token four fighters and twenty shuttle craft for the entire mission, but would carry a complete squadron of starfighters which would leave them when they left the solar system behind. All but three of the shuttlecraft would be left behind on the remote planet.

One evening, as David made his way through the vast interior of the hangar decks of the Excalibur making his final walk through, he almost missed one tank that was not quite lined up with the rest. He stepped closer bending at the knees to investigate when someone attacked him from behind hitting him on the head and slamming him to the deck.

CHAPTER 6

Marie was lined up synchronizing her shuttle to remain stationary with relation to the Excalibur waiting with her load of tanks to enter the starship. This was her last shuttle for the day, and she planned to be back on earth with her mother and daughter for the night. Her private com button on the control panel lit with an accompanying buzz. She pushed the button responding, "Ashton."

"Marie, we have a problem." Tom's voice quavered slightly alerting Marie to a sense of disaster. "We are giving you priority and will maneuver you directly into the hangar deck."

"What's wrong?" Marie couldn't keep the alarm out of her voice.

"David's been in an accident. We don't think it's serious, but you should be here. Dr. Baker is checking him out."

Marie guided her shuttle into position and waited for the tractor beam to take her through the hatch into the ship. Marie shutdown her engines and waited as the massive pressure doors to the pressurizing chambers slowly and methodically opened and closed in sequence keeping the ship's environment intact.

She wasted no time exiting her craft, making her way to the hospital ward. Tom met her at the entrance, "We don't know much yet, but Dr. Baker is hopeful. Some idiot was running amuck on the hangar deck and struck David. He's in a coma, but Dr. Baker says all signs are positive."

"Can I see him?"

"Come on in." He opened the door allowing her entry.

Warren Baker glanced up for a second and went back to his monitor for a moment before looking back to Marie. He smiled and spoke cheerfully, "Marie, I think he will be okay. You can hold his hand and talk to him."

Marie moved over to the bed and took David's hand and squeezed. After no response, she looked at Dr. Baker. "Is he really okay?"

"We don't know for sure, but his vitals are good. There is no pressure on the brain, and our scanners have found no major physical damage. I think he will recover soon, but don't be discouraged if it takes a little longer. He may be able to hear you, so just talk to him."

"All right. David, honey, it's Marie. I'm with you and Dr. Baker says you'll be okay. I love you. Please wake up and talk to me. Squeeze my hand or blink your eyes. Please don't leave me now," she begged. She continued to plead telling him how much she loved him.

After several minutes, Dr. Baker took her hand pulling her away. "Sorry Marie, but my monitor doesn't show any response. Either he doesn't hear you or can't respond. He probably just needs time to recuperate."

"But doctor, I thought you were an expert in this field." She had a little sarcasm in her voice. "Concussions are not that rare!" Her voice grew louder, "Dr. Baker is there something you're not telling me?"

"Marie, please! Doctors are human and the human brain is far too complex for us to understand completely. We know when the brain responds and we can relieve pressure, but for the most part, the brain is one of life's greatest mysteries."

She calmed a bit, "But, what is your best prognosis. I want the facts as straight as you can give them to me."

"I don't know! I've seen similar cases where patients have remained in a coma for years. Usually, it only lasts a few minutes or a few hours. When he comes out of the coma, he will probably be completely normal. If he doesn't recover on his own soon, we could give him something to help the body repair itself, but those drugs aren't usually effective in cases like this. All we can do is wait. Be positive, especially when near him. Other than that, all you can do is pray! Now why don't you go with Tom? I think he would like to discuss the problem before elevating it to the president."

Marie left the ICU and followed Tom to his command module near the front of the starship. Tom's office was a large room elegantly furnished with comfortable seating arrangements around a small conference table. The office also had an excellent exterior view directly to the front with large screen TV monitors which could be selected to view any exterior area. The optics were so good that it was difficult to tell which was real and which was the image.

Roger entered giving them a rundown on the situation. "We have the intruder isolated on the hangar deck. The team responded quickly and has sealed off the area. I don't think David was the target, but he inadvertently caught the intruder in an act of sabotage. The incident was recorded on camera and seen by the security team monitoring the area.

Marie listened intently before asking, "Why would anyone want to sabotage the ship. I thought this was a top secret project. Who knows what's going on?"

Tom answered quietly, "The president has kept the number of participants to a minimum. The five of us, David, you, Warren, Roger and I know but the remainder of those on board don't. Of course, we can't load the number of fuel tanks like we've done without someone getting some idea of the scope of the mission. The president said this project was approved by a Congressional Committee, so the leak could be there. The oil industrial complex has always had a strong lobby in Congress and anyone in that area would be prime suspects. We've got to double our security, but if they're determined, somebody is bound to get through. Once we get underway, we'll be gone so long that no one will remember us until we get back. But for now, the question is, what are we going to do if David is unable to go? Warren may not want to clear him for the voyage. What would you do in that case, Marie?"

Marie hesitated only for a moment, "I desperately want to go, but I can't leave without David, or my daughter. I'm sorry, but it's not fair, and I wouldn't be any use to you, and probably wouldn't be safe flying under those conditions. I won't go without him!"

Tom continued, "I appreciate your honesty, and I anticipated that. Considering the circumstances, my answer would have been the same. However, if we have to replace both of you, it could delay the mission for months. I suppose we ought to get on line with the president and give him the bad news."

Roger spoke up, "Don't be too hasty Tom! I see no reason why Warren wouldn't let him remain on board. Our facilities are as good as any hospital and the low gravity conditions are good for him. Marie, you wouldn't have any objections to that would you?"

"I don't think so. I might as well be working as sitting around home waiting for his recovery!"

A low frequency chime sounded on Tom's desk and Warren's voice was projected into the room, "Tom, David is recovering rapidly. He is out of danger and his reactions are normal. He will have a headache for a few days, but no other side effects. He must have a hard head! Marie, you can come back and see him now."

Marie returned immediately to the ICU unit and the meeting broke up. Roger went to check on the security team while Tom made a call to update the president. David was lying flat on his back not making any sudden moves. Other than the pain, his only obvious condition was the large goose egg on the back of his head. Marie wrapped her arms around him, kissing his eyes, mouth, and any other exposed facial area, repeated her declarations of love she had made a few minutes earlier.

The intruder was captured a few minutes later, but nothing they said could convince him to talk. By his demeanor, it was obvious that he feared reprisals from his employer more than any threats from any security forces aboard the Excalibur. His identification indicated he worked for ArkTex Oil Company but that was all they could determine. That didn't mean much considering the large number of fuel tanks provided by ArkTex. David was irate, and uncharacteristically, he ranted and raved about how he wanted some time alone with him and he would get the truth out of him, but it didn't do him any good as Tom turned the culprit over to the FBI and he was transported back to earth for trial. The matter was closed as far as the crew of the Excalibur was concerned.

Marie made one more shuttle trip and brought Laura back with her. She said her tearful farewells to her mother and left without relating how long she would be gone. In truth, she didn't know. Laura remained aboard the Excalibur while David recovered allowing her augmented crew of shuttle pilots to complete the task of loading the oil containers.

After a few days of recovery and light tasks for David, the executive council met again in conference at Roger's request. This time, Tom, Marie, and Roger were joined by David and Warren. There was an air of excitement and anticipation in the room as the long awaited date of departure drew nearer. Tom began, "We have almost completed our preparations and we should be ready to depart one week from today. Is that enough time for the rest of you? Roger, I know you have something to spring on us so I'd like to get reports from the rest of you first. Marie, how is your pilot force? Are you ready to bring them on board?"

"As good as can be expected. All the shuttle pilots will be involved in the airlift of the fuel tanks for about two more days. Most of the tanks are already in orbit and docked at the space station. The Starfighter pilots are ready and waiting orders to board. We'll be ready whenever you give us the go ahead."

"Good, David, how about your end of the mission?"

"Everything is going well. The power plant workers and navigation specialists are probably the most technical and are in place. The defensive forces who control the on board phasors and the protective shields remain in place from the original crew. They did take some time off, but they are back for the duration. Many of the workers who have been installing the tanks have been recruited for loading duty at our destination. I'm not so sure about keeping them since they are suspects as far as I'm concerned, especially those who worked for ArkTex Oil. However, we are ready!"

"Sounds good! But how do you feel?"

"Couldn't be better. I'm angry, but that little episode gave me the rest I needed."

"Okay, that leaves you, Roger. How are things going with the technical end?"

"Very well. We have the latest and most powerful propulsion units ever developed. If they can't push us beyond light speed, I don't know what will. They are capable of accelerating more rapidly than our bodies can physically withstand over long periods of time. On this first leg to Juliet, we will accelerate using maximum sustained g forces until reaching the half-way point and then immediately begin to decelerate, and that will give us enough data to project our ultimate speed and duration to our final destination.

After we leave the solar system and begin to accelerate, the real test for our propulsion system and the navigation computers will begin. Even a minute change in direction would result in missing our target destination by light years. Any course deviations will have to be made by computer, or we would probably collide with another body we couldn't see in time to avoid. Our biggest threat involves large asteroids. Our on board telescopes and detectors will be constantly feeding the computer with new data which the computer is capable of analyzing and using to alter our course, if they can be detected early enough. A glancing blow on the atmosphere of a small moon or asteroid would be like hitting severe turbulence in the Earth's atmosphere. We could expect severe injuries and perhaps fatalities. At multi light velocities, a direct hit on any object of size would be catastrophic and the entire ship would be destroyed. In effect, it would be similar to a nuclear blast. On the whole, however, distances are vast and there is little to avoid between Solar Systems, and our route will not take us near any other solar system until we get close to our destination when our velocity will be reduced. Like on earth, with the big sky theories on aircraft collision avoidance, all I can say, is it's a big empty universe for the most part."

When Roger paused, Tom spoke up, "All of us have volunteered knowing there would be considerable risks. I think the odds are in our favor concerning collisions. Roger, you had some other concerns. Please share them."

"All right. The load of crude oil we bring back will be a drop in the bucket compared to the total worldwide need, not to mention our ventures throughout the solar system and beyond. This is a grand and noble undertaking, but I think it could be a waste of several years of our lives. We will come back years older and completely out of touch with reality."

Tom's expression was serious. He had similar doubts and often wondered if the entire project should be scrapped. "Roger, I agree with you, but we don't see the whole picture. The Pioneer Probe can't be recalled, and if we scrubbed, they would be left up the creek without a paddle. President Gardiner shares your concerns and has researchers working on other possible solutions. I've gone over this again and again, but bear in mind; this was not intended to be the final solution. It's an exploration of the unknown. If it works, then we could plan a vast armada of ships or link several tankers together to bring back much more oil."

Roger smiled, "Don't get me wrong. I'm not sour on the project and I certainly see it as worthwhile. I just wanted to point out the fallacy of thinking we are going to solve the world's problems all by ourselves with this one mission. I want to carry it one step further with your approval."

"We're listening!"

"David, remember that little ditty I assigned my class when you came to see me at MIT?"

David was thoughtful before hesitantly responding, "Sure. Something about traveling faster than the speed of light and the previous night?"

"Yes, Einstein probably understood much more than we about light speed and it's relation to the dimension of time. Up until this point, nobody had a laboratory capable of testing those theories, because nobody ever traveled faster than light. Anyway, I think that is what Einstein's theory of relativity is all about. The Excalibur could be that laboratory. Imagine for a moment that we could build a time machine capable of returning to the twentieth century and not only encouraging the conservation of fossil fuel resources, but give them a means to do it."

Marie was skeptical but her thoughts were running wild in all directions, "Why the twentieth century? Why not earlier?"

"In the 19th century, Petroleum oil was discovered, but wasn't used much, until the internal combustion engine was developed. Until the late 1850s, people used whale oil for lamps and minimal other uses and it wasn't until a find in Titusville, Pennsylvania, of burnable petroleum that those ideas abruptly changed. In 1858, Colonel Edwin Drake was sent by the Seneca Oil Company to investigate the find in Pennsylvania. In Titusville he found reports about oil seeping from the ground were true, and he began devising ways to extract it for commercial use. That first working oil well might be the logical place to start, but in the next hundred years, progress moved ahead in leaps and bounds. Much of that progress was necessary and we wouldn't want to change any of it. Even more dangerous would be changing history by introducing technology beyond their political ability to adapt. I'm a twentieth century historical buff so my thoughts are prejudiced, but I think valid. During World War II, the tide of battle swung in the Allies favor due to heavy bombing of German oil refineries which resulted in Hitler's forces ineffective response with the fuel shortage particularly for their new jet fighters. Imagine the reversal if Hitler had the advantage of magnetic propulsion engines. We could give the advantage to the Allied Powers, and shorten the war, but it might result in a much larger impact on the future than we like. However until the late twentieth century, demand for oil was relatively low. There were many who warned about the shortfalls, but oil was plentiful, and not many cared. Consumption was high in the late twentieth century and the cost rose dramatically, but not when compared to a century later. Preserving oil, for the most part, wasn't practical until much later with the development of the electromagnetic propulsion units. If we could push that discovery back, say a couple hundred years, then we would have a plenteous supply of oil for all eternity."

David began to get excited sensing the potential he saw when recruiting Roger. "That sounds incredible, can we do it?"

"Don't know, but it's worth a try. Are you prepared to turn it up a notch?"

Tom looked around seeing approval on each face. "What do you propose, Roger?"

"Delay our launch and convert one entire deck into a research laboratory before converting most of it back to storage for the return trip. The lab should be capable of manufacturing electronic and other materials needed for research as well as all the test equipment required. I have in mind several top notch physicists and engineers who could be persuaded to join the project. All of them have top secret clearances and I think they would gladly make themselves available."

Tom tried to calculate in his mind how much delay that would cause, but gave up, "How long are we talking about?"

"Maybe a month. Sorry I didn't bring this up months ago, but the ideas took a long time to germinate and make their way through my thick skull. The basic idea first popped into my head on that first visit David made to seek me out when he told me that the speed of light had already been exceeded, but the concept was slow in developing. That idea in my mind, not the fact that we would exceed the speed of light, was the deciding factor in my decision to join you. How to accomplish it is not crystal clear, but is becoming more so all the time. If nothing more, I think my research would be invaluable to future scientists and physicists. I don't want to waste my time wandering in space for the next twenty years. If we can build a time machine, then it will have to have complete secrecy beyond anything the world has ever known. What better place to keep it secret than off in deep space where no one can talk?"

David was dubious, "How can we put the lab together without anyone knowing? And why would it have to be secret?"

"You four obviously have had no time to think about the concept, but in my field, it has been discussed thoroughly. Time travel could be extremely dangerous even if the best people were in control. How tempting for anyone to go back and help someone involved in a noble, but losing cause? Wouldn't some Jewish person want to try to stop Hitler and prevent the holocaust? Maybe some zealous person would try to prevent the Jews and Romans from crucifying Jesus! It has to be secret! We can build the lab without undue concern since the existence of a lab is rather routine in space. In fact we should not try to keep it secret; it would just lead to greater speculation. I've already given it a lot of thought and I know what we need. We can inform the president there is a minor problem with the propulsion units, and we need to replace a couple defective ones. Those units in all my experiences never fail, but we'll assume he doesn't know that. Maybe he would believe someone sabotaged them. It wouldn't take much modification; the decks are set up perfectly for that purpose. My people could procure the lab equipment without any leak and do any installation themselves after we are en route. Besides the lab equipment, we need the manufacturing capability to build electronic parts and construct probes that can be used for testing. We need to find machinists or engineers that can fabricate items using a wide variety of materials. I wouldn't want to skimp on our inventory of exotic metals and alloys, but I'm sure all of the excess would be useful for the colonists on the planet. Marie, you could deliver the equipment and supplies without any of the other crewmembers getting suspicious."

Warren had been silent up to that point, but he was bubbling over with enthusiasm. "We can do it! David could fake some headaches and I could put a hold on the mission for that reason alone. You remember what we said would happen if he wasn't physically able to continue."

CHAPTER 7

They postponed their launch for two months using both excuses for the delay. Roger recruited three noted physicists and several lab technicians, engineers, and machinists who considered it a once in a lifetime opportunity to work on any project headed by the famous Dr. Roger Dorn. One worked in the Research and Development Division of Westinghouse and the other two were faculty staff members who had worked with Roger at the university. The lab technicians were all Roger's former students, and most were in varying stages of earning advanced degrees in physics or electrical engineering. Roger believed most of them would earn their doctorate before the voyage ended. The machinists were recruited from the manufacturing site at the space station.

As the Excalibur pulled away from Earth's orbit, David requested all non-essential crewmembers to gather in the main auditorium on the second level for mission briefings. David, Marie, and Warren and made their way to the front after the conference room filled. The screens were filled with spectacular images from each respective end of the Excalibur. Toward the front, the distant stars were bright and steady, but the view in the rear was breathtaking as the Earth began to recede. The cloud shrouded continents were plainly visible but growing smaller by the minute. David, along with several other space veterans watched with fascination and delight along with the rookies. During their voyage to the edge of the solar system, they were promised spectacular close up views of Mars and Saturn as their planned track across the solar system to Space Station Juliet brought them close. The sights could be seen with the naked eye from the view ports or seen displayed on viewing screens available to all crewmembers in various places around the ship.

David waited until the space station became a small speck before taking his place behind the podium, "Commander White and Dr. Dorn are occupied with the departure, but they will get to know each of you personally in the coming months. It's my job to inform you of our final destination and the unique features of the mission. Our first stop will be at Space Station Juliet which is beyond Pluto's orbit to pick up some passengers who will accompany us to our final destination.

David flipped a switch and a three dimensional chart of the Milky Way filled the screen. He highlighted the Earth and a planet in a remote spot on the chart. "Our destination is this remote planet designated O-2113. As most of you realize by now, we are configured as a giant oil tanker, and hopefully, that planet will be our source of crude oil which is in short supply on Earth. That's the gist of our mission. For you amateur astronomers in the group, the nearest star is approximately four and a half light years from our solar system. That planet is one hundred and three light-years from Earth." He waited for the buzz of awe to die down, "We are not about to waste the several thousand years it would take at normal sub light velocity. That would obviously require some sort of suspended animation or none of us would be alive to reach our destination. That length of time is unacceptable. We are planning to accelerate constantly to the half-way point then reverse the engines to decelerate at approximately the same rate until reaching O-2113. Doctor Dorn, our science officer estimates we will reach at least Warp 35, and maybe slightly higher velocity. We are following a manned pioneer probe launched several years ago which will break new ground and send progress reports regularly. The last message indicated they were at Warp 2.1 and accelerating rapidly. Long before we reach Warp 35, we should receive confirmation that it is completely safe to do so."

Warren took his place behind the podium. He looked out at his eager audience and began, "We have been involved experimentally in suspended physical states or deep sleep states for some time and have a lot of data pertaining to laboratory animals, but little research has been done with humans except for short periods. If you are willing to take the risk, this may be the course you want to follow. We think it will be relatively safe and the rewards may be of value for many of you. The choice is yours. If you are interested in the suspended state or deep sleep mode, we will begin that immediately for those personnel not needed for the rendezvous at Juliet."

David stepped back to the podium, "The voyage to the edge of the solar system will be our shakedown cruise which will involve normal speeds. It will take a couple of months to arrive at Juliet so you will have at least that much time to make up your minds. Some of our starfighter pilots will be on alert for encounters with space pirates, and will remain that way until we leave the Solar System or until just prior to reaching Warp One. After that, we're on our own.

CHAPTER 8

The executive council met regularly, at first every morning, then more irregularly, but at least once a week. A couple of weeks after passing the planet Mars, Tom handed the council a message received from the Pathfinder. David read it aloud, "We are at Warp 2.5 and accelerating more rapidly than planned. The Pathfinder was turned broadside and the acceleration forces have been increased significantly without adverse effect on the crew and passengers. By turning broadside, we are now using acceleration forces in place of artificial gravity. The forces are only slightly higher than on the earth's surface and the artificial gravity simulator is no longer needed freeing more power for the propulsion units."

Tom turned to Roger, "What do you think Roger? Will that work for us?"

"It should work." Roger's mind was rapidly recalculating time and distance scenarios.

David expressed his impatience and disappointment, "I thought they would be that fast by now anyway. Why are they accelerating so slowly?"

Roger laughed, "They are accelerating faster than you think, but at that speed, it will be a long time before we know it. If their approach is practical for us, then we should cut our time en route dramatically. Maybe in half. The solution is simple; why didn't we consider it before. Obviously we think in terms of Earth's atmosphere and aerodynamic force components. Those don't apply. The probability of collision with space junk or maverick asteroids will increase, but not significantly, although I'll have to run that model through the computer."

"Okay, we have plenty of time before we reach light speed. The personnel on Space Station Juliet are anxiously awaiting our arrival, planning a reception in our honor, which my wife and I will attend. David will be in command during my absence. Marie, you can shuttle us to the station and bring the passengers aboard. I don't want any of our regular crew to leave the ship. Too many loose tongues and news of our mission would reach the space pirates long before we reach light speed. We will put our starfighter pilots on full alert as we approach Juliet and remain on red alert until we reach light speed. The greatest danger from the pirates will be in the solar system and particularly while we are relatively stationary at the space station. Roger, what's the latest ETA?"

"We should be there in under two weeks. We began our deceleration weeks ago."

"Marie, you and David should get with Kevin Haugen, the flight commander for the starfighters, and map out the alert strategy."

"We'll get right on it."

Marie paged Kevin and David joined her as they walked the short distance to the pilot's briefing room. David turned on the projection system and they watched again the spectacular view they recorded while they passed near Saturn a few weeks earlier. The planet had been close enough for the rings to take on definition of their own. In moments like that, space travel had its rewards. They sat together and David held Marie close as they watched as the particles making up the rings seemed to swirl as the irregular shaped particles caught and reflected the sun's rays. It was like watching a beautiful romantic sunset on Earth which seemed to go on forever.

They were interrupted in their reverie as Kevin entered the room, "Good morning Marie, David, you wanted to see me?"

Marie nodded, "Yes, Kevin, sit down. Can you believe this fantastic sight?" They continued to watch as she briefly described the rendezvous at the space station. "The Excalibur will be most vulnerable while orbiting Juliet, and we will require fighter protection. As soon as we slow to launch, we need to keep a portion of our force outside the ship on patrol and the rest ready for immediate launch until leaving the Solar System. Our intelligence reports are months old, but they indicate all known pirate ships have been relatively quiet recently and were last sighted near Jupiter which is a long way from our course. Even though we have no reason to believe they are aware of our mission or our configuration, we must be prepared. I'm sure they would love to capture some additional top of the line starfighters. If we could continue at top speed, we wouldn't have any trouble running away from them, but we must stop at Juliet. We will have to rotate the crews on and off duty while we orbit Juliet. Give me your candid opinion on those security plans."

Kevin was confident, "Don't worry, we have the best pilots and anyone tangling with us should have their heads examined. We have been practicing the latest defensive maneuvers in the simulator and all our pilots are well prepared."

Marie was more cautious, "Don't get too cocky. Those pirates may not have the latest equipment, but the element of surprise will be on their side. Our intelligence reports indicate they do have the latest stealth cloaking technology and we won't be able to detect them until it's too late to prevent an attack."

"True and there's always danger involving a surprise attack. We would not be here if we weren't willing to take that risk, but it won't be as easy as they might think. We will launch four ships and keep them in a high speed scissors formation at a distance of one to two hundred miles from the Excalibur.

At our speed, we can cover that distance quickly while keeping our surveillance active. We could cloak, but our speed will be our advantage. If they attack, they will have to uncloak for a few seconds first and that should be enough. While cloaked, they can't maneuver quickly and they will not be up to speed. That is the standard defensive stance for all the battle cruisers and it has been highly successful in the past."

"That would be sufficient if our mission weren't so critical and our total force so vulnerable." Marie protested.

"You wanted my opinion. That's it and I'm sure that would be sufficient, but we will not be satisfied with that alone. The most critical time for the Excalibur will be during the launch of the shuttle and the starfighters when our doors are open. After the launch, nothing can penetrate our shields. David, I think we should keep the Excalibur moving above cloaking speed until after we launch the shuttle. After the launch, you can decelerate below cloaking speed, cloak, and then move to a new position. We will continue to orbit your vacated position as a decoy while keeping surveillance on your new position. You can orbit Juliet below cloaking speed and they won't find you. Of course, you need to maintain a precise timed orbit and position. We don't want any collisions between our own forces and the Excalibur. Marie, before you leave the ship, we will launch our remaining starfighters which will not return to the ship. They will remain with us until after you have made a high speed rejoin.

David had a premonition that something wasn't quite right, but it escaped him. He held Marie even closer until his fears subsided.

CHAPTER 9

The interceptors had been in formation for twenty four hours when Kevin and three other pilots relieved the four who had been on station the previous four hours. While several thousand miles from Juliet, Commander and Mrs. White joined Marie in the shuttle craft ready, waiting until the remaining starfighters were launched. The shuttle was pushed out through the airlock and moved several hundred feet from the Excalibur using the powerful tractor beam most often used for the launches especially when underway at their speed. As Marie was given the all clear, she pushed the throttles forward moving the shuttle rapidly toward the rendezvous with Juliet.

As Marie began to slow the shuttle for docking, she changed her radio frequency and called, "Space Station Juliet, Shuttle One ready for docking."

The controller's voice bordered on hysteria as she shrieked her response, "Shuttle One! Break now! You have an unidentified fighter on your six."

Without hesitation, Marie shoved the throttles full forward while adding maximum input for a hard descending right turn. It was too late as the pirate fired his weapons at the first sound of warning, vaporizing a gaping hole in the side of the shuttle causing an explosive decompression. Marie and her passengers died instantly as trapped gases in their lungs and other body cavities expanded more rapidly than the gases could escape causing massive internal hemorrhaging followed by ruptures through the walls of their chest cavities. It wouldn't have mattered as the remainder of the shuttle vaporized as the renegade held his finger on the trigger.

Kevin was one second late as his Laser beam made contact with the renegade ship which was followed by an even stronger avenging blast from the Excalibur. The remaining renegade fleet of almost fifty fighters emerged from their cloaking and began to attack the Excalibur like swarming killer bees. The ensuing battle was fierce although short as the pirate forces made a major error in judgment attacking an impregnable vessel with its protective shield in place and within the deadly range of the Excalibur's Lasers. The renegade forces were disorganized with their leader gone and unable to regroup before being utterly decimated. Those pirates lucky enough to fly out of range of the Excalibur were systematically hunted and destroyed by the technologically superior forces under Kevin Haugen's command.

Another shuttle was launched to retrieve the passengers before the Excalibur and her crew pulled away from Space Station Juliet without her commander, his wife or Marie.

Laura, not quite three years old, couldn't understand what happened to her mother, but she sensed the sadness and misery in her father's voice. She clung to him crying, "I want my Mama."

David was heartsick, hardly able to keep his anger in check and keep the quavering emotions from his voice as he tried to comfort her. "Laura, honey, it's you and me now." He hugged her, kissing her, trying to drive away the hurt. "Mommy is . . ." He broke down sobbing, composing himself for her benefit. "Mommy has gone to be with Jesus. It's hard, but you will have to be the lady of the house. I need you to help me run this ship. Can you do that?"

"Mommy not coming back?" Her question was more a statement of simple understanding of the new state of her family. She did not understand, but somehow in a childish sort of way, she sensed the permanent nature of her mother's absence. "Why? How come her go away?"

"Mama didn't want to go, but some bad men hurt her; she is in a safe place where they can't hurt her anymore."

She quieted allowing David to lead her into the auditorium for the memorial service. She didn't understand evil men, and could only draw parallels with an association with naughty children. In her naive and innocent state, she couldn't conceive of any ideas of revenge, although as she heard the simple statements of other crew members in memorial, she sensed the bad men had paid for their misdeeds. She sat by her father's side in solemn dignity as the eulogies were read honoring her mother, Commander White and his wife Elaine. At that time, there was a sense of mission dedication ingrained within her to serve the ship which was now her father's to command and a loyalty to her country which she didn't know.

David wanted no time to grieve, and kept as busy as humanly possible. He invited Kevin Haugen to his private office, turning on him as he entered. "You are a disgrace to your profession! What happened out there is beyond my comprehension. I certainly don't understand defensive fighter tactics, but I thought you did."

Kevin stood without offering any excuses looking David straight in the eye until David's anger subsided. David continued, "I shouldn't blame you, but I have to direct my anger somewhere. And you did an exceptional job in cleaning up the mess. Let's leave it at that. Regardless of how I feel at the moment, I'm promoting you to chief pilot as you are the most qualified to take over that position. I have another task for you since there will be no flying until we reach our destination. I'm activating our Big Brother Security System and I want you to conduct the investigation."

David began the next Executive Council meeting solemnly, seething inside, holding his anger in check, "What happened is tragic; We made a tactical error in assuming the target was the Excalibur rather than the shuttle. I had a premonition, but didn't act on it. I don't know what we could have done differently, and it no longer matters, but I will be more sensitive to those types of feelings and seek counsel from you whenever I have doubts in the future. Some of you may think we should end this mission right now. That's not about to happen. Some of you may think I'm too young to take over the ship and grieving too much to make valid judgments. I am grief stricken, but it has not changed the facts. Commander White and President Gardiner both had confidence in me and my ability to continue. We planned for this eventuality, although I didn't think it would happen, but we will continue. We have a vital mission to perform and I intend to see it through to completion. Does anyone have any objections?"

Nobody objected and all expressed their confidence in him before he continued, "Roger Dorn is now my executive officer and will act as second in command. He will continue giving his experiments priority, but he will take part in all major decisions. Kevin Haugen will join us on the executive council, and take over Marie's position as flight commander. Roger, you can brief him on all research projects at your leisure. I'm not satisfied with the security aboard ship; I find it hard to believe those pirate forces would have attacked one lone Battle Cruiser risking everything they had, without being tipped off concerning our mission or our weaknesses. Because of the serious nature of our loss, and the possibility of saboteurs or spies aboard, I have asked Kevin to conduct an independent investigation. I hoped it wouldn't be necessary, but after consultation with President Gardiner, I am authorizing Kevin to activate our Big Brother Security System. The system was installed several months ago under Roger's supervision while he alone installed key components which I hope means that until this moment Roger and I were the only ones other than Commander White who were aware of its existence or purpose. It's a rather sophisticated, but simple system that monitors every activity, and I mean every activity aboard this ship with microscopic microphones and camera lenses. Does anyone have any questions?"

Warren Baker jumped to his feet responding heatedly, "Surely, you don't mean you have been spying on us since day one? What right do you have to do away with our individual rights and freedoms? I hardly know what to think or say about this, but I don't like it!

David's temper again rose to the surface, and he had to use all his restraint as he responded slowly in a controlled command voice, "Sit down, Warren, and take it easy." And then continued in a milder tone, "I don't like it either. If the survival of our civilization wasn't at stake, I wouldn't consider it. We absolutely have to know if we have any opposition on board. Roger and I have already spent hours with the central computer checking out Kevin's every activity since he came on board. He's clean. In fact we checked on each of you on the council in the same manner. Roger even checked on me, while I checked on him. Before we go any further, I must explain. We don't monitor your conversations or watch videos of anyone's activity. We simply let the computer do complete data searches and key in on certain images or phrases we think might be suspicious. I'm sorry if you object, but I don't have any choice!"

Warren calmed down, but was still agitated, "David, I don't like it. I'm a little paranoid about computers gaining control of our mission and our entire civilization for that matter."

David continued, "You, as a council can override me on this as it is a matter of stretching my legal authority, and I want this council to have a positive governing role in the operation of this ship. The president approved this surveillance, but even he doesn't have that kind of authority. If I wanted to be devious, I wouldn't have said anything. I assure you; we look at no video or listen to any conversations. Kevin will not do that either without at least two other council members present. His job will be primarily a computer search, bringing any results before the council before anyone will watch or listen. Unless you override me on this, Kevin will have the authority to proceed. I'm going to my quarters now, and you can discuss it in private. If I hear nothing to the contrary, we will proceed. The council will meet again tomorrow morning at O Eight hundred."

David walked out, going to check on Laura.

CHAPTER 10

Laura accompanied her father to the council meeting the following morning, sitting quietly and listening intently as they discussed the next stages of their mission. Roger was given the go ahead to turn the ship broadside to their direction of flight and accelerate as rapidly as feasible to and beyond Warp Speed. Nothing more was said in David's presence in opposition to Operation Big Brother.

Laura became a constant companion of her father following him throughout the ship as he performed his duties, except for her school time which gradually became more intense. She was a bright child and quickly grasped the ideas of command and protocol. David included her in all the executive council meetings even though he never knew how much she understood. As she grew older, she occasionally would interject ideas which David took seriously as did the other members of the council.

Two weeks later, Kevin found a computer match of several key words and phrases and David convened the council giving Kevin free rein conducting the meeting. He began speaking directly to the computer, "Computer, this is Kevin. Activate Big Brother and present audio and video on subject previously selected."

The computer voice was well modulated and even as it responded, "Verification for Kevin Haugen is satisfactory. Request the presence of two additional council members."

David responded, "David Ashton here," and placed his hand on the identification module.

The computer almost droned, "David Ashton verified."

Roger placed his hand on the module and added, "Roger Dorn here."

"Roger Dorn verified. Please verify that no one without access is present."

David replied, "All present are council members except Laura Ashton. She has my authorization. Continue."

"Accepted. Three matches have been found for Bill Moore. Video and voice and images will follow."

A holographic image of Bill Moore, their chief of security, in his private quarters appeared in midair in front of the council members. Bill was using a portable computer to make and record a series of tones. The image faded and Bill's image appeared in the communications center activating the recorder and a nearly inaudible muted tone could faintly be heard the same time as another authorized coded message was being sent by the communications technician. Another indistinct image appeared with Bill in a bathroom stall whispering instructions directing the attack on the Excalibur.

Kevin spoke as the images faded, "Computer, decode recording!"

The computer voice droned on, "Recording includes coordinates and time corresponding to the rendezvous of the Excalibur at Space Station Juliet."

Kevin asked, "Computer, are there any other matches?"

"None. Search continues!"

Warren Baker exploded, "Well I'll be Dad Gummed! And I objected to this computer search. What is this world coming to?"

David spoke, "That's interesting. Good thing we didn't have him doing the investigation. Kevin, I want every move of his monitored for now, but take no action against him. Instruct the computer to expand the search to include all visits to the Comm Center by anyone, and particularly Bill Moore, especially since our encounter with the pirates. I'd like to know his next plan of attack."

Roger asked, "What should we do with him?"

David responded, "Warren, I think you said the hibernation state experiments were going well. We will freeze him and he can face treason charges when we return."

Warren wanted to know, "Why not do it now?"

Kevin pointed out, "I'd like to freeze him, put him in a capsule and maroon him in space, but we have just begun our search and I don't want to miss anybody else that might be involved. We will keep a close eye on him mostly with the computer. It can monitor his every movement and if any key words are spoken, I will be alerted immediately. We will watch for any communications devices and keep an even closer eye on him if he goes anywhere near the Comm Center."

David's voice was calm, but serious, "Kevin, I think we heard you very confidently talk in the same way when you spoke about protecting the shuttle. I don't like the idea any more now than I did then, though I think you're right this time. I'm not blaming you, I think we all should have anticipated that attack, and should have taken appropriate actions to prevent it. We do need to complete the investigation before we take any action. I don't want any direct observation unless the computer finds a key match. Then we'll meet to listen together unless it involves immediate security of the Excalibur. Other than the security personnel, clear all personnel associated with Roger's Time Project first." Kevin nodded his understanding and David turned toward the others, "Roger, bring us up to speed on the acceleration."

"We have a bit of time before approaching Warp one, but we should pass that milestone within the next month. We have encountered no problems so far and everyone seems to be adjusting to the slightly higher body weights associated with the acceleration forces. If we could get everyone to remain in the reclining position, we could double that process."

"Well that's impractical. Maybe you could increase it slightly. Warren can monitor any associated health problems. Warren, how's your hibernation project coming along?"

"It's going well; We have half of the non-essential personnel participating. I've got lots of volunteers hoping to make this project part of their medical education."

CHAPTER 11

Roger was humming excitedly as he scurried around with last minute checks on his test equipment. They were several months past Warp speed, approaching Warp 5 and no one reported any adverse effects. He had constructed two identical test devices which would, if all his computations were correct, be able to move forward a matter of hours into the future. David and the rest of the Executive Council were present to watch the grand experiment.

He pushed a button on his computer terminal, and they watched as one of the devices buzzed and began to shake. Roger explained, "It will vibrate for a few minutes and then it will probably glow brightly and then disappear. If it works as planned, it will be missing for approximately two hours." The object began to glow slightly and vibrate more violently as it suddenly popped and crackled as acrid smoke poured from cracks in its side.

Roger shouted, "Take cover!" He grabbed Laura throwing her to the floor and covering her with his own body as others found shelter behind cabinets and other pieces of test equipment seconds before the device exploded with a blinding flash of light. Shrapnel flew in every direction destroying everything in the room in above the table level.

The automatic fire extinguishing system activated spraying the room in a chemical fire retardant and the room was cleared of smoke moments later by the air conditioning system. David reached for Laura asking, "Is everyone all right?" Laura was crying as he comforted her, but seemed to be okay.

Roger looked about the room shaking his head, "Sorry, David, we should have taken greater precautions. Not only did we destroy both models, we destroyed this part of the lab too. It could have gotten us all killed!"

Laura quit crying and David laughed as he looked at the destruction in the room. "Well, we certainly don't do anything quietly. All we've lost is some valuable time and we certainly have lots of that. I think we learned a lesson today, and nobody ever accomplished anything of this magnitude without occasional failures. Let's pick up the pieces and see if we can determine what went wrong."

A few days later, Kevin called another council meeting making his report. "The computer is finished with its initial search and has found five more suspects. One is Glen Talbot, one of Roger's people and that probably explains our little accident." Kevin activated the Big Brother program and the computer again requested identification from the members present. Four of the five were caught in the act of incriminating themselves, once during a planning session in a remote area of the ship. The fifth was a false alarm, and was exonerated. Kevin went on, "Roger, I understand Glen Talbot has been working on the time model?"

"Yes, he was a key man putting that thing together. Since you clued me in on this possibility earlier, I've already taken him off the project."

Kevin continued, "I've requested the computer to look at all of his work particularly on the project and maybe we can see if and how he sabotaged it.

David interrupted, "Roger, did he know the magnitude of the project?"

Not entirely, although he probably has his suspicions. Very few know exactly what we are working on."

"All right, Kevin, take a sufficient force of trustworthy guards and pick up all of them. Then I want you to expand the computer search to include any conversations about Roger's project outside the lab. Warren, go ahead and freeze them for the duration."

Their conversation was interrupted by the intercom priority alarm signal. David pressed the button and Larry Cole, a technician from the lab excitedly blurted out, "Roger, you better get down here quick. The device is back."

"I'll be right there!"

The entire council made their way down to the lab and found the device they thought had exploded, in the middle of the lab, a bit battered and scarred but mostly in one piece. Larry Cole could not explain except to say, "It wasn't there when I came in. I turned my back for a minute and when I turned around, there it was.

Roger was excited as he examined it, "It worked! It actually worked! I wondered why we couldn't find any pieces of this one after the explosion, but this explains it. You know we didn't actually see the explosion, because we were diving for cover, but it must have left as programmed except it went farther ahead in time than we thought."

David acted quickly, "Kevin, get cracking on those arrests. I don't want any more leaks in this project." He turned to Larry, "Did you speak to anyone else about this?"

"No sir!"

"Good, keep it under your hat. Roger, is it possible the intercom has been monitored by anyone other than us?"

"Of course! Anything is possible, David. It's not likely, but we have to assume they heard."

David turned back to Kevin, but he had already left.

CHAPTER 12

Roger easily found the cause of the explosion when examining the device. He explained, "I found minute traces of high explosive plastic all the way inside the core. I suspect there was enough explosive to have destroyed the entire ship killing us all. I am kicking myself for allowing the entire council, including Laura, to be present for the test."

David responded, "Don't worry, you're only human, and you had no reason to suspect anything like that. But why weren't we killed?"

"That's the beauty of it. The damn thing worked! The timing for the detonation must have been slightly off. I think it blew at the same instant the device departed our time. Any explosion is not as instantaneous as we think, even though it occurs over a very small fragment of time. We felt only the beginning of the blast. The device must have been traveling faster than light through time so the remainder of the blast was dissipated in an apparent elongation of its exposure; hence the device was not harmed substantially."

Warren remarked, "Pure luck, and I thought you were in the genius category. Now can you explain how it works?"

Kevin laughed, "If he could, none of us would understand it anyway."

"True!"

"All right," David continued, "now that it works, what are you going to do for the remainder of the voyage?"

"In theory and concept, it works. But we have to find out how to control it and make it work on its own without this ship already moving at warp speed plus. We have our work cut out for us!"

David added, "By the way, we got an urgent message from Pathfinder. They had a near miss with an uncharted asteroid. The data has been plugged in and if necessary, the computer can make course corrections. They were small enough to narrowly miss it, but we probably wouldn't have been so lucky. If we could stay on their path, you would think it would be safer, except that the universe is not static and that particular asteroid will be nowhere near our path when we get to that point."

CHAPTER 13

"David, it's taken us nearly two years, but we're almost half way. As near as we can compute, we have reached Warp 100 and it will soon be time to begin our deceleration phase."

"Thanks Roger. It's too bad we couldn't have gone this fast from day one. Is there any way you could have miscalculated? At these speeds, we could skip right past."

"There's always the chance of error, but several of us did the calculations separately and the computer agrees with us."

"All right, what now?"

"First we stop accelerating which I've programmed the computer to do within the next few minutes and then we will coast at Warp 100 for about two months. During that time, we can shut off the main thrusters and turn the artificial gravity back on. That will be accomplished gradually enough so nobody will have any difficulty adjusting to the reduced gravity. Anybody who has complained about the high g forces will have two months of bliss. This plan allows us to rotate one hundred eighty degrees and begin deceleration at the precise second required. While the thrusters are off line, we can do a little preventive maintenance. I don't expect any problems, but if they fail while we are at this speed, we will be lost in space with no way to slow down."

David braced himself expecting some type of body adjustment while the sight of crewmembers jumping around jogged his memory, "Roger, where's Laura? Isn't she usually with you at this time?" Roger had been teaching her about the ship and how it worked. Laura was only five years old, but she already showed genius level aptitudes in her studies far beyond her years.

"She's with Kevin. I haven't been able to have much time with her since Kevin took her into the simulator bay. She wants to be a pilot and Kevin says she does very well. She should be along soon."

"Gee, I thought she just wanted to get away from her Dad. Although I'm glad she has shown interest in something."

The door into the control room opened with a bang and Laura came in, full of energy seeing how far she could jump like a kangaroo instead of walking. "Daddy," she exclaimed, "look, how far I can jump. I can almost fly."

David bubbled over with joy as he caught her and threw her toward Roger. She squealed with delight as Roger caught her. "I am flying. Do it again!"

David caught her as Roger tossed her back. He held her a moment, "Darling, I hear you are flying in the simulator with Kevin?"

Kevin came in on cue and Laura ran over to him and playfully hit him in the chest. "Kevin, you told! I wanted it to be a surprise." She came back over to David, "Daddy, I want to be a shuttle pilot like Mommy!"

Tears flooded his eyes as the pain and emotion of Marie's death burst again to the surface. He fought hard to control himself as he took Laura's hand and headed for his private quarters. He walked almost all the way before he could find and control his voice. "Laura, you can be anything you want to be, and I will help you. But I don't know if I can handle even the thought of you being in danger like Mommy."

She held his larger hand in both of hers and comforted him as if she were the adult. "Daddy, Warren says you have not faced

Mommy's death and until you do, you will be sad." They both looked deep into each other's eyes as she continued, "I can see how much it hurts and I promise I will learn all you want me to learn, but I want to keep learning with Kevin too. Can we continue this way and see how it goes?"

David could hardly believe his ears sensing so much wisdom coming from his daughter. "All right Laura, but I need to have a talk with Kevin. By the way, he didn't tell, it was Roger."

He cornered Kevin a short time later intending to chastise him, "Kevin, what's going on? Who gave you the right to teach Laura about flying behind my back?" He couldn't even convince himself that Kevin was wrong, but he tried.

Kevin shrugged, "David, you know as well as I that neither you nor anybody else aboard this ship can say no to Laura about anything. Besides, I can't see any harm in letting her fly the simulator. We have only been at it a couple of months, and already she can fly circles around me in that thing."

"But you're a starfighter pilot. What are you doing in the shuttle simulator?"

"It doesn't matter, she flies both equally well. I think I can beat her in a dogfight, but I don't know how long I can say that. All the starfighter pilots are learning to fly the shuttle. I don't see much use for starfighter pilots for the rest of the mission and we are short on shuttle pilots. The simulator is so good; they will be seasoned pilots by the time we reach our destination. We originally planned to spend more time and only shuttle during daylight hours. But, the way I see it, with the amount of oil we must transfer, it will take too long unless we shuttle around the clock. We have been practicing the mission in darkness, and most of the pilots are doing very well. Of course, it will only be night on the planet surface. In orbit, it won't matter. I think weather conditions could be more limiting than darkness, although we won't know much about the weather until we get there. I highly recommend we shuttle around the clock."

David pondered the idea for a moment, "Good idea; I can't even remember how long we took to ferry those empty bladders on board and every moment counts. How much time do you think we can save?"

I don't know; it depends on the amount of gravity on the planet before we can determine how many bladders we can take on each trip. If we worked only during daylight hours, I think it would take between four and six months. We can cut that in half and probably more with the additional pilots."

Roger joined in their conversation and seconded that recommendation. "David, I don't know how long we want to spend on the planet, but the more time we spend, the less time we will have to construct a ship capable of going back through time when we get back to Earth."

David agreed, "Thanks Kevin, you're right on and I guess you can continue to let Laura fly. I guess the only difference between her and normal kids, is the size and price of her toys. By the way, Roger, how are you coming on the time machine?"

"Okay if you want to change the subject. Actually, it seems to work well, but I don't know how to control it! We have sent it forward many times, successfully, I might add. But back in time is another story. The real problem is we have no way of testing sending an object back and seeing the results."

"But that's what we've got to do to change the past!"

"Don't forget, we've got to get back too. I don't think we will find those answers until we build the thing and put our lives on the line testing it. I'm willing to take the chance, but I wouldn't want to make any guarantees. Everyone working on the project with me is willing to take that gamble too."

"Well, if there's a chance it will work, then we don't have much choice. I'm with you Roger!"

"Thanks for your vote of confidence. I am certain it can be done with relative safety, but I wouldn't hazard a guess as to whether we can get back to the same world we left. If you remember when we first began discussing the problem, we didn't know how many pasts, presents or futures there are. We might return to a completely different and parallel future."

"That's not so bad. We would be alive and it would be quite an adventure."

"And you're the man who complained because his daughter wanted an adventurous career."

"She's too young to make that kind of decision."

Laura spoke up, "I have an idea that could work!"

"And what would that be?" Roger asked courteously.

"Well you could remind yourself to send it back two hours from now, and then all we have to do is look around and it should be here."

Roger laughed out loud, "By Golly, you've got a point. Let me think about that for a while, but it's certainly worth a try!"

CHAPTER 14

"They did it!" David opened his weekly executive council meeting with those emphatic words. "We got another message from the Pathfinder crew. They struck oil! Apparently it's a huge oil field and they should have no trouble filling our tanks." The Excalibur was still about one light year from O-2113, and slowing through Warp twenty. "I guess that means the discovery occurred at least a year ago so they will have plenty of time to pump out the oil we need. They say the planet is almost identical to Earth geologically and climate wise and has abundant resources with food sources readily available. I suppose by this time, they have already established some sort of farming."

"It will be good to eat normal food again!"

The entire council was excited as David made the announcement throughout the entire ship. When he finished, he asked, "Roger, how are we doing on our trajectory?"

"Not bad considering our ETA is a year away, but we need to make a correction or we will not be able to stop until we are about a half light year beyond the planet. I think we should do a wide swing around the planet as we are decelerating, and then we wouldn't have to increase the G loads. We probably could increase the G loads slightly, but it's not necessary. Maybe we weren't able to pinpoint our positions as accurately as we thought. However considering the distance involved, that error is not large."

David turned to Dr. Baker, "How about it Warren, can we do that safely?"

"I think we could. The acceleration deceleration forces haven't affected anyone adversely and we are now used to the higher amounts. But if it's not necessary, I would rather we didn't."

"Okay, Roger, make the wide swing."

The remaining time fled by as the entire crew was busy cleaning up last minute details. Those who had opted for the deep sleep mode were now being slowly reawakened except for their prisoners who would remain catatonic until returning to Earth. The passengers who joined them at Juliet were digesting the latest information reported from the Pioneer crew and were planning their colony establishment. It seemed that the planet had been uninhabited from a human standpoint, but there were many different types of animal wildlife that were similar to species on Earth.

Dr. Baker was quick to warn against possible diseases that could devastate their colony before it got started. He, assisted by his medical students, planned exhaustive tests to determine how healthy the planet would be. He would be bestowing advanced degrees upon many of his students, some of which were planning to remain on the planet.

They were well below Warp one when the planet became visible as a small speck in the sky and two way communications were established. At first contact, the communications center patched David into the link with the Pathfinder leader. David opened the communications, "Pathfinder, this is the Excalibur. Greetings from Earth. We have been receiving your regular transmissions since, well it seems like forever. Over." The distance was still considerable and each transmission and reply had a built in delay of several minutes.

After the delay, the message came in loud and clear, "This is Mike Wells of the Pathfinder. It's good to hear another voice from Earth. Welcome to the new world. We knew another ship was to follow, but we were at a loss as to how long it would take. We have an abundance of oil. Is the situation still desperate at home? Over."

"Situation still desperate. However, our ship is large enough to fulfill requirements for several years. We also bring you a group who will establish a colony that is if the planet is big enough for you and them too."

"Enough and to spare. The mountains are majestic; the water is clean although we have already despoiled part of this pristine world by drilling for oil. If we don't spoil it entirely, it will be a thing of beauty for a long time. It's paradise! The temperatures are moderate except at the poles and there are few natural disasters. We have seen evidence of earthquakes or should I say planet quakes, but storms are mild. I hope you plan to spend some time with us."

"We will be there only long enough to unload our cargo and passengers and to take on the maximum oil that our tanks will hold. That could be several months."

On her seventh birthday, David allowed Laura to join Kevin in the cockpit of one of the shuttles that would carry the first party to the surface. She made the most of it and Kevin let her do much of the flying. "Just like the simulator," he said. And it was except she thought it was much easier. She orbited the planet from lower altitudes at high speeds sending sonic booms reverberating through the mountain valleys. They enjoyed the scenic view, but for posterity and future earthbound researchers, everything was recorded with high resolution cameras and all sorts of probes for temperature, winds, pressures, and sensors to determine the presence of all known elements. As the scientists from the Pathfinder had indicated, the atmosphere was ideal, almost identical to that on the earth with the same balance between, oxygen, hydrogen, carbon dioxide, nitrogen, and most of the other inert gases. In sharp contrast, the only exception was that they found little pollution.

CHAPTER 15

Kevin and his crew of pilots immediately began to shuttle the empty containers to the surface and return full loads back to the ship, a process would go on around the clock for several weeks. Most of the remaining crewmen were pressed into service moving the full tanks from the hangar deck and securing them in the various storage areas throughout the ship. Kevin organized the group rotating schedules to allow for ample rest and relaxation, and for all who desired to spend off duty time on the planet. Laura flew many of the trips under Kevin's direct supervision. He reported to David that Laura could fly the missions by herself, but David wouldn't allow that much latitude even though Laura pleaded again and again to be allowed to fly solo. He was adamant and finally quieted her by handing out his ultimatum. "If you don't quit that incessant begging, you will not fly at all! I don't want to hear anything more about it. I must admit, you have the skill, but you lack the years of experience that all the other pilots have. You will have years to become a pilot like your mother was. Enjoy your flying with Kevin."

Within the fenced in boundaries of the colony established by the crew of the Pathfinder, everything was safe and civilized. It was like living on the western frontier of the United States in the eighteenth and nineteenth centuries. There, the colonists fled to safety behind stockades from wild animals and the ferocious Indian tribes that were often on the warpath. On this planet, there were no known natives to contend with, although much of the planet had not been explored. However, there were uncharted continents with many unknown species of wild animals, large and small, but some of the colonists regaled them with tales, describing their encounters with wild beasts as ferocious as lions and tigers and compared their temperament with that of grizzly bears. Most of their tales were grossly exaggerated, but the forests were alive with insect infestations which were more of a nuisance than a hazard, although there were many bee-like insects with venomous stingers as long and hard as thorns. They were not a problem when left alone, and undisturbed.

David spent as much time with Laura as he could visiting various areas around the planet observing and photographing animals in their natural habitat when he could pry her away from flying with Kevin. There were vast canyons, majestic mountains, and broad winding rivers, but look as hard as he might, he found no signs of civilization. He knew he was keeping one of the shuttle craft and a pilot from the work of loading the Excalibur, but he thought the exploration and photography expeditions would be invaluable when he returned to earth and reported on the planet, and it allowed the off duty crewmembers to see much of the planet. He was not a naturalist, but he was becoming proficient with the camera, while using their shuttle craft as protection from the elements and wildlife. Many of his crew and colonists accompanied them, and they spent hours in the evenings around a campfire reminiscent of wagon trains of the old west where they circled the wagons and spent the nights in the protection of the ring of wagons.

David enjoyed these expeditions and the encounters with nature, but that was secondary to his interest in the reactions of Laura and the other children to the new world of enchantment. He lamented the fact that he hadn't had the foresight to bring explorers and photographers from the National Geographic along, but there was always the next trip, and he didn't think it would take much convincing to get them to come along.

They spent hours observing the antics of a colony of monkey-like creatures who after the first few moments of alarm, ignored the human trespassers and went about their life as usual. Laura was fascinated and wanted to know more about them, and kept asking how they compared to monkey colonies in Africa. David became more and more aware of the isolation of deep space, which was the only world Laura knew that could not be seen on a computer screen or visual computer output. But he was glad Laura showed interest in something other than flying.

This world, he vowed, would remain as pristine as possible avoiding the pitfalls of the industrial revolution that had plagued the earth as the development occurred with the resultant waste of natural resources. This world would never know the sweat shops that plundered the innocence of children and spawned the violence of the emerging labor unions, and the modern world as he knew it today. It wouldn't be a Utopia with complete absence of crime and violence, but he hoped they would benefit from the lessons of the developing civilizations of the Earth.

He would have been thrilled to remain and insure those high ideals would become reality, but that was not his destiny. He had chosen his mission which would change history. He wanted to stay out of the politics of establishing the new world, but he was realistic enough to know his report back to the President would have to include specifics on the needs of the colony.

Roger spent hours in the lab working on his time project until he solved the problem of initiating the time sequence without first being at and beyond warp one. He took Laura's advice and soon began to send the device back and forth to himself a couple hours in the future. Under laboratory conditions, he could control to the precise minute when the object would arrive although he had no idea how long it took for the object to travel to the new time. He was proficient at it and it was like playing ping pong with himself. Only then did he relax and spend more time on the surface with David for the remainder of their stay.

CHAPTER 16

President Albee welcomed David and Laura into the oval office. "David, I am most impressed with your success. The oil you brought back should be sufficient for several years if we use it conservatively. You accomplished your mission in less time than I imagined, but it's a long haul for any crew. Admiral White would be proud. I must ask, do you think I should send the Excalibur back for another load?"

David thought carefully before answering. He didn't want to disappoint the president, but he didn't want to make another trip either. "Thanks, Mr. President, for your confidence in us. I don't think you have much choice and you need to send the ship back. The ship performed flawlessly, and I think we need to support the colony on that planet even if we didn't need more oil. The Excalibur could carry an enormous load of passengers and supplies especially if they were placed in the sleep state Dr. Baker perfected. The planet is ideal for tourism or permanent settlement."

"Do you really think voyages of that magnitude on a regular basis are safe for those kinds of enterprise? Not to mention the economic cost of such ventures?"

David kept a straight face as he replied, "Enterprise . . . . that ship was from Star Trek. We were on the Excalibur!" The president only grinned, so he continued, "Not exactly safe, but it's bound to get safer as we gain experience. The probability of a catastrophic accident in deep space is a reality; however I consider it safer than any voyage taken by the early Apollo missions to the moon. My concerns are not as much for the voyages as to the governing or managing of the settlements and those that will follow. As for the economic impact, I'm not an economist, but when I look back at all the benefits of the space race from the beginning, I see far more benefits than cost. And of course, traveling at multi light speeds opens up the possibilities for even wider exploration of other solar systems."

The president smiled, "I will take that under advisement. Do you want to command a return voyage?"

"No sir!" David replied promptly and emphatically, "Once is enough for me. I'd like to work on another project. Roger Dorn and I have some ideas which may provide a better solution in the long run."

"Oh, care to share them with me?"

"Not yet, but if funds are available, we will make it worthwhile."

"Good enough. I have every confidence in you and Roger. I will appoint you to manage the project and give it the secret code name, 'Manhattan II Project.' Bring me your recommendations as soon as practical."

David could only stammer, "Yes Sir!"

"Okay, but I do have conditions . . . . I am concerned with your daughter's education; the reasons are all important and will soon be apparent. She must be in school, and I think I have the perfect solution. I know a young woman who could be of great help . . . Brenda Kay Brockway. She lives near your mother in law in nearby Springfield, Virginia and is more than willing for Laura to stay with her if she wants to go to school in Washington. There are plenty of great schools in the area for gifted kids. Laura could then spend some time with her grandmother too."

David had already been considering placing her in a good school but had been undecided. He looked at Laura, seeing the doubt and dismay on her face, "Laura, what do you think?"

"But Dad," she protested, "you need me! Face it; you wouldn't know what to do without me." Eleven year old Laura sensed she was facing a losing battle, but she would not give up without a fight.

David looked at the President hopelessly, "I don't know. She could be tutored privately, and she has been deeply involved in our project from the beginning."

The president spoke gravely with a purpose not to be denied, "David, if you want to head up this commission, you, like me, have little choice. I need you to take some time by yourself and get your life back in order. Your social life is sadly lacking and spending all your time with Laura doesn't help, and it doesn't help with Laura's development either. She needs a mother figure. But, the choice is yours." He turned to Laura, "Laura, will you give her a chance? Let me tell you about Brenda." They both nodded and he continued, "She was an astronaut and flew a shuttle like your mother and knew your mom in the early days. She will be available to shuttle either of you back and forth to your project, as often as is practical and I think she might even be able to teach you, Laura, how to fly, if you like. Although she works directly for me, her first priority will be to support you and your father's mission."

"But, I already know how to fly!" Laura was on the verge of throwing an uncharacteristic tantrum.

David was troubled, not wanting to leave his daughter for any length of time, but he desperately wanted to head up this mission. He asked, "Why would this Brenda, what's her name, want to do this? What's wrong with her?"

"Nothing! She's perfect for both of you. She lost her husband and child in a tragic accident which she is not at liberty to talk about. I told her about Laura and I think she would be very good for Laura. No child, not even Laura can make up for her great loss, but it would help. Brenda left NASA, but she has the required clearances, knows the details of your project, and is dedicated to your success. As a favor to me, please consider her."

David looked doubtful and began to wonder what was going on. How could anyone know the details of Roger's project? Was there another leak? He was afraid someone tied close to Marie's former life would be too difficult for him, let alone Laura. He didn't know if he wanted Laura to take flying lessons from anyone. But the president would not relent, "David, as I said, you don't have much choice. Why not meet with Brenda and talk it over; then you can make your decision. As I understand it, your project will not require your full time presence on site. You will need to spend time in Washington since many of the people you will consult are here and have already been working on similar solutions. And you could help me get a crew ready for the Excalibur to return."

David protested, "She couldn't know the details of our project."

The president smiled, "Things aren't always what they seem. Believe me when I say she can help you immensely."

David looked at Laura who with bowed head nodded with resignation, "All right, we'll try it. When can we meet her?"

"She's waiting outside." He buzzed his secretary asking her to send Brenda in.

Brenda, a tall young woman with closely cropped dark hair walked in. She wore glasses with thick black frames that hid her upper facial features. When she opened her mouth to speak, they could see a couple of her front teeth were larger than normal and slightly crooked giving her a lisp when she spoke. She stopped and stared at both of them for a moment as if she couldn't help herself and then walked over to Laura, smiling, "Laura, you look just like I pictured in my mind. You look a lot like your mother did when we first met."

David gaped for a moment thinking he saw a ghost of Marie until she opened her mouth, and turned away at the mention of Marie, but Laura perked up, "You knew my mother when she was my age?"

"Yes, we were neighbors. I was younger, but we hung out together. When she joined the astronaut corps, she was my idol and I wanted to do the same. Without her, and her inspiration, I probably would not have chosen that lifestyle. We could have some great times together. Would you like to go to my house and check out the neighborhood?"

"Are there any kids my age?"

"Probably. And lots of kids your age going to the same school."

"I have never known very many kids. There were a few on board the Excalibur, but they didn't associate with me very much.

"Well, you'll have your chance." She turned to David and spoke quietly and carefully, "David, I'd love to care for her while you are busy, if you approve?"

David felt some strange emotion nagging in the back of his mind wondering how she already knew of the project when he had just been appointed himself. He could see Brenda was different than Marie, but she had an uncanny resemblance if she didn't open her mouth. Her hair color and what he could see of her eyes was different too, but there was something about her besides the president's ultimatum, that drove him to accept her offer. "All right, Brenda, I guess I don't have much choice, but . . . ." He became deadly serious, "You'd better treat her well and . . . . Love her!"

"I will care for her as my own daughter when she is with me and I won't interfere when she is with you. The president will make sure of that. I'm not going to mollycoddle her, but she will have a loving home while she is with me."

Laura left her father with the president and went with Brenda. As they closed the door behind them, Brenda whispered, "Don't tell your father, but I think he's handsome."

Laura giggled, "I think you're pretty too, but why didn't you get braces when you were younger and have your teeth fixed?"

"Well, aren't you the most straightforward young lady? I like your openness, but we're going to have to work on your lack of tact. You've got to learn to be a lady if you're going to work with your Dad on the time project."

Laura's face showed only a little embarrassment, "I'm sorry, I just blurted that out. I will try not to ask so many personal questions."

"No problem. Ask as many questions as you like. My teeth weren't like this when I was young. I had a little accident while flying and it's been like that ever since. It doesn't bother me anymore and I consider myself lucky; I wasn't scarred in any other way. Actually it's my disguise. Without it, I would look too much like another lady I know."

They reached the transport car in the lower part of the White House and Laura observed closely as Brenda punched in their destination on the control panel. When underway, she asked, "Can you really teach me to fly? You know I already know how. I do pretty darn good in the simulators, and with the shuttles, but you're talking about a different type of flying, aren't you?

"Yes to both questions. I have access to an antique airplane that must be five or six hundred years old, and it's probably been rebuilt more often than I would like to count, but it's fun. It's a Piper J3 Cub and it'll probably be around another five hundred years. We'll start with that and then you can graduate to more complex aircraft. You haven't really learned how to fly without wings and aerodynamic controls. I suppose we could do it all in the simulator, but it wouldn't be near as much fun."

"But, weren't those models powered by gasoline engines? How do you get fuel?"

"Hey, I thought you were cooped up on that space ship all these years. How do you know about all that?"

Laura looked indignant, "I may have been isolated, but I can read. Besides the computer libraries on board the Excalibur have excellent historical reference to almost every aircraft ever built, and I've looked at all of them."

"Touché! However the J3 we will be flying is not quite original. It is, except for the engine and even that has a close resemblance. Unless you look under the cowling, you can't tell the difference. It has an electro magnetic rotor, but it simulates the real thing. You have to treat it like the original and even the sounds are authentic. If a pilot from the twentieth century didn't know about the engine, he would even think he was in the real thing. I hope you will learn to love that airplane as I do."

Laura beamed with joy, "Oh, I'm going to have fun! When can we go flying?"

Brenda laughed, "Let's stop at home first and get something to eat and then maybe we can introduce you to the real world of flight later this afternoon. The weather is great and we might as well take advantage of that. We've got to get you enrolled in school soon though. Tomorrow night, we are supposed to attend a dinner at the White House in honor of your father and his crew so maybe we should do some shopping in the morning."

"Don't you have to go back to work? I thought government workers had to punch the time clock."

"Well, not all of us. You and your father and the time machine are my work! My job is rather different and how much I have to do will depend on your father since he will be the mission director. It's something I want to do, particularly since the president requested me for the job. The government has provided me with all my needs since my husband's accident so I don't need to work."

"What happened?"

Brenda's smile vanished, "Sorry, I can't talk about it. Maybe someday, I can tell you all about it. It's just that it happened when we were working on something top secret."

"I understand; Daddy has drilled into me that same level of security on our project. I'm glad I can talk to you about it though."

"So am I honey. So am I."

Brenda's home was actually a modest sized apartment in a large complex. She apologized as they entered. "It's not a grand estate or anything like that, but it's comfortable, cozy and convenient. It's not easy finding a place anywhere near Washington these days."

Laura never lived anywhere off the Excalibur and anyplace on solid ground suited her fine. "It's great and I will have my own private room. Thanks Brenda, for everything."

"You're welcome. And maybe you already know about your grandmother's home. It's a real gem and I know you'll like it there."

"Oh, I'd almost forgotten about her. Will she accept me or, I mean, what is she like?"

"She's the most wonderful woman I know who has been waiting years to see you again. You stayed with her for a time before you left. Of course, she misses your mom, but she'll never let on how much it hurts. I don't know if your Dad will want to visit her or not, but they used to have good rapport."

She skipped alongside Brenda excitedly as she replied, "You sure seem to know a lot about my family. Sounds like you know more about them than I do."

"President Albee made it my business and I have spent quite a bit of time with your grandmother preparing her for your return. Until a few months ago, she had given up hope of ever seeing you again. The news of your mother's accident was a real blow to her."

"Maybe we should go see her today and give up on the flying?"

"Can't, she's not home; she went to a beauty shop. She wants to look her best when she sees you and we will go over there later tonight."

"It's beautiful, but awful crude. It doesn't have any instruments. How can you fly it?" Laura excitedly walked around the old aircraft looking at each feature with curiosity. Are you sure it's safe?"

"Of course, but it's only as safe as the pilots that fly it. It's totally VFR, but I suppose you don't know much about that. It's almost a lost art, but there are many pilots who work hard keeping it as a viable alternative, if only for sport. There are areas of dedicated airspace for this type of sport flying and we will use one of those. As for the instruments, you're going to learn to fly by making your own. The only instruments you need on the panel are the altimeter and airspeed indicator. Of course the tach and oil pressure were pretty essential for the good of the old engines. The attitude indicator is something you want to be able to rely on if you ever need it when flying VFR. More than one pilot has bought the farm when they lost their outside reference when the weather turned bad or the sky was too hazy to recognize the horizon. For now, I want you to get to feel the aircraft by the seat of your pants. The tach is for reference of the power setting and the oil pressure is not real. But, they are there because after flying this, you can fly the real thing and then it's important to keep those in your crosscheck. Today, let's go up and let you get a feel for it, and that way I can see if you have any aptitude for flying."

"Get me in the simulator, or get me on the shuttle, and I'll show you!"

"Oh, I know you can do that, and with that ability, you can be a good average pilot. But, we need to know if you have what it takes to be the best and that's why we are going to fly today."

"Why?"

"The president wants my recommendation by tomorrow. Your father doesn't know it, but if you have what it takes, you will have a major role after his project becomes operational. The time machine is only the vehicle to take you back to the past where you can make a difference, but you have to make the difference by modifying and test flying aircraft from that century. That's why you have to learn to fly this way. You're going to be our agent in the twentieth century. That's why we are taking the time out to fly today."

Laura stopped dead in her tracks, and exclaimed, "How do you know all that? All that information was kept Top Secret and only a few of the crew from the Excalibur know anything about that."

Brenda grabbed her arm, pulling her toward the open door, "Come on, we're burning daylight. I've probably said too much already, but that's why it's so important. Let's get this thing in the air so I can make my report to the president. By the way, keep this under your hat, your father will know soon enough.

I'm only going to show you once and then we'll land and you can do it." Brenda demonstrated how to start the engine, check it out, and properly preflight the aircraft. She taxied to the runway stressing the importance of proper flight control adjustments for the wind. She spoke briefly about the requirements for engine run ups and magneto checks required before the advent of the electromagnetic engines before taxiing to the end of the runway. Soon they were in the air where Brenda made good on her promise to help Laura make her own instruments. She trimmed the aircraft for straight and level flight and asked Laura to draw with a grease pencil, a vertical line in the center and a horizontal line across the windscreen corresponding with the horizon. "That's your attitude indicator. Keep the vertical line straight up and down, and the horizontal line on the horizon and you'll do fine. Use it until you get the picture, then you won't need it any longer." Brenda demonstrated a perfect landing and asked, "Are you ready to give it a try?"

Laura could hardly hold her enthusiasm in check, "I'm ready!"

A few minutes later, she had her chance, and bounced into the air. At first she couldn't keep her altitude within five hundred feet nearly making herself sick, but she improved rapidly in the next twenty minutes. She bounced five times on landing but managed to get it on the runway. Brenda's only comment, "They say any landing you can walk away from is a good one!"

Laura was subdued the rest of the afternoon. She wasn't used to failing in anything she tried and she was learning one of her first lessons in humility. Brenda didn't say much as she prepared to take Laura to see her grandmother. Laura was pleasantly surprised to find her belongings had been already delivered and stowed in her room, but she was at a loss to decide what to wear that evening. She carried two sets of clothing out asking, "What do you think? I don't know what to wear."

"Either of those will be fine for tonight, your grandmother won't care, but we've got to get you something decent before tomorrow night. Go ahead and get dressed, we don't want to keep her waiting!" Brenda wondered how hard it must have been for Laura without a mother's touch after she had left the scene and thought, 'If I had been there, she would have had lots of pretty clothes made especially for her.'

Laura's grandmother's house was only a few blocks and they walked. Brenda walked through the door without knocking greeting the older lady, "Hi Mom, are you ready for your granddaughter?"

Laura didn't have time to think about it as her grandmother rushed to her and enfolded her in her arms. "Laura my baby!" She didn't say much more as she could hardly control her emotions. She held Laura for a few minutes before leading her into the kitchen where she served freshly baked cookies and milk. "My how you've grown since I last saw you. Let's see, you were about two years old I believe. So young to have lost your Mama and so far from home. Whatever did you do all those years?"

Laura felt right at home and chatted about everything aboard the Excalibur except for any reference to the time machine. Brenda sat watching, munching her cookies, but not saying much. Grandmother listened with fascination, occasionally interjecting a question. She led Laura into another room and opened a closet full of girl's clothing. "These used to belong to your mother. You can take what you like. Maybe some of them will fit. You're tall and lanky like your mother was."

Laura exclaimed in glee, "They're beautiful. Look at this!" She pulled out a red party gown with gold thread woven into the fabric."

Brenda watched with amusement as Laura's grandmother exclaimed, "My daughter had a taste for the exotic too. She was way too young to wear anything like that as you are. But, no matter, your father will probably let you wear anything you like. Too bad your mother isn't here to teach you how to be a lady, but I suppose Brenda can do the job, if she can stay around long enough."

Laura picked several articles and changed into one to wear for the rest of the evening and Brenda programmed the house computer to have the rest delivered to her apartment. Time passed quickly as Laura became acquainted with her grandmother, but Brenda finally suggested they start for home. "You know the way and can walk here as often as you like; it's quite safe even after dark. Of course you can use public transportation anytime you like."

As they were walking, Laura asked, "Why do you call her Mom? You're not her daughter are you? You couldn't possibly be my aunt, could you?"

"Heavens no! Your mother and I were close and I was at your grandmother's almost every day. I've called her Mom as long as I can remember. You don't mind do you?"

"No, of course not." She hesitated for a moment before asking, "Can I call you Mom? I know you're not old enough to be my Mom, but . . . ."

Brenda wrapped her arms around Laura, not wanting to ever let go, and replied with tears in her eyes, "I'd love that! But, maybe your Dad would object?"

"Too bad! Serves him right for going along with President Albee when I didn't want to stay here. I get along with Dad and I love him, but I've wanted a mom a long time."

"I've wanted a daughter a long time too. I'm so glad you're going to be staying with me." They hugged each other as if trying to make up for all the lost years. "Oh, and have you changed your mind about staying with me here in Washington? I love you, Laura."

"I love you too Mom, and Yes, as my father says, I'm in hog heaven!" She was happy for most of the evening, but when she remembered her flying that afternoon, she lapsed back into a subdued mood.

The next morning, they spent hours shopping, getting all the necessities along with several outfits practical for school. That evening, Laura insisted on wearing the red dress that had been her mothers. It fit perfectly and Brenda was pleased.

They arrived at the White House on schedule and met David as they got off the transport. He had been there a few minutes, but waited for them. He almost didn't recognize Laura and marveled at how beautiful Brenda looked in her evening gown. He took her arm to escort her into the White House dining room, while Laura took his other hand.

The room was filled with cabinet members and a few select Congressmen, former President Gardiner, along with Roger and Warren with their wives. The president paid high tribute to David and his crew. "My hat goes off to David Ashton, Roger Dorn, Kevin Haugen, Warren Baker and Laura Ashton who is the heart and soul of this team. I wish to acknowledge to all of you here tonight that this group along with the rest of the crew on the Excalibur, sacrificed nine years of their lives to make it possible for each of us to continue to live in this nation without worrying about a shortage of oil. They have also been part of a team that for the first time traveled faster than light. Their journey took them over two hundred light years distance and in all estimations their mission was a complete success." The president's tone changed to a somber note, "We remember the sacrifice of Gladys Ashton, Thomas White, and Annette White who died while attempting to accomplish that mission."

After dinner, the president waited patiently for the room to clear and allow the secret service detail to secure the room. He asked all to be seated and began, "You members of my staff and congressmen have been wondering, I'm sure, what I've been talking about. What's this, you wonder, about an oil shortage? And you, the crew from the Excalibur have an impressive technological advancement to share in regard to time travel."

David protested, "But sir, you couldn't know about that!"

"I know, but I do! I have appointed you, David, to be the project manager to build that time machine Roger has developed. You see the trouble with time machines is that once they've been used, you never know whether you are in the past or the present. Roger, your theories and time machine worked to perfection and we have eliminated the oil shortage problem. Please, stay with me on this for a moment. You congressmen are living in a different dimension of the future than you, the crew of the Excalibur, or maybe it's all one and the same. I don't know, but your future has been secured. I say that, but it will only be secured if we do the same thing we are doing in that other dimension of time, if there is another dimension. That's why you distinguished members of congress are here."

He had their attention and everyone was listening with awe and wonder, "Let me back up a moment. Nine years ago, President Gardiner sent David and his crew deep into the Milky Way to get as much oil as they could possibly bring back in their starship. President Gardiner did that because the world as he knew it was running out of oil, and he didn't have any other choice. You may ask why we didn't know about that. Because, in our dimension of time, that is no longer the case because David and his crew were successful. They went far beyond what we asked of them and invented a time machine which had, with further development, the ability to go back in time five hundred years and make it possible for our ancestors to conserve oil so we would have an abundance today. That time machine has not been built yet, but it did go back and was successful!"

Senator Young threw up his hands in exasperation, "Sir, you're not making any sense, if something has not been built then it couldn't do what you say it did!"

The president continued, "President Gardiner, in the present dimension, acted for a different reason than he did originally, but the result was the same and the crew of the Excalibur didn't know the difference. I am acting the same as I did in the original dimension, but with a different motivation because now I have the benefit of hind sight. I know how the mission was accomplished and we will do it again just as we did before, if there is a before, even when we have no awareness of the other dimension of time. I have invited you members of congress who hold key positions on the finance committees, here tonight to present a formal request to fund a top secret mission, which we will call the Manhattan II Project. The projected cost to build the Manhattan, a time ship to go back to the twentieth century is two hundred twenty-three trillion dollars."

Senator Young laughed, "You're out of your gourd if you think we are going to authorize that kind of money on a project as dumb as that! You have no way of knowing what is happening in other dimensions of time, even if it's possible."

The president was deadly serious, "Oh, I know, and I have ironclad proof; I think you will agree once you've seen it. Over five hundred years ago President Daniel Dugan was the recipient of the Manhattan Project and with his help, the mission was accomplished. The original planners foresaw the meeting we are having tonight and set us up for the project to continue especially if it was successful as it apparently was. They planted an egg in the Oval Office which hatched during President Gardiner's term in office. David Ashton and his crew placed a strongbox in Dugan's Oval Office set to open five hundred years later. That box contained the plans for the Manhattan and the proof you require. I have sealed documents from every president in the intervening years authenticating their guardianship of that box."

The president paused and pressed a button under the table. The door opened and an aide wheeled in a black strongbox and then left securing the door behind him. "This is the box which President Gardiner opened." He looked over at President Gardiner for confirmation.

Former President Gardiner nodded, "What President Albee has said is true. The box opened on schedule and I sent the Excalibur on their original mission. I flat out lied through my teeth, telling them how we were running out of oil. They went on that mission with the belief that if they were unsuccessful, then our civilization would burn itself out. I found all the information which the president has given you, and had to put on a performance that should have won me an Oscar. I sent the earlier Pathfinder Probe out with the same degree of deception."

President Albee continued, "The box has an inner box which is set to open tonight with all of you present. In fact it cannot be opened unless the majority of you are present here tonight and authenticate by voice. I want each of you first to confirm the box is sealed. He pulled a small computer out of the box and turned it on. The voice authentication procedure which they were all familiar with began. The President, each member of his cabinet, and each congressman present was called and authentication was complete with a ten number combination given by computer voice. A panel slid open on the box revealing the code panel. The president keyed in the correct combination and the box opened. Another computer was removed from the box and turned on. Holographic images appeared in the center of the room, images of all those present from the other dimension. Each man's image presented his case and each of those present was convinced.

President Albee's image appeared giving final instructions, "Remaining in the box are documents from each of you in your own words telling the complete story, and instructions for each of you. Your mission is simple, build the Manhattan according to the plans provided. David Ashton should command the mission, assisted by Roger Dorn and Warren Baker. Laura Ashton will remain in the twentieth century to complete the mission as described. She should be prepared to introduce electro magnetic engine technology and assist President Dugan making this technology a reality in the twentieth century. The Manhattan should be completed and the plan should be executed on the prescribed time schedule. Each of those involved in the mission are not to be given full details to prevent any change in a mission that was successful!

In the twentieth century, President Dugan, at our suggestion, opened a trust fund administered by the Solar Magnetics Corporation. That initial fund was begun with a 25 billion dollar investment over a twenty five year period, provided for by hefty licensing fees paid to SMA. After that initial period, fees continued to be collected at a reduced rate and as you know, fees are still collected on every electro magnetic engine manufactured and that fund continues to grow. I'm sure you are aware of those funds, but had no idea why the fund was set up. Today that fund contributes trillions of dollars annually supporting the Federal budget. Over the years, several politicians have attempted to use the principle of those funds for other projects, but the strings are tight and that proved to be impossible. The Solar Magnetics Administration controls those strings and I'm not certain they even know why, but it's in their charter. As long as the fund balance is sufficient for the Manhattan Project, then the excess earnings are available to balance the budget, and the fund will remain substantial even after the Manhattan Project is funded. Part of the trust fund has already been used to fund the Excalibur mission and of course has more than sufficient funds for the Manhattan Project! One word of warning—If you do not authorize the expenditure of these funds for the Manhattan Project, that fund will no longer exist and you will probably have great difficulty trying to balance the budget! And on top of that, we would then be faced with an acute shortage of oil. I don't know how long it would take

CHAPTER 17

Laura, David and Brenda left for home with their own packages, but waited to be alone before taking time to read their instructions. They rode together as far as Brenda's apartment when she asked, "David, do you want to come in for a few minutes?"

He followed her inside commenting, "You have a real nice place here."

"Thanks to President Albee, I couldn't have found it without him. You're always welcome here with Laura."

David sat down across the kitchen table from Laura, "Brenda, I'm puzzled, I understand almost everything that went on tonight except for your part. You're a mystery. What is your role?"

Brenda answered cautiously, "I've known the president a long time, but really I just work for him. It's convenient since I knew your wife and your mother in law; consequently, President Albee can get a lot of miles out of me. He knew Laura needed a top notch pilot, which I am, to get her prepared, so here I am."

"Mom," Laura hesitatingly began, "you know I couldn't fly worth a hoot. Why didn't you tell the president I couldn't do it?"

"What did you say?" David exclaimed. "Have you allowed Brenda to take your mother's place already?"

"Daddy, be reasonable. Brenda calls Grandmother Mom, and I think it's a rather nice thing to do. Besides," she rationalized, "if I'm going to be living with her, it'll help with the other kids." She turned back to Brenda ignoring any further objection from her father, "Well, what did you say to the president?"

"I told him that any daughter of mine would make an excellent pilot to fly twentieth century airplanes. You didn't do as badly as you thought. Most of my students couldn't get airborne by themselves the first time, let alone land it. You do have the aptitude Laura."

"Thanks Mom. Now I think I will go to my room and read my package. Good night Daddy."

"Good night Laura." He stood and kissed her, proudly watching her leave the room before turning to Brenda. "What a kid, huh?"

She stood and led him into the living room where it would be more comfortable. "She's the best and she will be a hero for all time. You have every right to be proud of her."

"I guess since you are going to be her Mom, then I'd better see if you are the right person for the job." He drew her into his arms, kissing her tenderly. The embrace grew more passionate as she responded eagerly to his advances. Suddenly he abruptly pushed her away, "I'm sorry Brenda; this won't do. All I could think of, when kissing you, was Marie. Your face, your features, everything was Marie as if she only left me yesterday. Please forgive me."

Brenda was tempted to throw him out and tell him never to come back, but she controlled her emotions putting on her poker face, feigning indifference, "Don't let it bother you. You kiss pretty well, but you're too old for me." She laughed leaving the room allowing him to find his own way out.

Laura opened her package and began reading:

"Your package is the smallest which is indirectly proportional to your role which is the largest. The original mission featured a delicate balance between your intervention and preventable non-intervention. Your goal is to change only one aspect of the past which will have significant impact on the future without disrupting our world. The fewer details you know, the greater your probability of success.

Prepare yourself by studying physics, engineering, electro magnetic propulsion, aerodynamics, and medicine. Brenda Brockway will prepare you to fly and evaluate twentieth century aircraft, and will be invaluable to you during your time of preparation. In the twentieth century, you will assist an agent you and your father select to present electro magnetic engine technology to Aircraft and Automobile industries to enable them to conserve fossil fuel resources.

You are restricted from sharing any technology except in research and development toward the introduction of the electro magnetic propulsion units. Every action you take in the twentieth century could result in disastrous consequences in our time. From your study of history, you will know of momentous events in your new time that you could alter by issuing warnings. You must resist those interventions even though you will be tormented knowing a great many lives could have been saved, but instead, you must stand by and do nothing. That will be difficult as it may go against your grain of decency and compassion, but you must remain strong in this area. For example, if you grabbed a child to prevent him or her from running into the street and getting run over by a car. That intervention could start a chain reaction that could alter the course of history. We do not expect you to go to that extreme, but we want you to be aware that every one of your actions in the twentieth century could create paradoxes that would make tremendous changes in our life in the world. A better example would be the terrorist attacks on the World Trade Center on September 11, 2001. You must not interfere although you will suffer as the nation suffers on that day of infamy.

If you accept this mission as your own, then you must agree to remain single, never marrying any man from the twentieth century.

David found his way out and went quietly back to his hotel brooding on the loss of his wife, but remembering her more vividly than any time since the accident. He thrust the memories out of his mind as he began to read his instructions.

"David Ashton will command the 'Manhattan', a time ship built under Roger Dorn's supervision, according to the plans provided in this package. You will assist in preparing your daughter to remain in the twentieth century to carry out the mission, as she has been instructed. Her directions are included in your package. The remainder of these instructions are for your own use and should only be shared with Roger Dorn and Warren Baker as you deem appropriate. Your daughter will need to be the only contact with persons from the twentieth century except as directed and she will not have any knowledge of the rest of the plan except for her conviction that the mission was and will be successful."

David continued to read all the plans details before locking his plans in the safe in his room. He fell asleep wondering, "Twelve years here and four more aboard the Manhattan and then I will lose my daughter as I have lost her mother. The world is so unfair!"

CHAPTER 18

Laura and Brenda were inseparable in the days and weeks that followed except during school hours, and David found very little time he could be alone with his daughter for any extended period. He accepted this new status with few regrets after seeing how Laura was blossoming under Brenda's care and supervision. A few months later David asked Brenda to join him and Laura on a surprise vacation trip travelling northward along the East coast to Maine and beyond and then down the St Lawrence Seaway into the Great Lakes. Neither Brenda nor Laura knew what to expect, and he only told them to bring clothes enough for an extended sea cruise and any files or information she would need for the project in the next couple of months. He unconsciously welcomed Brenda's presence whenever he wanted time to be with Laura. This was an unexpected bonus as he realized he would be able to spend more time with Brenda. He watched the gals chat as he imagined it would have occurred between Laura and her mother. A gradual change had come over him since Brenda came into their life as the natural healing process began working its wonder on David's personality. He didn't realize his progress, but had to acknowledge it as Warren and Roger both made comments to that effect. He gradually began to feel alive while doing something other than working on the project for the first time in years.

His paychecks from the last nine years had accumulated untouched, with interest. He found it hard to believe the total of his bank account balance. Laura's expenses over the next few years in private schools would be considerable, but the government would pick up the tab for most of them since it was almost completely in preparation for the Manhattan Project. Each of the Excalibur crewmembers found themselves in a similar financial situation with money to burn. Kevin Haugen convinced David, Roger and Warren to join him in leasing a hundred foot yacht which would be a perfect vacation getaway vehicle.

Kevin Haugen and Warren Baker with his wife, Aimee would be along for the trip, but Roger Dorn decided he would sit this one out as he was preoccupied with checking out sources for materials needed in the construction of the Manhattan.

David watched with amusement as the girls explored every inch of the yacht with excitement. He wasn't immune either as all the comforts of home were available, and it was almost like being back aboard the Excalibur with ample, but smaller living quarters. David joined the captain in the cockpit while the rest of the party sat on the forward deck near the bow while the yacht easily pulled out of her moorings under her own power and slid smoothly out into the Chesapeake Bay. They ran slowly while the captain got the feel for it making sure everything ran smoothly. Soon, he opened the throttles; the yacht responded rapidly getting on plane, rising a few feet above the surface on the hydrofoil. David soon went down on the deck and joined the rest of the group. He found Kevin standing close to Brenda sharing some little bit of information and felt a twinge of jealousy.

As he approached, Brenda threw her arms around David and gave him a lingering kiss, "Thanks for such a wonderful surprise!" She exclaimed. "It's wonderful. Now where are we going?"

David, thrown off guard by that totally unexpected gesture, felt a stirring of memories of earlier, similar expressions from Marie. He couldn't quite place those memories and after a moment answered, "We're going to sail up the coast to Maine and beyond, then travel the entire length of the St Lawrence Seaway all the way to Chicago. We'll stop at all the major cities and attractions along the way and relax and enjoy ourselves."

Brenda was amused, "But, what about the project? Isn't anybody going to work?"

"Sure! You are! We've got all the latest communication equipment aboard and you can work to your heart's content." He chuckled, "Seriously this will be a working cruise and although we may occasionally leave the ship and even take a shuttle back to Washington for a meeting or whatever; we will work hard. We will conduct business aboard ship, but we can take all the time we want to relax and enjoy ourselves. Roger is off working but will probably join us for at least part of the trip. Kevin and I will be going back to the Excalibur shortly helping the new crew get ready for another trip. The president okayed your absence as long you keep in touch with him on the video phone. I don't know why except he wants to see your pretty face as often as he can."

"He probably wants to be sure I keep you in line!"

"Probably."

"Maybe I'd better go check out that equipment and you can have a few minutes with Laura."

"Okay, but don't take too long. The cook will have our dinner ready soon and we don't want to keep him waiting."

David let her go as he watched Kevin join her heading for the communications room. He took his daughter's arm and began walking aft. Laura beamed with joy, "She's great isn't she dad?"

"Oh, yeah. It's a great boat and I want you to have a wonderful time. Maybe next summer we can take a cruise down to the Caribbean."

"I wasn't talking about the boat, Dad," she replied indignantly, "I meant Brenda. She's the best. It would be great if the two of you could . . . Well, I mean I would love to have her for a real mother."

"Get serious Laura. She told me I was too old. Besides didn't you see her walk off with Kevin? We will be going back in time and unless you change your mind, you'll be staying there and who knows if I'll ever get back."

"Hmm . . ." she mused, "I suppose you're right. That would be asking a lot. She already lost one husband." Laura hadn't given up, but would let it go for now.

"Has she said anything about what happened?"

"Nope, she talks about everything else except him. I don't even know his name."

"I suppose it doesn't matter. She is rather cute. If she would take off those glasses and get her teeth straightened, she could be a real knockout."

"Dad . . . . Don't make fun of her. She said her teeth were damaged in the accident. I've wondered why she doesn't get her eyes operated on though . . . Maybe I'll ask her."

"I'm not making fun of her. I would never do that. I like her too much. But it doesn't make much sense. Teeth don't grow bigger after an accident. Maybe she is trying to hide something . . ."

They met Brenda coming around the corner and their conversation stopped abruptly. She joked, "You must have been talking about me. My ears are ringing."

David took her arm as they headed toward the dining room. "Nope, that's the dinner bell."

"Okay, keep your secrets. We've got more serious things to discuss anyway. Roger will be expecting our call in a couple hours. He said he has some business to take care of."

After dinner, they met in the conference room. Roger gave his preliminary report via video conferencing, "David, I've got a line on all the structural materials we need. The same contractor used previously is available. They built the Excalibur and I'm sure they can build the basic airframe without too much interference from us. I think you can handle the airframe contractor, and I'll concentrate on the electronics. The electronics, which is the heart of the systems, will have to be built from scratch and I want to supervise whoever works on it pretty closely. That ship, like the Excalibur, is going to be our home away from home for a number of years."

David replied, "Good, that's what we expected. I will insure the airframe is built like a tank. I don't mean to have it armor plated, but it has to take whatever stresses we put on it without failure of any structural component. First we need to find a good location to set up shop. The president has offered a couple sites to evaluate. The first is an abandoned military base out in the middle of the Nevada desert. It's out in the middle of nowhere, with no access except for an old interstate highway that hasn't been used for years. The second option would require more work, but it could provide better cover. It's an old silver mine in Colorado with underground space which could be enlarged to suit our purposes. We could re-open the mine since it has pockets of low grade silver and might be profitable using the latest equipment."

Laura asked, "Why don't we build it out in space like the Excalibur?"

Roger replied, "We could, but it would be difficult to keep secret. And of course that would mean it was manufactured differently than we did it earlier. I suppose that doesn't matter, but we need to keep everything as close to the original as possible. We want the outcome to be exactly the same."

David continued, "Roger, on Monday, Kevin and I are going up to the Excalibur. I'll meet you in Denver on Tuesday morning at nine."

Roger replied, "I've got the lab from the Excalibur dismantled and all the test equipment ready to ship. Kevin can shuttle it to the site when we're ready. I'll see you on Tuesday."

David turned back to the girls, "We have a couple of days together. Let's make the most of it. Do you want to go with us or would you rather stay aboard and continue your vacation?"

Laura laughed, "You go right ahead, Daddy. I've spent enough time aboard the Excalibur."

"How about you, Brenda?"

Brenda shook her head negatively, "Thanks, but I'll keep my feet on solid ground." She chuckled as the boat hit a swell and rocked slightly. "I would like to see what it's like aboard the Excalibur, but it'll wait."

"But the president said you would be available to shuttle us anywhere we need to go."

"If you really want me to, I will, but he didn't mean you couldn't use other transportation."

"I'd love for you to go with me, but I guess you should stay with Laura; I imagine we'll get along without you. In the meantime, let's enjoy our little cruise." He put his arm around her and they took a leisurely stroll around the ship.

On Monday morning, David and Kevin left the boat while moored in the New York Harbor. Brenda, Aimee and Laura joined them in the runabout with the intention of doing some shopping in the Big Apple before continuing up the coastline. Warren decided to stay aboard and relax.

As David and Kevin boarded a shuttle to take them to Andrews AFB, David said, "Kevin, the president is offering you a choice. You can stay on the Manhattan Project with us or become the Executive Officer aboard the Excalibur.

Kevin reacted with surprise, "You're serious! I was wondering what I would do during the construction of the Manhattan. I'm sure, for you, it's an exciting project, but I don't think I'd be satisfied being out of action. I need to keep my hand in the flying end of it. I'll have to think long and hard about another trip though."

"Take a good look around today and we'll wait a couple of days for your decision."

"Who is the commander going to be?"

"I don't know. The president wouldn't say. Would that have anything to do with your decision?"

"Maybe. If you were going back, there would be no hesitation. I would go in a minute."

"Whatever your decision, the president will back you. The commander, whoever he is, has never travelled beyond the speed of light, so I'm sure he would welcome your expertise."

Their visit aboard the Excalibur was short and everything looked to be in proper order. The ship was undergoing a complete two year inspection and preventative maintenance cycle and would be ready to depart immediately afterward. They were renovating one deck level to accommodate a much larger number of passengers.

The next morning, Roger joined David and they met with an agent for the owners of the silver mine. The site was isolated and the out buildings made it look like a ghost town from the old West. Although shabby on the exterior, most of the buildings were constructed using weather proof materials and were in great shape on the inside. The agents were highly motivated sales personnel, eager to unload this piece of property which had been highly unprofitable in recent years. They didn't use any high pressure tactics, but were enthusiastic touting the value of the silver in the ground and the rising price of precious metals on the world market. As they approached the main shaft, one apologized, "Sorry, the electricity has been off for quite some time and none of the equipment has been inspected recently. Check your portable lanterns now because it will be awfully dark in there until we get the generators on line."

David and Roger had been silent up to this point, but David couldn't resist the jibe, "Looks like the owners should give this thing away. It's probably a liability anyway. Other than the terrific view of the mountains, I don't see much value in anything here. How much are they paying in taxes?"

"Minimal. If it was a working mine, it would be different. The last few years it operated was mostly at a loss. They aren't going to give it away, but I'm sure we can come to agreeable terms."

David and Roger didn't reply as they were led deeper into the mine. After he turned on the power units and checked them out, the agent resumed his tour, "This is the main level. In its prime, millions of dollars' worth of silver was taken out of here every day. This area has been cut out of solid granite except for the silver, and doesn't need much climate control. It's almost always a constant fifty five degrees in here with very little moisture." He picked up a silver streaked rock, "As you can see from this sample taken from this area, silver was abundant. But look at the walls now, there's not a trace of the metal. The company expected to hit a larger lode of silver, but never found it."

David and Roger were more interested in the size of the excavated cavern and found it to their liking. Roger turned to the agent, "I don't see any signs of support. Has the mine been tested for stability? I wouldn't want to be in here if there is a chance of a cave in."

"Not much chance of that. It's been tested frequently with no signs of instability. The ore taken from here apparently was in a pocket. The remaining rock is solid. Deeper in the mine, there are signs of additional pockets of ore, but it's nowhere as rich as was found here."

David remarked, "It's obvious the mine was well maintained, but I'm not sure that we'll be able to find a significant amount of ore. If we do make an offer on the property and begin operations, we would require an escape clause."

"We would expect that. We think the owners would be agreeable to a reasonable down payment with annual payments dependent on finding ore."

Roger and David followed the agents through the mine finding an occasional trace of the precious metal, but nothing significant. They went back to the surface, inwardly intrigued, but outwardly noncommittal.

They waited to discuss the merits of the site until they were on a shuttle to Reno, Nevada. David was far more impressed with the possibilities than he showed for the agent's sake, "What do you think, Roger? Is that location ideal or what?"

"I think so. Although, we would need to cut an exit path for the Manhattan. It wouldn't help to build it without a way to get out of the mountain. Too much is at stake to rely on their reports of stability though. Even if our reports come back the same, I think we should reinforce the walls and ceiling with high grade steel and concrete."

"Maybe we should take a tour of the military site under the mountain in Cheyenne. They have occupied that site for several hundred years without a problem."

"If you'd like, I will go there and see how they do it."

"Okay with me, but you sound like you've already decided without even seeing the other site.

"We will be spending years at whatever site we choose and I don't relish the thought of spending that much time in the desert. The scenery here is spectacular and the air is so fresh and clean."

"At the Nevada site, we'd have to do a lot of excavating before going underground, and what excuse would we give?"

Roger thought for a minute, going over the project in his mind, "We wouldn't need much of a cover story in Colorado. We could operate it as a mine for all exterior purposes. That would even give us excuses to come and go as often as we like. Even so, we could get a shuttle in at night without anyone the wiser, although it would probably be best if we didn't try to do anything outwardly secretive."

In Reno, Army General William C. Marshall met and escorted them to the other site. General Marshall was the opposite of the land agents at the mine. He ushered them around the site with obvious disdain, "Not much of a base here anymore. The only thing going for it is its remote location. I don't know what you'd want with this place unless you're doing something highly secretive." He looked closely at them for a minute, "Haven't I seen your face in the news recently? You look familiar. I know; you're from that spacecraft, the Excalibur, aren't you?"

"There's no keeping secrets from you is there?"

"There was a decent story on you circulating around the Pentagon. Traveling faster than light makes you as famous as General Yeager when he broke the sound barrier. Congratulations."

"Thanks."

"There's nothing around here except snakes and lizards. It's none of my business but I guess you must have plenty of pull. My orders to support you came from pretty high up in the Pentagon. What are you planning to do here anyway?"

David laughed, "Right the first time. None of your business. We were going to do some research on some materials not welcome around populated areas, but I'm not convinced the desert is the best place anyway. That hangar over there is about the only thing on the site of any value." He pointed to the one building that wasn't in need of immediate repair. He turned to Roger, "Maybe we should take our project out into space. The moon might be more hospitable than this place."

CHAPTER 19

A month later David joined Kevin and the girls aboard the yacht moored in the Detroit River. In spite of her resolve to berate David for his long absence, Brenda was overjoyed to see him again, but restrained herself quietly welcoming them back aboard giving David a hug and a lingering kiss that ended way too soon for either of their tastes. Brenda and Laura were pretty much on their own as Warren and Aimee left a few days earlier. Laura was full of enthusiasm relating all their experiences from New York to Detroit. David asked, "Well, what was the most impressive sight in all your travels?"

"Niagara Falls! You should have been there. I know Mom would have enjoyed herself much more if you had been there."

Brenda reddened, "I think not. He's too involved in his work for me. I think Kevin would be better company. He's been a gracious escort for us when you were gone, David."

He ignored the jibe, knowing Kevin would be soon be absent. "We've got a few days off now so let's enjoy ourselves. Tonight, I want to take you to a Detroit Tigers baseball game, and tomorrow morning we will be at one of the most unusual places in the whole universe. Mackinac Island is a unique place where there are no modern vehicles except for fire engines and ambulances. It's a small island no more than five miles across, but the major mode of transportation is horse and buggy or bicycle."

"Have you been there, David?" Brenda asked wistfully.

"Yes, my wife and I spent our honeymoon there."

David was silent as if remembering pleasant memories mixed with unpleasant ones. Brenda broke the silence, "I'm sorry David. I keep putting my foot in my mouth. If you'd rather not talk about it . . ."

"David smiled, "No, that's not it. I thought it would be hard, but I have nothing but pleasant memories of Marie. I have mourned long enough; It's time to live again. I was thinking of how much it rained when we were there. Now, I think Kevin has an announcement to make."

Kevin stood and became serious, "I don't really want to, but I will be leaving the project and joining the Excalibur crew for another trip to O-2113 as the Executive Officer. I'm looking forward to the trip, but I will miss all of you."

David shook his hand, "We'll miss you Kevin, but this is a great opportunity for you. By the way, who's the commander?"

Kevin shook his head, "Sorry David; I can't say. The president was adamant. He asks that you not try to find out as it might adversely affect your own mission. He said, 'Someday, you will know and that should be sufficient."

"Okay, you can keep your secret. I admit I'm curious, but when President Albee says something like that, there is a good reason."

He turned to Brenda, "I guess one of the crew will take me back to shore, will you accompany me?" He hugged David and wished him good luck.

Brenda left with Kevin promising to be back shortly for their conference meeting. Kevin put his arm around her shoulder, possessively leading her toward the launch. He sat beside her, drawing her closer and kissed her. She tenderly returned the kiss, sincerely wishing him well on his new assignment. Kevin began to demand more and Brenda pulled away. He held on to her hand and pleaded, "Brenda, please don't reject me. I'm falling madly in love with you. Would you come with me aboard the Excalibur? We could stay for the entire trip or re-settle in the new world."

Brenda drew back, "Sorry, Kevin. It can't be. I'm committed to David."

"But, he will be leaving you and you know he will have no time for you once the project begins."

Brenda took off her dark framed glasses and took her hand from his, "I have no choice, but time is on my side. Say hello to your commander for me. I flew with him a long time ago. I know you will have a very enjoyable trip."

Kevin's mouth dropped, recognition coming slowly, "It's you isn't it?"

"Yes."

"David doesn't know who you are, does he?"

"No, it's hard but I think he's falling in love with me anyway."

"He'd be a fool if he doesn't! And how about Laura?"

"For her sake, she must never know!"

They thoroughly enjoyed the baseball game although David and Brenda spent more time holding hands and watching each other than the game. Laura quickly became excited with the game and interrupted them frequently asking questions about how the game was played. Laura had read about baseball, but never experienced anything like it. A pop fly came close to their position once which caused a little excitement, but they weren't able to get the ball. Hotdogs and soft drinks were their banquet for the evening.

When they returned to the ship, David gave the captain the go ahead to proceed and after they were underway gave Brenda and Laura his update. "We are now the owners of a silver mine in Colorado."

"What for?" was Brenda's quick response.

"Why do you care? Aren't you going with Kevin?" He couldn't help himself as he gently teased her. He had felt very close to her the entire evening, but every now and then, a twinge of jealousy overcame him.

"David," She began all the while shaking her head, "It's not like that. We shared some memories from when I knew him a long time ago. You know the astronaut corps has always been a close knit group."

David was relieved, but kept his thoughts to himself as he answered her question, "Well it was a silver mine and we are going to make anybody aware of any activity in the area think it's a profitable working mine once again, even if we have to haul ore in from somewhere else."

Laura asked, "But Dad, how are we going to work on the project with all that activity going on?"

"We need to do a lot of excavation to enlarge one of the caverns so we do need to move a lot of rock. The mining operation will only be our cover, not of primary concern. And we can hire plenty of other people for that operation, so none of us need to be involved."

The next morning they docked at Mackinac Island where David rented a carriage pulled by a team of horses. Laura was fascinated by the horses, since she had never seen an animal larger than a dog up close other than the wild animals on O-2113. She laughed with glee seeing the canvas bags hung behind the horses. The driver explained, "It's unnatural, but the local laws are very strict and we are required to keep the island as clean as possible."

They started off with the horses moving at a slow plodding walk which got even slower as they climbed the small hills. Laura urged the driver to go faster, but he just smiled replying politely, "Sorry, these horses work too many hours to wear them out running them. The authorities watch us pretty close and would slap us with an animal abuse charge quicker than you can say Mackinac Island. It's not far across the island and we'll trot going downhill. After this trip you can rent a bicycle and go as fast as you like."

"But I don't know how to ride!" Laura complained.

"Nothing like the present to learn." David laughed, "Sit back and relax. You'll get the hang of the bicycle in a few minutes of expert instruction from Brenda."

Brenda snorted, "Ha! You can do the honors of that yourself buster. That is if you can ride yourself."

"Well, I haven't ridden since I was here before. Marie and I rode around the island several times. But it's just like flying; once you learn, you never forget."

They entered a wooded area darkened by the overhead foliage blocking out the sun. Brenda leaned back against David laying her head on his shoulder. He put his arm around her and it felt good. He had no illusions about his future with Brenda, but for the moment, he wanted her to enjoy the vacation. Laura stifled a giggle when she saw them.

The ride ended at the Grand Hotel where they ate lunch, then sat quietly on the long hotel porch sipping lemonade enjoying quiet moments together. Laura wanted more action and David agreed to go cycling with her. David showed her how to ride and she was soon pedaling like a pro while David and Brenda had a hard time keeping up with her along the trails. They didn't care; they were taking their time enjoying each other's company. They stopped for a walk up to the old fort and watched the drama of a reenactment of an early eighteenth century court martial. Laura watched with excitement, but David and Brenda were more interested in each other.

At the end of the day, David left boarding a small aircraft for the flight off the island to the Emmet County Airport at Pellston where he could board a shuttle on his way to Colorado. He didn't want to leave, but he thought he was getting too close to Brenda and he didn't know how he could fit that kind of relationship into his plans.

David and Brenda saw more and more of each other over the next few years, but there was always something between them that left them a step apart each time they got together. They held each other, kissed frequently, but when it became serious, they would back off for a time. They talked regularly over the videophone mostly on business. Brenda was disappointed, yet knew that a closer relationship should not develop between them.

She kept herself occupied while honing Laura's flying skills in all types of aircraft and becoming a real mother to her. Laura earned her pilot's license and Brenda found some older aircraft from the National Space and Flight Museum that were flyable. They were all equipped with Electro Magnetic Engines, but they utilized wings for lift and were controlled aerodynamically. It took all the power the president could wield, but the director of the museum finally relented and cooperating fully allowing Brenda to fly and instruct in the aircraft she requested. It only took a few flights in each for Laura to feel comfortable with them. One of the most interesting aircraft they found was the original DC9 that had been modified with the first Electro Magnetics engines in the twentieth century. It flew like a dream and Laura quickly became proficient in it. They flew several different aircraft, but the simulators were utilized extensively for most of the rest of her training. The remainder of Brenda's time was occupied by President Albee with continual updates from the project, although she often shuttled to various places around the country in support of David and Roger.

CHAPTER 20

Roger had the benefit of data from the safe which confirmed the experiments he had conducted during the voyage of the Excalibur, but he didn't know details of what would occur along the way. He had lingering questions that nagged at the back of his mind, but knew they could proceed with confidence. He thought if the cycle continued, there would be an infinite number of voyages even as there are an infinite number of pasts, presents, and futures? Or would they all become one and the same? In the final analysis, it didn't matter. They had already changed history, but he instinctively knew they weren't just going through the motions, and this trip and the earlier trips if there were such a time dimension as earlier, would probably be the same as if they merged into themselves and became one.

The testing of the Manhattan took several weeks after attaining orbit as each system was subjected to a battery of test objectives with the Manhattan away from the mountain stronghold under its own power. Brenda watched from inside the complex as the countdown included bringing the time machine to the brink of sending them back into time and David and Laura out of her life perhaps for all time. She wondered if she would ever see either of them again. She remained on pins and needles until the Manhattan returned back to their mountain stronghold where it would remain until the launch.

Although the Manhattan itself was a complete self-contained community, the complex deep within the mountain contained a small city with all the support needed for day to day operation. The personnel in the complex would not be able to provide any support once the voyage began, but they had enormous responsibilities prior to the launch. Those support members would not have any extended time off during the voyages, but would immediately prepare for the Manhattan's return which might be only a matter of hours or even minutes after their departure even though those aboard the Manhattan would experience years of their life before returning. Most of the crew were technicians, professionals in aircraft and spacecraft maintenance who would monitor the Manhattan's performance particularly in the power plant and propulsion areas. They could work on the airframe of the Manhattan, although not much work was expected in that area. They were capable of modifying many different types of twentieth century aircraft and couldn't wait to get their hands on them. During the last couple of years before launch, they had procured a number of antique aircraft, which they had torn apart panel by panel, and put back together again and again. They would spend hours en route studying the blueprints and designs of several different models and be ready when called upon.

Although many of the crew remained aboard the Manhattan, David and Laura exited the ship to spend their last evening with Brenda. It was a difficult time for Brenda, who had to say good bye to Laura for all time. For Laura, it was just as hard, Brenda wasn't her real mother in the biological sense, but for all other purposes, she was more than a mother; she was her companion and friend. She loved her far more than she thought she could possibly have loved her real mother, although how could she know. Laura also felt that Brenda would be a perfect stepmother if she could leave the two of them by themselves for a little while, and so she made her excuses and went back to the ship.

David agreed as though he read Laura's mind and didn't put up any fuss when Laura left for the evening. David didn't waste any time calling the manager aside requesting the perfect romantic setting at the site restaurant where the entire crew that desired to leave the ship would eat their last meal off the Manhattan for several years. Everyone at the restaurant, and everyone who could be there from the site bent over backwards to insure this was a memorable evening for the crew. Most of the personnel on the site were aware the Manhattan would be going on a long voyage, but that was all, other than knowing their destination was Top Secret. In reality, only a few of the onboard crew knew the entire story. The site supervisor who would be left behind to manage the site during their absence wanted everyone to be a part of this historic event, but he also wanted to provide the perfect evening for David and Brenda. He found a private room and provided a candlelit dinner with all the trimmings.

David seated Brenda close to him where they could hold hands, embrace, and share an occasional lingering kiss as they ate their meal. There wasn't much in conversation as they quietly enjoyed each other's company. David waited all evening and finally got up the nerve to ask, "Brenda, I think you know . . . I love you . . . . Will you marry me?"

Brenda kissed him deeply and he thought he had his answer. She broke off and looked him directly in the eyes, "David, I do love you and I want more than anything to be your wife, but I can't . . . . I think you're in love with Marie and I don't think you will ever forget her and your memories would always stand between us."

David protested even knowing he would never forget Marie and he would always love her. He couldn't even look at his daughter without seeing and thinking of Marie, but he also had a deep love for Brenda. He begged her to reconsider, but she adamantly refused, "If you stop and think for a minute, you know I can't marry you. It's too late, and even if we could get someone to marry us tonight, I don't want to spend only one night with my husband. You are going to be gone a long time and there's no way I can go. The president has told me in no uncertain terms that I can't marry you and he wouldn't allow it for reasons you couldn't know now but someday may understand."

"Are you seeing someone else?" He couldn't look her in the eyes as he thought about her being with Kevin.

"No, David, I love you and have never even looked at anyone else since the first day we met. I have loved you longer than you know."

He was relieved, "I don't understand, but I have to accept your reasons. Will it be okay for me to ask you again when we return?"

"Yes, David, but I don't think it would work then either."

"Darling, I think you're wrong and I will never stop trying to win your love."

"Oh, I hope not, but you have already won all I have to give."

CHAPTER 21

The Manhattan hummed and vibrated slightly as the countdown continued past their previous tests. For those in the control room observing the ship on their monitors, it glowed brightly for a brief moment after reaching its orbit before it disappeared from their sight. Inside the ship, the vibrations ceased, and the hum diminished as the ship began a slow rotation in a clockwise direction which the crew soon became accustomed to. Roger reported, "Everything is normal, but I have no way of knowing the exact dates we are passing through. In approximately four years the computer will initiate the arrival in the last few years of the twentieth century. When we arrive, we will have to ascertain the correct year before we begin."

David and Laura both earned their doctorates while en route with few distractions. David's degree was in human resources, while Laura earned hers in physics studying electro magnetics with Dr. Roger Dorn. She spent much of her time with Dr. Baker learning as much about the medical field as he could teach her. She wasn't planning on practicing medicine in the twentieth century, but she didn't want to be left without recourse when encountering diseases which were no longer a problem in her time. She spent hours in the simulator keeping current on several types of aircraft known to exist in the twentieth century but primarily concentrating on passenger aircraft produced by Boeing, and Airbus. She enjoyed flying small business jets that could easily be modified with the electro magnetic technology.

Keeping busy helped the time pass quickly although she spent many hours relaxing with her father and they often chatted together with David sharing memories of her mother and family histories. Both cherished these moments knowing they would end all too soon. One evening, Laura asked, "Dad, I thought you were going to ask Brenda to marry you. What happened? Did you chicken out? You haven't mentioned her for months."

"No, I didn't chicken out. She said no . . . . We both told each other of our love, but she refused. She even said she wanted to be my wife. That's why it doesn't make any sense to me, and she really surprised me when she said President Albee would not allow it."

"I love her, and I know you love her and I really wanted her to be my stepmom. Why would the president make that restriction? Did he give a good reason?"

"Well, yes, I guess to him it was anyway, but it didn't make any sense to me. He told her it didn't happen on the original voyage back in time and changing that could drastically alter the success of our mission. She really was your stepmom in every way except being married to me. Does that make sense to you?"

"I suppose it does in much the same way I have been told I cannot marry anyone from the twentieth century. Suppose I were to marry one of our ancestors. Would that alter the family tree enough to jeopardize our existence?"

"That's the theory anyway."

"It doesn't make sense! If I did marry and then I ceased to exist, then I couldn't marry could I?"

"Your logic is off a mite, I'm afraid, but it doesn't change the fact that we have orders to the contrary. Even if you existed, you might not be the same person?"

CHAPTER 22

The Manhattan arrived in the twentieth century as predicted and the computer initiated the sequence to stop traveling back farther in time with precision. They were in orbit above the earth as they had been before initiating the leap through time. They had been secluded within the ship for almost four years without seeing anything but a blur when looking out viewing ports. Children born while en route saw, for the first time, sights of the world beyond the inside of the Manhattan.

Their first few weeks in orbit were spent intercepting news stories and analyzing the political situation throughout the world, and then narrowing their analysis to the United States, correlating their findings with their history data banks. They easily had access to all mainframe computers and could access any other computer without difficulty. They were looking for the best place to start and for the best individual that could be their agent in this century working side by side with Laura. The surveillance equipment aboard the Manhattan would make George Orwell's 1984 a reality if put in the wrong hands. In their time, controls had been stringent making sure the equipment was not used in that manner. But, the equipment here in the twentieth century was not subject to those controls, except for the authority of David Ashton, the commander. He was in fact the supreme commander, and had the power to subjugate the entire world to his control. He had no offensive weapons, but he could use many different energy forms to gain the upper hand. He had a strong tractor beam that could move huge objects, defensive shields, and mind altering stun beams that would render adversaries helpless. He could control all communications and intrude into all computer systems, which could in effect control the world. He had the technology to manufacture weapons of mass destruction beyond anything seen in the twentieth century. Although these temptations passed through his mind, he paid them no heed and went about his mission professionally.

They looked at a wide spectrum of men and women who would make suitable candidates, but were biased toward the military since they seemed to have closer ties to the government and were subject to government control. They observed military pilots in several squadrons looking for flying ability, attitude, and leadership abilities. Their council met to evaluate the final candidates where they allowed Laura to choose the one individual she felt best suited for their purposes. After narrowing the list of candidates to a few, they stepped up their surveillance on those individuals. They observed each candidate flying their respective airplanes, working with other crewmembers, watching their relationship with the command structure, and their treatment of individuals inside and outside the military. David and Roger already knew who was chosen and would make sure Laura selected the same person. Laura in this time dimension had the same data available to her as the Laura of the other time dimension, and she made the same decision validating their choice.

Laura announced her choice, "Major Brad Anderson is a C9A Nightingale pilot assigned to the 11th Aeromedical Airlift Squadron at Scott Air Force Base, Illinois. He is one of the most experienced instructor pilots assigned to the unit, with over 7,000 hours of total flying time and almost 3,000 hours in the C9 after flying several other types of military aircraft during the latter months of the Vietnam War and subsequent assignments. He has combat experience in Vietnam flying the F4 Phantom and now enjoys flying a more humanitarian mission transporting military patients to and from hospitals all across the United States. I observed his treatment of co-workers and his masterly approach in getting the job done professionally. He is polite and respectful of all he makes contact with, and has a great sense of humor. On top of all that, he is an expert pilot, unmarried, and has nothing we can see to keep him from dedicating himself to the mission."

David chuckled and remarked, "Actually, he wasn't my first choice. He's a little bit on the stubborn side, but he's a good choice. He'll do fine even if we have to knock him over the head to convince him to cooperate with us. Now we wait until we can grab him out of the sky. It won't be long as he is scheduled to fly a mission two days from now originating at Scott AFB which is scheduled to fly to Andrews AFB. I think we should grab him when he has the least number of patients on board. Will you be ready?"

Laura replied enthusiastically, "I'm ready now, but I can wait."

David turned to Roger and Warren, "How about you? Is everything ready?"

"Everything's a go in sick bay," Warren replied.

Roger was just as positive, "Everything with the ship is in tip top shape. We can put them on the beam any time we want. As soon as we get their itinerary, we can plot their course and take the Manhattan out of orbit and arrange the rendezvous. It's fine for us, but his unit will have fits when their aircraft comes up missing."

"That's okay, it will take place like history has already recorded," David replied.

"You mean you knew all along whom I would pick! You set me up, didn't you?"

David chuckled, "Yes, but that's all I'm going to say on the subject.

Two days later, they were ready. The aircraft was scheduled to fly first to Little Rock AFB in Arkansas and then on a direct flight to Andrews AFB. Roger reported, "The flight from Little Rock to Andrews will probably be our best bet. They will have a critically injured patient aboard and because of that they will have only four other patients, no passengers, and a crew of eight. That number should be manageable. They will be at the relatively low altitude of FL190 or nineteen thousand feet for their patient's best chance of survival. That aircraft is capable of maintaining sea level pressurization at that altitude. We won't need to be too concerned about equalizing pressures and that area will be generally free of other traffic."

"Okay," David replied, "let's get to work and intercept them soon after they leave Little Rock." David and Laura monitored their progress as Roger managed the speed and altitude changes, navigating to the rendezvous point waiting until the C9 came closer. Dr. Baker placed all the crew and passengers except for Major Anderson into a hypnotic trance as Roger ordered the large doors opened. They grasped the aircraft with their powerful beam, taking all control away from Major Anderson and guided the aircraft into the Manhattan. When the aircraft came to a stop on the hangar floor, David projected his voice into the cockpit of the aircraft, "Welcome aboard the Manhattan, Major Anderson! Have no fear . . . we have no intention of causing you any harm."

Major Anderson picked up the radio mike, demanding, "Who are you? What do you want?"

David's voice remained calm and unruffled, "No need to shout; we hear you plainly. We'll explain as soon as you come inside."

"What happened to my crew?" Brad asked taking into account the unresponsive trancelike nature of his copilot and flight mechanic.

"No need to worry; they're fine."

"What about my patients?" His tone was cool and disapproving with a hint of desperation. "I have a critically injured patient who needs to get to Andrews Air Force Base ASAP."

"It's too late! Your patient will die if you don't cooperate immediately. We can give her the care she needs. Please shut down, and allow us to help."

Laura and Doctor Baker waited until Brad, sensing his helplessness shut down the engines, opened the door and allowed the Manhattan crew to begin. Dr. Baker entered first asking permission to treat the patient. Brad knew he had no choice as his entire crew was in a trance and his patient needed immediate care. He stood to one side as Doctor Baker began to treat the patient, Dana Higgins.

Laura addressed Brad, "Welcome aboard the Manhattan, Major Anderson."

Brad was distracted and bewildered. He found himself stammering, "What did you say?"

Laura flashed him another bright smile and replied with a trace of humor in her voice, "I welcomed you aboard the Manhattan. Your patient's getting the best care available; she'll be fine. Please follow me." She turned and left the aircraft expecting him to follow.

Laura led Brad through the airlock into the interior of the ship directly to her father's office. With pride, she introduced David, "Major Anderson, meet my father, Dr. David Ashton, commander of the Manhattan." She left the room closing the door behind her.

David gave Brad a firm, enthusiastic handshake and spoke with the same warm, friendly voice he had used earlier, "Welcome aboard, Major Anderson."

Brad needed a moment to find his voice and instinctively reacted, demanding, "What right do you have hijacking my aircraft, drugging my crew, and bringing me aboard this ship?"

"Please, take a seat. I will explain

Irrationally, Brad shouted, "I don't want a seat; I want answers. What happened? Where are we?"

David sat back, relaxing with a hint of a smile on his face, and a twinkle in his eye, "If you'll allow me, I'll answer all your questions. May I call you Brad?"

Brad didn't look relaxed nor was he ready to comply. He sat in one of the plush chairs and replied belligerently, "Of course, if it will get me some answers."

"Brad, we need your help. You are on a spaceship which you might describe as a UFO. We need contact with your government, and we have selected you, if you are willing, to provide that contact."

Brad interrupted, "What right does that give you to hijack my aircraft, and drug my crew?" He was repeating himself, but he didn't care.

David paused, "I'll be the first to admit we acted high handedly. I apologize for the inconvenience, but no harm done."

"Oh, how nice," Brad interjected sarcastically. "You think you can get away with anything you like, if you sweet talk your way out of it."

"No. We will not hold you against your will. It's up to you."

"All right, let me out of here!"

"There's no lock on the door; not that it would do you any good. We are in outer space several thousand feet above the atmosphere. It will take time to get you safely back to your altitude and back on course." He let that sink in before pleading, "Brad, we can save your patient's life with our advanced medical knowledge. And we hope you will help us."

Brad didn't answer immediately; he was thinking, and watching a large second hand on the wall clock, silently ticking off the seconds. Would I, or is he playing God, interfering with the natural order of things? Is this guy on the level? It seemed like a dream—so real, yet beyond belief.

After a few moments of silence, David spoke, "Brad, my daughter, Laura, and I took a great risk bringing you aboard. You may be contaminated with strains of disease that our immune systems can't handle. We are risking death, and complete failure of our mission, and all we ask of you is to listen to our story. Then, you can make your own decision. But if you want to leave, we'll not stand in your way."

Brad felt ashamed of his hasty reactions. He thought of the young lady who brought him here. He remembered the lengthy and thorough decontamination procedures the early astronauts went through after returning from simple missions to the moon. He could see in his mind's eye the lovely Laura dying a slow, painful death, knowing he might be the cause of it. He answered, "You're right. I was being hasty, and I really want to hear your story."

"Good, we were counting on that. We have been watching you, along with many other pilots, for several weeks, and have selected you as our number one candidate. You are an experienced pilot and a dedicated professional officer; with our help, we believe you can gain access to the leaders of your country, the military, and your president, and effectively present our proposals to them, insuring the success of our mission."

"Now wait a cotton-picking minute! I'm a loyal American. I will not be your spy."

"Brad," he chuckled, "we're Americans too, and we feel the same way. We wouldn't want you for this mission if you felt any other way."

"What do you mean, you're Americans? That's hard to swallow!"

"It's true! Considering your generation's science fiction literature, and so many recent mysterious UFO sightings, I'm sure you must have some concept of who we are, or where we came from."

"Yes, but you don't fit the image I have of little green men."

"We are time travelers. Recalling your ideas of time and relativity, I'll say we have travelled a long distance. We are Americans, representing the United States government from the year 2603."

Brad hesitated; he had dreamed of the possibility of time travel, even fantasized about it, read books on the topic, and could partially comprehend the inherent possibilities. "I didn't think it was possible. If true, how can I do anything you can't do yourselves?"

"We are doing something that has never been attempted before. We don't know if we can accomplish anything without help. We don't know! Remember the name of our ship, the Manhattan? Do you recall the Manhattan Project?"

"Certainly, it was how we created the Bomb! Has there been a nuclear holocaust?"

"No, but, in our time, we are desperate for a solution to a problem as serious as your government faced during World War II. We created the 'Manhattan II project,' like President Roosevelt authorized the 'Manhattan project,' and our president in the future allocated a huge amount of our country's resources to go ahead with the project. It's a monumental task, hence the name. The major difference is: our problems are rooted in the consequences of your actions in our past, rather than from an external force, but the danger to our society has far greater consequences."

"Are you blaming us for your problems?"

"No. It began in your century, and has gone from bad to worse. We can no longer survive without a change of some sort. We are taking a great risk in trying to improve our future by interfering with our past. Worse case; if we change the past, we or the world as we know it will not exist, and then our mission will end in failure. We are fully aware of the risk involved when anyone interferes with the time continuum. However, if we don't, it won't matter, our future, at least the civilized part of it, is doomed."

Brad interjected, thinking out loud, "Changing the past, even in some insignificant way seems like it could have enormous consequences, particularly if someone important lived or died. It's what our science fiction writers call the butterfly effect. As far as I know, that is totally fiction."

"Truth is stranger than fiction. However, you're getting the idea; the probability of some catastrophic event occurring is high! That's why we need your help. If we did it all ourselves, the impact on our civilization could be staggering. But if you or one of your countrymen accomplishes our mission with help from us only when needed, we think the impact—in theory at least—might be lessened. We have several theories with probabilities of success that our best minds have been working on, but we know little more about it than you."

"Let me get this straight. You and the United States government in the year 2603 are willing to jeopardize all life itself in this monumental experiment you call Manhattan II?"

"Right on! This may sound threatening; I don't mean it that way, but we will not allow anyone to stand in our way and stop us from accomplishing our mission! If you won't be our agent voluntarily, then we will find someone who will!"

Brad wanted to be part of this adventure, no matter what the consequences, and didn't hesitate any longer. "What is this terrible problem that will destroy your civilization?"

"We have run out of oil!"

Brad felt a twinge of guilt for being a part of his wasteful generation, "I admit; there are many prophets of doom today concerned with what we leave behind for future generations. We use oil products and gasoline as if there were no tomorrow. But what can we do?"

"We don't expect you to change overnight the way you use your natural resources, but we hope to interject an attitude of conservation at the highest levels of government, which should help immensely over a six-hundred-year period."

"I see, I suppose you want my decision now."

"Yes, I know this has been fast and furious, but I've told you enough for an intelligent decision."

"I'm not sure I believe you, but I sense in this a big challenge, and just this morning—which seems like ages ago—I made the decision to change my present job and seek out new challenges. I will help you if I can."

"Good, now I can tell you, your patient Dana Higgins is responding well to treatment, and her recovery should be remarkable. Will you go now with my daughter to the hospital ward, and get a checkup so we can protect ourselves from any diseases you may have brought aboard. The rest of your crew is already there."

CHAPTER 23

Laura Ashton was thrilled at the prospect of guiding Major Brad Anderson around the Manhattan. She was totally stricken, tongue-tied, and head-over-heels in love since the moment she saw him in person. The improbable happened; Cupid's arrow pierced her heart with unerring accuracy. Of this she had no doubt. Her very being was filled to overflowing with incredible overpowering love. Never in her wildest imagination did she dream it could happen to her. She didn't believe in love at first sight, but she supposed that her love had developed gradually over the past few weeks during those times she observed his behavior, his manners, his conduct, and seen all the qualities that made him her first choice. She had been completely unaware, but she had no doubt in her mind. With difficulty, she had been able to resist the fluttering of her heart, and stoically lead him to her father's office without revealing any of her inner turmoil. She had never felt such wonderfully strange feelings before, probably because she had been so deeply involved in the Manhattan project over the years, and had little time for thoughts of romance. All her time and effort for the past sixteen years had been devoted to her studies, and her inputs into the project. But she was twenty-eight years old, and even though they had proven that a person could travel through time, there was no known way to stop the aging process—at least, none she knew about.

Her surveillance during the past few weeks hadn't prepared her emotionally for meeting him face-to-face aboard the C9. She thought she was mentally ready, and even though he was her choice as the best candidate, shock ran through her entire body, as she was caught off-guard by the sudden vibrancy of his being. He stood there, devilishly handsome in his uniform, and her traitorous pounding heart shouted, telling her there could be no other. She was speechless, but took advantage of his reactions, letting him believe she had the air of calm and self-confidence as she turned her back, and led him from the aircraft.

As she waited for her father to finish his session with Brad, she couldn't help wondering if his strong willpower, and his ideals that she had admired, might clash with their plans, making it difficult for him to cooperate. Some of the same qualities that made him her first choice could be personality traits that might cause him to refuse.

It was a welcome relief when her father gave the signal to escort Brad to the hospital, which meant her father had been successful. She opened the door as Brad approached, "I'm glad you've decided to join us; please come with me."

"How did you know?"

"I didn't, but I hoped you would. We have observed you for some weeks now, and I think we'll make a great team. If you refused, he would have sent you back to your airplane with someone else. He knew how much I supported you as our first choice."

"What do you mean we'll make a great team?"

"I'm going with you, and together, we will carry out the mission."

"In that case I'll do what I've wanted to do since I first saw you."

He pulled her roughly into his arms, weaving his fingers into her hair, pulling her lips hard against his as he kissed her possessively. She reacted with surprise and shock as she pushed against him, trying desperately to resist, but soon found that to be futile. Her calm facade shattered from the hunger and intensity of his kiss, and her own longing. She found herself responding involuntarily, enjoying it, reacting exactly like she pictured it in her mind, since the moment she first walked onto the C9. She melted against him reaching up, her arms encircling his neck, pulling closer, molding her curves to fit his body.

As suddenly as he grabbed her, he pushed her away. Her face turned a thousand shades of red with embarrassment, as she deeply felt his rejection, but she maintained her silence, deep in thought, as she guided him toward the hospital.

As Brad entered the hospital room, he felt the day's brightness dim, figuratively turning to night as Laura departed, leaving him alone to face the medical staff. He walked almost the entire length of the ship, but couldn't recall any details. At first he had been engrossed in their conversation, but even more in the way she walked, and the sound of her voice, so that nothing else seemed to matter except for that one moment when he forgot himself, and succumbed to sheer instinct. She was without doubt the most beautiful and desirable woman he had ever met. And now he had ruined any relationship that may have developed between them; even so, he was hooked, and had little power to resist. He had forgotten for that brief moment how he might have transmitted a fatal disease to her unwittingly. Just the thought of what he did caused him to pull back and release her suddenly, not realizing the deep sense of rejection she felt. He reacted with a startled expression as his thoughts were interrupted. "Major Anderson, welcome aboard our ship and to the ship's hospital. Please relax and we'll have you checked out before Laura comes back to show you your quarters. I see she has captured your heart, like the rest of us."

Brad was brought back to reality remembering his crew and their patient. "Doctor, did you treat Dana Higgins, or do you know anything of her condition?"

"Yes, she is recovering rapidly. She had severe trauma, but she will be all right in a couple of days. However, I can tell you she wouldn't have lived another fifteen minutes without the care she received here. I have no need to brag, but we do have the finest facilities and the latest medical equipment on board this ship."

"Thanks, you don't know how much of a relief that is. How about the rest of my crew and the other patients? Can I see them?"

"Your crew and patients are fine! They are resting comfortably in the next room under observation as you can see through the window." He pointed toward the adjoining room. "They are in a hypnotic state but can continue normal functions, as well as keep up some sort of physical exercise while they are staying with us. Dr. Ashton will explain, but basically, we don't want them to remember anything. They will be in a dream world while with us, and probably wouldn't even recognize you. As soon as I finish with you, we will take them to their quarters where they can have some privacy and rest. By tomorrow, they will be able to get around and eat with us in the dining hall. You can talk with them, but don't expect any real intelligent conversation."

"And the other patients?"

"Their medical histories are interesting to me. Many of us have never encountered any of these diseases before. You see, long ago, we wiped out most forms of cancer, arthritis, and similar forms of viral disease. It may make your task more difficult, but with your permission, we will treat them, and in most cases, if not all, affect a cure."

"I don't know how it could make my mission any harder, but go ahead if you can help them."

We need to check you over, so please step over here, and lie down on the table. This machine here will give you a complete painless body scan, and if you have any abnormalities, it will pick them out. We also need to get some blood, tissue, and urine samples to get a thorough check on you. It'll only take a few minutes."

Brad relaxed as Dr. Baker took a vial of blood, nearly as much as had been the usual practice in the Air Force physicals he had undergone in the past. Dr. Baker explained, "We plan to send one of our crew with you, and she will need to be inoculated against many of your common diseases that could otherwise kill her. We think your blood has most, if not all, of the antibodies needed to produce the serum. I hope you don't mind. I'm sure you won't miss this little sample."

"Well, I don't see how it would do any good to object. You've already done it." He amazed himself thinking of how much trust he had already placed in Dr. Ashton and his staff. He actually submitted voluntarily to what could have been labeled medical experimentation. Wasn't that the very thing that was usually reported in UFO encounters?

"Just relax a little while longer; we'll have your tests completed, and we'll show you the results immediately. Ah, this little computer can really crank out fantastic diagnoses in a hurry. Your heart looks good, and there's no problem with your lungs. Looks like you're one of the few in your time who doesn't smoke."

"I never have."

"Good! You have a slight hearing loss in the very high frequency ranges. I suppose that's normal for pilots who spend a lot of time around jet engines. Just a little buildup or hardening of your arteries; we should be able to take care of that with a short drug treatment, and that will greatly reduce your danger of heart attack, if you will take it for a couple of weeks. You have some nearsightedness in your right eye, which we can correct, if you desire."

"Doc, you mean you can read all that from this little machine! That's incredible!"

"Sure, and it's pretty dammed accurate too."

"Okay, patch me up, and make me good as new."

"Your blood sugar looks good, and you have no known blood diseases. I see you have never had the three-day measles.

That could have been a problem at your age, but I see you have been vaccinated."

"That's amazing, what can't you do?"

"Oh, there are many areas of medicine we are researching. There are many mysterious parts of the brain that we can't begin to touch. Some of the rarer diseases and mental disorders baffle us to a great degree, and as the evolutionary process continues, we regularly discover new diseases as they develop. I just need a urine sample, and we'll be through. We don't have to worry about you anymore—you are not carrying any bacteria or viruses that need concern us."

The physical over, Dr. Baker gave him the drug in horse-capsule form, and told him to take one a day for the next two weeks. Laura appeared, almost as if she had been waiting outside the door. The sun was shining again and he couldn't help but notice; she kept a little more distance between them as they made their way along the corridor.

He, too, was wary, and ineffectually tried to make casual conversation, "Gee, Miss Ashton, how can you anticipate so easily, and so exactly, when I'm finished with another phase of my initiation, or whatever you call it?"

She answered in an exaggerated professional manner, "Dr. Baker was helpful, and gave me advance warning; we work together very well as a crew."

"I sure like the way you conduct physicals! It takes hours to complete a physical in the Air Force. Although most of the time is spent waiting to see the doctor. And then, I feel like most of their tests are invalid. They certainly don't, or won't tell me anything like your doctor told me after less than ten minutes."

"Maybe he should keep you a little longer. He didn't take time to check your mental health . . . . By the way, are you hungry?"

He ignored her barb, "I didn't notice before, but I think I could eat a horse!"

She looked bewildered, "A horse! You don't eat horses, do you? There wasn't anything like that in any of the history files we studied."

Brad laughed out loud, and their tension seemed to evaporate as he explained, "Nah, that's only a figure of speech. But, surely you don't trust our history books."

Before she could respond, David walked around the corner, and caught sight of them, "You two must be getting along very well, that's the first time I've heard you laugh all day. We knew you had a good sense of humor, and we're certainly glad you can laugh after everything you've been through."

"Thanks, I'm not so sure how well we're getting along, but to keep my sanity, if I have any left, I need my sense of humor."

David introduced a few of the other members of the crew as the dinner was served. Each course of the dinner was exquisitely prepared and delicious, though Brad had no idea of what most of it was. "What is this we are eating?"

Laura chuckled, "You don't really want to know, do you? It might be horse!"

"Brad," Dr. Ashton interrupted, "It's time for the evening news. Would you like to see yourself on TV?"

"I would like to know what the reaction to all this has been back home." Brad had almost forgotten about the aftermath of his aircraft's disappearance.

"We are receiving signals direct from several of your satellites, and we'll project one of the network's broadcasts on the wall screen."

The familiar CBS television news program appeared in sharp detail on a screen that covered the wall. There was a picture of a C9 breaking apart with a question mark superimposed over it. The broadcast began:

"Tonight, an Air Force C9A, a hospital version of the McDonnell Douglas DC9, is missing and feared down in a rough area of the Great Smoky Mountains in Eastern Tennessee. The aircraft was last heard from at 10:46 Eastern Standard Time this morning when it disappeared from the Memphis Air Route Traffic Control Center's radar. The aircraft carried a crew of eight with five patients on board. Among them was a critically injured patient, the daughter of an Air Force General. The aircraft was receiving a priority routing direct to Andrews Air Force Base when the incident occurred. We now switch to our KMOX correspondent reporting live from Scott Air Force Base near St. Louis, the home base of the C9s. This is Stan Newell live from Scott Air Force Base; we have Captain Jerry White, the information officer with an official statement—

A C9 with thirteen aboard on a routine mission from Little Rock Air Force Base to Andrews Air Force Base disappeared this morning at approximately 9:46 Central Standard Time and is officially listed as missing. The FAA has launched a full-scale search and investigation, but we have very little information at this time. A list of names of crew and passengers will not be released until next of kin have been notified. I'm sorry; I have no further information at this time."

[Stan Newell continued] "We have been informed that this is the first domestic aeromedical airlift aircraft that has been lost in the history of the Air Force. The 375th Aeromedical Airlift Wing had one accident in 1971 involving the C9A; however, at the time it was not carrying patients. They have also informed me that they have not given up hope that the aircraft will be recovered. Search and rescue teams have been up since early afternoon, but have not found any sign of the missing aircraft."

The scene switched to the national news showing the remains of a small sports car.

"This picture graphically proves that lightning does strike twice in the same place. This is what's left of the critical patient's automobile after her accident involving a tractor-trailer last night in the Ozark Mountains of Southern Missouri. Officials at Little Rock Air Force Base hospital tell us that the driver sustained near-fatal injuries and was aboard the C9 en route to Andrews Air Force Base."

CHAPTER 24

Laura couldn't sleep, spending the night tossing and turning, filled with emotional turmoil. Morning came as she came to one undeniable conclusion; she didn't want to live her life without Brad Anderson, and would do anything to stay with him. She wasn't angry with him; at first she was angry with herself, but no longer. She had momentarily lost control of her body, which betrayed her with Brad, but when she was perfectly honest with herself, she was glad she responded the way she did, and would always treasure that moment, no matter what the final outcome. She could still feel the sensation of the pressure of Brad's lips, and yearned more intensely to go with him than she ever dreamed possible. She didn't want to leave her father never to see him again, but she was ready and couldn't wait to get started.

She went to her father's office to share the early morning with him as had often been her custom, either in the early morning or late evening when she relaxed from her studies. She bubbled over with excitement as she spoke of Brad. "Isn't he everything we wanted for the project? He's the best, and I think I could fall in love with him in a heartbeat!"

David had to control himself, knowing he had to tread carefully. He didn't want to throw a damper on Laura's reactions, but he must. "You have to be extremely careful. This is entirely new territory, and nobody knows how much we will change history. We think your presence will disturb the past enough as it is, but remember your promise to President Albee. Your marriage to anyone in this century is simply impossible!"

"I know—," Laura stammered. It was as though he had read her mind. "Who said anything about marriage? I already made my choice when the president told me I couldn't, but it's not going to be easy. If I didn't have those high ideals Brenda instilled within me, I could just live with him. That wouldn't be going back on my promise." Her heart saddened, skipped a beat, and her spirit dropped as she tried a new tact even though the tears were impossible to suppress, "If all the men are as egotistical as Major Anderson, I won't have any problem. Anyway let's make the most of our last few hours, and spend some time together."

David thought again of Brenda, and thanked his lucky stars that she had been there to have that kind of influence on his daughter. After a moment of reflection, he pushed aside his thoughts on Laura's romantic problems, knowing how they would complicate the mission, and replied, "That will be difficult. We have very little time. We will meet with Major Anderson in a few minutes and then we will both be busy. If we don't get to work, we may never be able to get back home."

Brad was ushered from his sleeping quarters to the dining room for breakfast and on to Dr. Ashton's office by another member of the crew, and he began to wonder if Laura was purposely avoiding him. He asked his guide, but she couldn't say, except that Laura had something she needed to do.

Upon reaching David's office, he heaved a sigh of relief finding Laura there, but he was concerned seeing her face flushed and huge tears streaming down her face. His heart skipped a beat wondering if her state of mind had anything to do with his actions, and if she had discussed his despicable behavior with her father. It was too late to change that, he thought, waiting for Dr. Ashton to speak. "Good morning Brad," David ignored the traumatic nature of the situation, "Laura is going to sit in with us if you don't mind. She will be going with you. You will agree we need one of us to go with you as soon as you see the rest of our plan. How do you feel this morning?"

"Great, I slept like a log."

"Dr. Baker had something to do with that. Have you reconsidered?"

"No, I've thought about it, I dreamed about it, but I don't have any intention to refuse unless . . ."

"Unless you learn we aren't what we claim, or we ask you to be involved in something you consider morally wrong, or some traitorous act, is that it?"

"Yes!"

"Good, you won't find any reason to doubt us. I anticipated your answer, and we have already begun a procedure that would be hard to reverse, and would make it difficult for us to put you back where you were yesterday morning."

"You mean the medical treatments Dr. Baker mentioned?"

"No, your doctors will just have to wonder." He paused for emphasis, "More crucial, we have begun to modify your aircraft, which would be difficult, if not impossible to reverse or for you to explain, especially with your memory of this experience erased."

"You're doing what?" Brad was beside himself, "I can't authorize that! And I'm sure you didn't run it by the Air Force."

"We've watched you operate for weeks now and we have great confidence in you. You've stuck your neck out, but nobody will object, all things considered. You'll be surprised what you can get away with, if you carry a big enough stick."

David turned on the video displaying the engines. Laura, completely composed, began, "We are replacing your turbojet engines and auxiliary power unit with what we call electromagnetic propulsion units, completely hidden in the tail compartment. The engine pods will contain only the compressor which will be used for your pneumatic bleed air requirements, and a drive for the accessory section." The scenes constantly changed as she talked to illustrate the main features of the new assembly.

"You have already begun this installation?"

"Yes, Boeing Aircraft which bought McDonnell Douglas provided copies of the original DC9 plans. We prepared these components to fit nicely in your aircraft. A more time consuming task," as the picture changed to show the cockpit and the electrical panels, "is the installation of different cockpit instrumentation. We're not replacing wires, but we have to sort them out and use individual wires for different purposes. In place of your engine instruments, we are installing a simple power indicator which displays a percentage of available power in use. We are including some sophisticated navigation and communications equipment, in case we run into difficulties." She paused waiting to assess his reaction.

"Why are you doing all this?"

David interjected, "These units don't require fuel. They directly convert a small amount of the latent or potential energy available in existing force fields to usable thrust. We just harness the energy, changing it into a controllable vectored force."

"Wow! Fantastic! Why didn't we know about this energy source?"

"Actually, you did! The existence of the force has been evident naturally in countless ways. Much of the earth's weather patterns are controlled, or maybe I should say are uncontrolled demonstrations of this same force. I don't understand the theory any more than I really understand how electricity can be generated by energizing a simple magnetic field. But it does work, and it will be the answer to our problems, if you can introduce it now as a safe alternative source of energy."

"But it's like getting something for nothing! That can't happen, can it? Everything has a price!"

"Let me illustrate. The earliest men saw swift-running streams and recognized the danger and power of the rapid current. It wasn't until someone invented the water wheel and harnessed that force that the river current became a powerful friend. Look at today's hydroelectric plants; they cost you nothing to operate, and save billions. We tap the same source earlier, before it's converted through rain or snow that falls on the mountains."

"What's the cost?"

"It means change! People will have to adapt like farmers switching from horses to tractors."

Brad ignored the social problems, rapidly thinking of numerous applications. "How much energy can we get from these engines?"

"The units for your aircraft are small-scale models of the same engines that power the Manhattan. We are giving you 20,000 pounds of thrust per engine. That's an increase of approximately 50 percent, and should prove more than adequate. If installed in the engine pods, there would be a problem with asymmetrical thrust, but since they are installed in the tail compartment, your C9 will become a center line thrust aircraft."

"It sounds like an awfully powerful engine, much more than needed."

"True." Laura interjected, "But, the DC9, like many early turbojet aircraft, is grossly underpowered considering your operations in and out of critical runway situations, particularly where high altitude and high temperatures are involved. Your margin of safety will increase significantly with the reduction in weight, and the tremendous power-to-weight ratio. Other than the fuel savings, it will reduce runway requirements dramatically and increase payload. It will revolutionize the way you operate. As a bonus, it will remove the most hazardous nature of aviation and that is the explosive fuel air mixture that can turn your aircraft into an instant fireball in an accident, making aircraft travel significantly safer."

"Have these been tested on similar aircraft?"

"Yes," David replied. "All our modern aircraft have this type of engine installed, but they greatly differ from a DC9. That's another reason why we need you. This modified aircraft will need to be test flown. Laura will be your copilot. I think you've always wanted to be a test pilot, haven't you?"

The images on the screen switched to a metal box-shaped object the approximate size of a standard office safe. Laura continued, "This is the most important part, and the key to the success of our mission. The entire plans and specifications for building the Manhattan are inside that box."

"Wow! Are you are going to trust me with that responsibility!"

"No," David laughed, "we don't trust anyone! The box is sealed, and the seal can't be broken, nor can the material be damaged. You probably can't even find the opening! It's the ultimate in strongbox construction."

Laura continued, "The box has a time-lock set to open in the year 2572 by the President of the United States. Our job is to get it to your President, convince him of the importance of establishing safeguard procedures, and insure that it is in the hands of the President of the United States in the year 2572."

"Why not take it back, and give it to him?"

David patiently replied, "First, we may never get back. Second, if we get back, we may arrive in an entirely different future. Third, we plan to arrive long after the president will need this information. And fourth, we don't know how all this will work out, but we are confident because we did arrive in your time as planned. It boils down to the chicken or the egg theory; did we start the process by sending this box to President Gardiner to begin the process, or did he start the process in 2572 by sending us to you? In essence the box is the egg! The Manhattan is the chicken!"

CHAPTER 25

"Brad, I want you to get with our engineers, mechanics, anybody who will talk with you. Get a good grasp of the systems and devices we are adding to your aircraft. Before you go, though, I'd like to talk with you alone."

On cue, Laura left, and after a moment of silent thought, David began, "It's going to be a couple of weeks before we get your aircraft modified, and I expect a few more days of flight testing. We have an excellent simulator where you will become fully proficient before you launch, although, you'll not find it difficult to fly. You'll be busy, and I may not get another chance to talk with you man to man. I may be a silly old fool, but I have to ask you to look after her. For Laura, it will be like living in a completely different world, and she is my only daughter; I have no one else. Her mother died when she was quite small—"

"So that's it! That's why she was crying. You'll lose each other in more ways than one."

"Yes, but please understand. Last night it looked like you two already had some sort of disagreement; I don't know why, and that doesn't matter. She's vulnerable, and I think she may fall in love with you, if she hasn't already. There's no question that she will give everything she's got to make sure this mission is successful. But she is innocent and extremely naive when it comes to men. She never had the opportunities that girls her age have grown up with. She has devoted her entire life to this project, and it means more to her than her own life. All I ask is—take care of her for me!"

"I—don't know what to say—I already care for her, and I will do what I can—"

"Brad—what I have to say now is difficult for me, and may be harder for you. Laura knows she can't marry anyone from this century. I'm asking you to be like a brother. Don't hurt her!"

"I don't understand." Brad felt an icy chill of darkness settling in around him and could only shake his head thinking, what a waste!

"She can't interfere with her own ancestors. Think about that for a moment."

"But I'm not one of her ancestors!"

"How do you know?"

The next two weeks sped by, faster than Brad thought possible, as the aircraft was modified and readied for flight. His mind was filled to overflowing with new ideas, technology, and wonder. The simulator was amazing, giving him unparalleled reality. He no longer had to spend time with fuel issues. He could hold as long as required for weather to clear without running out of fuel, and he could fly nonstop anywhere in the world. He hadn't been this excited about anything since his early days in pilot training, and was only beginning to grasp the impact on the history of the world.

The first test flight was planned for daybreak, far out over the Atlantic. To reduce the chance of being spotted, the Manhattan would run interference for them making the aircraft undetectable on radar, and invisible to the naked-eye.

After launching on the tractor beam, the Manhattan crew released their hold, leaving them in level flight just above stall speed. As Brad pushed the throttles forward, he felt powerful acceleration forces pushing him back into his seat as if he were back in a fighter aircraft lighting afterburners, without the thunderous roar. The aircraft accelerated rapidly from near stall to redline in a matter of seconds. He started to ease back on the throttles, but they were already coming back on their own as Laura laughed, "Surprised you! They are programmed to prevent exceeding redline speeds unless overridden. I guess you knew that from the simulator, but it really is different in the aircraft no matter how good the simulation is."

After a couple of hours putting the aircraft through its paces in several test maneuvers, he was ecstatic, "Laura, this thing really flies great; we probably won't even need any more test flights. It's so amazing considering, I can hardly tell the difference between what I'm experiencing now compared to what I saw and felt in the simulator."

"That may be, but my father will not release us until you've made at least a couple of takeoffs and landings, and we can't do that over the ocean."

"Isn't your father concerned that we might prang it on one of those landings?"

Laura laughed again, "He's seen you fly, but then, you forget the tractor beam!"

"Would you like to fly?"

She responded enthusiastically, "I thought you'd never ask! It's great to be out here feeling free as a bird after being cooped up in the Manhattan those many months. Let me see what this bird can do!"

It didn't take long for Brad to see she was an expert pilot as she entered a shallow climb, and began a slow barrel roll which she completed precisely on the exact heading she started, and with an imperceptible change in the rate of climb. She pointed the nose almost straight up pushing the throttles full forward. The aircraft responded beautifully, continuing to accelerate in the climb until reaching 30,000 feet where she began releasing back pressure and easing the power back, allowing the aircraft to level smoothly at 37,000 feet.

"We could play with this thing all day, but we'd better get these required checks completed. Go ahead and fly, you're doing a superb job. Where'd you learn to fly anyway?"

"I learned in a simulator on board a spaceship on a long voyage way beyond our solar system. After we returned to earth when I was about 11 years old, my friend who I considered my real mom taught me on a piper cub. She was a former astronaut who insisted I learn to fly the right way. She knew I would be on this mission and she wanted me well prepared. Actually, we obtained this very aircraft from the Air Force Museum and I got the chance to fly it. It seems strange though since at that time this aircraft did not have the engine pods installed. Maybe it was modified again later."

The heat shimmered off the desert, making distant objects almost fade out of sight as the early morning temperatures had already exceeded the ninety-degree mark. The modified Nightingale had taken to the skies shortly after dawn, this time using the Rogers Dry Lake bed as their runway. Brad picked the spot thinking there would be little traffic if they stayed far enough from the main runway at Edwards Air Force Base in southern California. With the Manhattan close by, keeping them separated from other traffic and invisible to the naked eye, they each made several takeoffs and landings, testing the flight characteristics in each of the normal and abnormal configurations. The only visible trace of their presence was an occasional cloud of dust that may have puzzled an experienced observer, had one been watching as they touched down on the dry lake bed. The modifications worked perfectly as the aircraft was rock-steady throughout the touchdown and landing. Brad marveled as their short-field landings stopped the aircraft in less than 1,000 feet and with minimum braking, and their takeoffs were completed in about the same distance. Laura remarked, "Our engineers say the landings with such a light aircraft are much improved because of the zero thrust you can set on these hummers, and, of course, the center line thrust."

"They sure are a great improvement. I think even my grandmother could have flown this baby."

"Maybe my grandmother will."

CHAPTER 26

David ordered the Manhattan positioned over the mid-Atlantic in preparation for the launch of the C9 for the historic return to Andrews Air Force Base. David and Roger watched intently, as Brad and Laura planned their strategy occasionally interjecting a suggestion. They planned to reenter the United States from the mid-Atlantic off the coast of Puerto Rico, approximating the flight path the C9s flew on a weekly scheduled basis, land at Andrews Air Force Base, conceal the aircraft, and meet with President Dugan. They wanted no surprises, yet they desired maximum control over the situation to give them a chance to get off to a flying start. They decided Brad should make two calls, one to the president, and the other to the Scott AFB command post. Brad had no illusions about his ability to cut through the red tape and talk to the president, but David assured him it was a piece of cake. Their plan was a calculated risk, but the fewer people knowing about the return flight, the better their odds of success. He thought they should have bluffed their way into landing at Scott, but they needed access to the president, and David convinced him it would be better to land at Andrews and get through to the president as soon as possible.

Their first call bypassed White House protocol, and connected Brad directly to the president's interphone. The buzzer sounded on the president's desk, and he picked it up, expecting his secretary's voice on the other end, answering casually, "Yes."

"Mr. President, this is Major Brad Anderson; may I speak with you?"

"Major who? How'd you get on this line?"

"I'm Major Brad Anderson, the aircraft commander from the C9 medical evacuation aircraft that disappeared a few weeks ago."

"You're who?" Brad had his attention. "Is this some kind of joke?"

"No, Sir! We will be arriving at Andrews Air Force Base just about three weeks late."

"What happened?" he demanded.

"I'm sorry, I can't discuss it over the phone, and there is more I need to talk to you about privately."

"Have you been hijacked? Is somebody coercing you to make this call?" He sounded concerned.

"No Sir! That's not it, but I'm not at liberty to say why or where I've been. It won't do any good for you to ask any more questions at—"

"Ridiculous! I'm the president, I demand to know! Where are you?"

"With your permission, I will be arriving at Andrews at 1400 hours this afternoon. For national security reasons, we must hangar the C9 and keep it from public view."

"That may be difficult considering. Hold on a minute." Brad waited patiently, overhearing the president giving orders to his secretary, "Major Anderson, what you are telling me is impossible, I won't deal with terrorists, or insubordinate military officers."

"Sir, I can't explain over the telephone, but I assure you, I'm not dealing with terrorists; I insist and I must have your cooperation. For national security reasons I must see you, in person, alone, before I can say more."

"I'm sorry, I can't accept those arrangements," he stated, stalling for time. "I think you should start by telling me the whole story."

"I'd like to. Believe me I would, but I can't. All I can say is the future of our civilization hangs in the balance. The people I'm working with will stop at nothing short of complete success for this mission, and I know you will be one hundred percent behind us as soon as we have an opportunity to speak with you!"

"I can't see you under those conditions. I can't even be sure of your identity!"

"I will speak with the duty officer at the Scott Air Force Base Command Post and with your permission, they can make those arrangements. They will also verify my identity. I'll be in touch—good-bye sir." He disconnected without giving the president a chance to say any more.

Brad turned around, "He didn't believe me. I'm afraid I wasn't very convincing."

"That's to be expected. If we don't succeed at first, we'll try again. Let's hope your friends at the command post will listen, and we can get through to the President that way."

At Scott Air Force Base, the same NCO who had been on duty the morning the aircraft disappeared answered, "Good morning, Scott Command Post, Sergeant Walter, may I help you, Sir?"

"Morning, Sergeant Walter, this is Major Anderson."

"Major who?" Her amazement was evident. "What are you doing on the phone? You're dead! We already had a memorial service for you! Are you a ghost?"

She kept rambling on until Brad broke in, "Hold on! You know who I am, and you know I'm alive. I waited until I knew you were working this morning; I wanted you to be the first one I talked with," Brad added to humor her a little, and hopefully settle her down.

"Where are you? What happened? Is everybody okay?" When he hesitated and didn't speak for a minute, she turned to the officer on duty, "Sir, I think you better handle this!"

The duty officer, sensing her confusion, picked up the phone, "This is Major Sparks, may I help you?"

"Bob, this is Brad. I'm glad you're on duty today." Major Robert Sparks was an old friend of Brad's; they had been buddies in Vietnam. "I know this may be a shock to you . . . Sorry about that, but we're on our way home!"

Major Sparks hesitated a moment before responding joyfully, "It's good to hear your voice, Brad! Best news I've heard all year, but you've lost me! What happened? Where are you?"

"We've been through a fantastic experience best described as one out of the twilight zone; maybe someday I can tell you all about it. I'm more excited than I've ever been before in my entire life. I'm really sorry I couldn't get back to you sooner, but you're the one I need to talk with. You know my voice, and I know I can count on you."

"Sure, but you know you've already turned this base upside down. You don't know how many friends you have until the worst happens. I don't know if we can take any more."

"I know, and I'm sorry about all the fuss. We are okay, and will be arriving at Andrews in a few hours. I talked with President Dugan, but I couldn't convince him. I told him I would be calling here; I'll bet you will be getting some high-level calls pretty darn quick!"

"I don't doubt that for a minute. Did you know he was here at Scott for your memorial?"

"Yes, I've been watching the news! At least he is aware of everything that has happened up to this point, and that should make him easier to deal with. Listen, unless your recorder is down, you should be getting all this on tape, so please don't interrupt until I finish. I can't give you many details, but I do need your help."

"Sure, Brad, the recorder is working fine, go ahead."

"I don't know if you will be questioned about it, but if you think it might be important, we could go through the identify verification procedures?"

"No, that's not necessary, I know who you are. We don't have that information here anyway. I would have to go through the squadron to get your file."

"Okay, this is important. We are not in difficulty, and everyone is in excellent physical condition, including Dana Higgins, our urgent patient. I need you to keep this secret. Nobody, I mean nobody, except those absolutely necessary! Talk it over with Colonel Brandt, he will understand. I know this line is not secure, but nothing is perfect. If all goes as planned, we will arrive at Andrews at 1400 today, and we need to hangar the aircraft immediately to keep it from the public's view. More importantly, I urgently need to speak to President Dugan privately. Those are the things I've already tried to convey to him, so far without success. Do you understand all that?"

"I understand, and I wouldn't have believed you either if I didn't know you so well, but why?"

"It's a matter of national security, and I need your cooperation on this. There is no danger to anyone; I have not been hijacked, and these are not terrorist's demands. But, I need you to understand that the aircraft must be hangered, and guarded so that no one can enter it without my knowledge. I also need a flight plan filed. If you will file a standard six eighty-one flight plan from Rosy Rhoads that will more than suffice."

"That's a big order Brad, I'm not sure we can do all that."

"Bob, I'm counting on you. I'll be ready to pick up that flight plan in less than an hour."

CHAPTER 27

Laura spent a few minutes with her father while Brad went to the aircraft to complete the preflight inspection, and assist Dr. Baker boarding his crewmembers and patients. David was acting his role making sure Laura understood how little time they had if they were going to be able to return to their time, but to Laura it was all too real. He had a hard time keeping a straight face as he allowed Laura to join Brad in the C9.

The strongbox containing the top-secret plans for the time machine was stowed in the forward cargo compartment. The rest of the storage areas were filled with spare engines, parts, and the equipment Laura needed for the introduction of the new engines. She had a wealth of technical information stored in the massive memory banks of her computer which she carried with her in a small attaché case. David insisted that she keep back up files stored with the other equipment in the forward storage compartment, even though from his perspective, he didn't think she would need them since their portable computers were 100 percent reliable.

As they passed several miles to the north of Puerto Rico, Brad descended to 17,500 feet, turned on the transponder to the VFR code 2100, and attempted contact with Miami Air Route

Control Center, convinced all arrangements were completed. "Miami Center, Air Evac six eight one."

"Air Evac six eight one, this is Miami Center, go ahead." was the immediate reply.

"Miami, Air Evac six eight one, four zero miles southeast of Grand Turk at one seven thousand five hundred feet heading three two zero. Request clearance to Andrews Air Force Base."

"Cleared to Andrews Air Force Base, direct Grand Turk, as filed, climb and maintain flight level three five zero. Squawk six eight one one."

"Roger, cleared to Andrews, direct Grand Turk, as filed, climbing to flight level three five zero, squawking six eight one one."

"Report Grand Turk to Miami Radio on one three five point one five."

"Roger Miami."

Brad pushed the throttles forward slightly and eased the nose up as they began their climb, flipped on the autopilot, and began to relax. "Easy as pie, no problems here, we'll arrive at Andrews right on schedule."

Brad observed Laura closely sitting silently, trancelike, morosely, berating herself for something beyond her control. But even her sullen disposition could not detract him from the love he felt or his resolve for his life with her. He needed to take her mind off her father, "Laura, how about checking making sure we arrive over the outer marker on approach to Andrews at exactly 1353; we want to make our arrival as close to the time I gave the president as possible."

Laura spent a few minutes toying with the computer and connecting the auto throttles that would control the proper speed to arrive on time. Unable to concentrate more than a short time, she sat in silence a few minutes before confiding, "Brad, I'm afraid." She lost a little more of her assurance and composure. "I hope Dad can make it back okay. I don't know how things will turn out. I feel so out of place, and so alone."

He wanted to hold her as he reached across the console, taking her hand to reassure her, "Don't worry, I'll be with you every step of the way; you can't drive me away. You're not alone, and your father will be fine. You've got to believe that, and since there is no way you'll ever know for sure, you should only think the best. I know he will have no regrets; he made a major contribution to our civilization's survival. Remember him that way. You'll do fine; hang in there."

"Thanks! I'll try not to embarrass you!"

"You couldn't; it'll probably be just the opposite. By the way, we are entering the United States in the normal way on this flight plan, and the customs agents will probably want to meet us. We'll just have to fake it. Do you have customs in your time?"

"No! And that's no longer my time!"

"Good, now snap out of it and let's get on with our business. You've sulked long enough!" He relentlessly continued, "It's a good thing your father can't see you now. Your father had a great deal of faith in you. Have a little in him!"

"Yes, Sir, Major Anderson!" She responded angrily.

"Well, that's better! I thought for a minute you had given up. Let's get back to work."

"Here we are swinging the Tacan at Grand Turk," she announced.

"Thanks; go ahead and give them a call." He flipped the VHF radio to 135.15 for her.

"Miami Radio, Air Evac six eight one, Grand Turk, flight level three five zero."

"Roger, Air Evac six eight one, radar contact."

"Gee, they didn't have radar down this far last time I was here. I guess they are getting more modern all the time."

"A far cry from modern; it all sounds primitive to me. I'd better go back, and check on the patients and see how the crew is doing; they should be waking up by now."

Brad busied himself with checking over the new navigation equipment, comparing the computer-generated maps on the newly installed CRTs with the islands gently passing by far below them. The islands were some of the most beautiful in the world as seen from the air. The colors around the islands varied from deep blue to light shades of pale green looking inviting for scuba diving or sailing. They were beautiful and he thought he could watch them forever, but he was glad he was going home.

Laura quietly returned, "They're doing fine; your copilot Jon can't understand why it's so quiet back there."

"The C9s are normally quite noisy the closer you get to the engines near the tail compartment. If the engines are a little out of sync, the throbbing vibrations can get to you. I hope he doesn't get too curious before we get to Andrews, and wonder why he's not up here."

"Right now he probably couldn't even force himself to stand. His mind is a bit sluggish, just beginning to function."

"A few more minutes and we'll be over Bimini and from there on over Miami and back in the States."

"Wow! It's beautiful down below. After four years without being able to look outside, I can't get enough of it. Of course the Manhattan has viewing ports in the command center, but while traveling through time, it's a blur."

"What did you do during those four long years?"

"It didn't seem that long; there was always something to do. I did a lot of studying with Dr. Dorn and Dr. Baker, a lot of exercise, and of course a lot of waiting. I'm sorry now I didn't spend more time with my father."

"Tell me about your mother."

"Not much to tell, I don't remember her; she died when I was two. My father says she was beautiful, and he's always saying he never remarried because he could never find another woman that could compare. He did find someone though, but he hasn't been able to convince her to marry him. She was my real mother."

"Sounds like your dad and I have a lot in common. There's always something between us and the women we love." Laura didn't respond; he continued, "My mom and dad are living, but Mom is in pretty bad shape. She is completely dependent on

Dad, but he has a pretty strong faith in God, believing that she will be completely healed someday."

"What's her problem?"

"She has a form of crippling rheumatoid arthritis which has kept her confined to a wheelchair for over twenty years."

"I'm sorry, that's a long time to suffer. We don't, I mean they don't have that problem in the twenty-seventh century; Mom died during that long voyage I told you about. She was an astronaut and died during a pirate attack on her shuttle. My father won't talk about it. I think he blames himself."

"Hey look out there, traffic at about eleven o'clock?"

"It's two aircraft flying in close formation. Are they ours?"

"This close to Miami, I hope so; probably interceptors sent to check us out. I don't think they mean any harm, but to be on the safe side, why don't you get your dad to turn on the force field. I don't want to be shot down before our mission begins."

She coordinated with the Manhattan, "Okay, it's on."

The radio suddenly came to life, "Air Evac six eight one, Miami Center, you are being intercepted by two Air Force F15s; they request you come up on frequency three three five point two."

"Roger, Air Evac six eight one."

By the time Brad tuned in the UHF radio, the F15 Eagle fighters were clearly visible, making a slow turn to come up behind them. "Air Evac six eight one, this is Topper three one flight, how do you read?"

"Five by."

"We have been ordered to look you over and escort you to Homestead Air Force Base!"

Without hesitation, Brad came back, "Sorry, Topper, no can do. You're welcome to look us over, but we will not land at Homestead!" His heart skipped a beat or two as he realized the critical nature of his position.

The lead fighter edged a little closer but encountered too much turbulence as he approached within 500 feet of the C9 and could come no closer—stopped cold by the force field.

The fighter pilot turned his camera on and pulled back coming alongside on the right. He could see nothing unusual and dropped back with the other fighter. "Air Evac, we had our look and insist that you follow us to Homestead."

"I can't do that!"

"Then we insist you turn around, and go back."

'Go back where?' Brad was beginning to think he hadn't communicated as well with his friend Bob as he thought.

The silence was punctuated by cannon fire as the lead fighter fired a volley across the nose of the C9. "Air Evac, that was a warning; we mean business, and will not allow you to proceed any farther!"

The C9 continued on its present course, as Brad had no intention of going back.

"Final warning, turn back!"

As Brad hesitated and didn't respond, there appeared a large orange ball of flame, and all three aircraft vanished from Miami Center's radar screen. The Sidewinder heat-seeking missile barely cleared the launcher before exploding upon contact with the protective shield surrounding the aircraft. The lead F15 was immediately engulfed in the fireball and destroyed, sending fragments of the aircraft falling into the sea far below, disappearing without a trace. The second F15 after colliding with the debris, tumbled toward the ocean surface out of control, leaving no opportunity for the pilot to eject.

CHAPTER 28

Brad glanced over at Laura who was as pale as a ghost, and visibly shaken, "Sorry, we lost the first round, let's go back to the Manhattan, and initiate phase II."

"Brad, how many more lives will be lost before we convince them we are serious? And how long will it take?"

"I don't know. But, this mission is far too important to stop now! The bigger question might be; how will the death of those interceptor pilots alter the future chain of events in your life? Could one of those pilots be your ancestor? It's incredible; I can't believe they would fire on an unarmed aircraft with the red cross emblazoned across the tail. I should have turned around instead of disregarding their orders. Maybe we should have landed at Scott AFB, it would have been much easier."

"Don't blame yourself, Brad. The easiest course is not always best. What's done is done; we can't change that. At least I don't think we can."

Brad began to suspect something else was bothering her, "What's wrong, your concern is not for our safety is it?"

"No, it's my father and his crew. This may delay them until it's too late."

"I'm sorry. We may have to resort to more drastic measures. Hey, chin up! I'm learning to place a lot of faith in Roger; he'll take care of your father and the crew."

"I hope so," but she didn't sound convinced.

As soon as they were back aboard, David announced, "Good news! Roger has been refining the computer program that creates the prediction profile. We have more time. He says we will return in about ten years. Roger has seldom been wrong before, and his ideas are sound, although his calculations are sometimes off. By the way, you shouldn't be too concerned over the loss of those interceptor pilots. Our computer search revealed those same two pilots were lost in a mysterious accident in about the same time frame."

"Does that mean we can't change history?"

"It might confirm that we on the Manhattan are no longer the original chicken! But, let's get started on phase II; Brad, we are going to reconnect you with the president. Your task won't be any easier, but you have more ammunition. Your first priority hasn't changed, and that is to convince him, you must reenter the United States, land at Andrews Air Force Base, and speak to him in private."

The atmosphere was tense inside the Oval Office; the president was furious, taking out his frustrations on his staff. General Williams, Chairman of the Joint Chiefs of Staff, was giving them a brief rundown of the events surrounding the C9 incident. "Sir, we don't know for sure; I'm sorry to admit, but we think our interceptors shot them down."

"They did what?"

General Williams squirmed uneasily in his chair, "Sir, according to Miami Center's tapes, the C9 was ordered to follow the interceptors to Homestead Air Force Base, and refused. They were given the option of turning around, and disregarded that order also."

"Who authorized you to shoot them down?"

"I had no such authorization. We simply don't know why they fired!"

"What do you mean; you think they were shot down?"

"We lost both fighters, but have no word on what happened to the C9 after all three aircraft vanished from radar. The Navy responded looking for any evidence of a downed aircraft, but has found nothing."

"I did approve your plan to escort them to Homestead, and now maybe that's the end of it. Get back to the Command Post at Scott, and see if you can put a lid on it. I suppose the major networks are already broadcasting the full story."

"I clamped down on Miami Center, and information has been sketchy for the networks as a result. Since it happened over international waters, it's easier to keep secret. I don't know how long we can continue to do so though."

"Why?"

"Well, it's too close to Cuba! You know how we broke the news to the world when the Soviets shot down that Korean airliner. We don't know how much the Cubans were monitoring."

"That's just great! Any suggestions?" The silence that followed was interrupted by the president's intercom. He answered with agitation, "I told you I didn't want to be disturbed!"

"I'm sorry Mr. President, this is Major Anderson, and I urgently need to talk with you."

"It's him!" Surprise and alarm showed on his face as he began ordering his staff, "Get this traced!" He turned back, "Major Anderson, why didn't you follow those interceptors, and land at Homestead?"

"I've already told you this is a matter of national security, and I need the protection of the aircraft as well as an opportunity to speak with you privately."

"I couldn't allow that, and now as your Commander in Chief I demand that you tell me where you are, and what the devil is going on!"

Brad replied with calculated reckless anger and contempt, "What would you do if I told you? Send more interceptors to finish what they started! You have jeopardized the lives of far too many people who are trying to help us, and now you have committed one of the most despicable acts imaginable. You ordered the shooting down of an unarmed aircraft with the international symbol of the hospital red cross, and you demand to know what's going on! I'll tell you what's going on! You have sent two innocent pilots to their death. At what point will you see reason, and meet with me. That's all I ask!"

"Major Anderson, calm down, I didn't order your aircraft shot down, and you are way out of line! You disobeyed a lawful order and those pilots had no other choice!" He turned to his aides. "Have you got this call traced?"

"No, Sir; we can't trace it beyond this room!"

"Major Anderson, what do you have in mind?" He didn't know what else to do or say, except to keep him talking in hopes that further trace action might help.

Brad forced himself to speak with a calm and restrained voice, "All right Mr. President, for now I accept the fact that you didn't order us shot down. I am planning to land at Andrews, and will do so with your cooperation tomorrow morning at 1000 hours. I'd like the aircraft hangered, and guarded until after I meet with you."

"I'd rather you landed at Homestead, and then we will talk about it." This was a compromise he hoped would be accepted.

"Mr. President, I can't do that. I wish I could, and I'm sorry, but I can't explain."

"Okay, land at Andrews, and then we'll talk." The phone went dead in his ears before he could continue; he turned to his staff, "He will try again tomorrow at ten. Let's get together on another plan."

CHAPTER 29

Early in the morning, the C9 launched over the Atlantic two hundred miles east of the Delaware coastline. As they approached the FIR (New York Flight Information Region) Brad checked in, "New York Center, this is Air Evac six eight one requesting entry clearance at point Champ." They were 150 miles east of the ADIZ (Air Defense Identification Zone) expecting to be delayed at least that long in getting a clearance to proceed.

"Air Evac six eight one, we have no flight plan on you. State your destination and type aircraft."

"New York Center, our destination is Andrews Air Force Base and we are an Air Force Charlie nine alpha. Contact Andrews Air Force Base for our flight plan and authorization."

"Roger, squawk code six eight one two, and standby east of Lynus.

"Roger, we will hold east of point Lynus."

They didn't have long to wait before two more F15 fighters appeared on their radar coming from the southwest. "Laura, let's get the shield back on and see what's up."

"Okay, it's on."

"Air Evac six eight one, Washington Center, contact Bearcat one two on three three five point eight."

"Roger, Air Evac six eight one." Brad tuned in the UHF radio, "Bearcat one two, Air Evac six eight one."

"Air Evac six eight one, this is Bearcat one two flight, we have been instructed to escort you to a landing at Langley Air Force Base. Follow us please."

"Unable Bearcat, we are landing at Andrews."

This time the fighters didn't wait, but began firing their cannons directly at the C9. Promptly, the Manhattan crew flipped the switch, and the C9 vanished from sight.

Brad turned to Laura, "I guess this means phase three."

Back aboard the Manhattan, David sadly commented, "I had a hunch that wouldn't work. But, the next phase should convince him. By the way, Roger has informed us we have about thirty days to spare to return safely within the parameters as planned."

"I'm glad to hear that, Dad." Laura hugged him tightly.

That evening at 8:03 Eastern Standard Time, every television satellite channel broadcasting to the nation instantaneously went blank for thirty seconds, with the sound replaced by a steady high-pitched tone. Immediately following, a broadcast emanating from the Manhattan began as a picture of the C9 filled the screen. "We interrupt this program to bring you this special news bulletin."

"This United States Air Force C9 aeromedical airlift aircraft was reported missing three weeks ago. The C9 is no longer missing, but the crew experienced a strange encounter that could best be described as one out of the 'Twilight zone.' Yesterday, just before noon, the scene you now see occurred off the east coast of Florida as the crew attempted to return to Andrews Air Force Base."

The picture changed, showing the entire sequence of the C9 being intercepted by the two F15 Eagle fighters. The images, clearly and dramatically showed the missile being fired from the lead F15, and both fighters destroyed while flying through the fireball—the explosion of the missile occurring long before reaching the DC9. The voice continued,

"These two fighters and their pilots, under the knowledge, if not under the direct orders of President Dugan, were lost while firing a missile at an unarmed hospital aircraft, with the red cross clearly visible on the tail. Why? Ask President Daniel Dugan. Again this morning the same aircraft was fired upon by two more fighters as depicted here."

The screen showed the two F15 fighters firing cannon shots, and the C9 disappearing from sight.

"This morning, the fighters fired without warning after President Dugan gave his assurance that he did not give the order for the aircraft to be shot down. We must ask: Why? I say, ask President Dugan!"

The screen went blank and after twenty seconds of steady tone, the regular programming resumed.

President Dugan's anger became a scalding fury as he shouted, "Why? Who prepared that damn broadcast? Why? I'll have someone's head for this! General Williams, I specifically gave you orders to escort that aircraft to Langley, not shoot it down!"

"Sir, I don't know why they fired, except the C9 crew must have refused to follow the fighters. Obviously, someone disobeyed orders!"

"That broadcast reported the aircraft was fired upon without warning!"

"I have no way of knowing if that's correct. Maybe they heard of yesterday's disaster, and wanted to be sure they succeeded."

"I told you; I specifically gave orders not to shoot it down! I want to know who changed those orders!"

The buzzer sounded on the president's desk, "Yes, what is it?"

His secretary in the outer office nervously replied, "Sir, the switchboard is lit up like a Christmas tree, and Senator North is here demanding to see you."

"Send him in—"

Senator North of Illinois, Chairman of the Armed Forces Committee barged in demanding, "What the hell is going on around here? You of all people, after what I heard you say at Scott Air Force Base a couple of weeks ago. You damn well better have a good explanation!"

"Calm down, John, I'm as baffled as you are, and I sure as hell didn't order that aircraft shot down."

"Then why are all the major networks broadcasting that story?"

"John, yes, I knew what happened yesterday morning, and yes I spoke with Major Anderson last night, but I swear to God I had nothing to do with it being shot down. General Williams, here, better have some answers."

General Williams began hesitatingly, "As far as we know, the aircraft was fired upon yesterday simply because the crew would not follow the interceptor's orders to follow them to Homestead Air Force Base. Today's, I don't know. Maybe—"

The buzzer interrupted them again. "What is it now?" the president demanded into the intercom.

"Mr. President, this is Major Anderson and—"

The president interrupted, "What the hell was that broadcast all about? I never heard of such nonsense! Why didn't you land at Langley as ordered?"

"Sir, I think we have been through all this; it seems I can't trust your word! I'll ask you again, why did you have those interceptors fire at us today?"

"Major Anderson, I regret that you were fired upon, but you've got to believe me, I didn't order it."

"We hold you directly responsible, and unless I miss my guess, the entire nation will after tonight."

President Dugan was getting uptight, "I hope you know the chaos you've caused! How did you accomplish that little charade?"

"Sir, how did I connect myself to your telephone? How did I prevent them from shooting us down? Where am I? You keep asking those questions; I want to tell you, but I will only do so in private for reasons of national security. If you don't believe national security is at stake, then go outside and see what kind of riots are already going on in the streets of Washington."

"All right, I believe you, now what do you want?" The president spoke as though defeated.

"I want the same thing I've been asking for these past three days. If you think I should trust you to guarantee our safety, I will land at Andrews tomorrow. Will you allow us?"

"Yes, land at Andrews, and I will personally send fighters to escort you."

"All right, we'll be ready. Good night, Sir."

The president turned to General Williams, "These are my strict orders, send some fighters up to escort that damn C9 to Andrews, and under no circumstances allow them to shoot at the aircraft. I repeat under no circumstances. I'm holding you personally responsible."

Senator North quietly asked, "You really don't know what's going on, do you?"

"No, Senator, I don't, but I'm sure as hell going to find out."

CHAPTER 30

At precisely 1000 hours, Brad landed the C9 at Andrews Air Force Base under fighter escort without further incident. A "follow me" vehicle met them at the end of the runway, leading them directly to one of the hangars. Brad shut the engines down, and allowed the aircraft to be towed inside, making sure the hangar doors were closed before opening the aircraft. The hangar was placed under heavy guard as President Dugan ordered, and Brad received no resistance when he demanded that everyone stay away from the aircraft, including maintenance and medical personnel. Laura escorted his original crew and patients off the aircraft to waiting ambulances, while he closed and sealed up the aircraft, giving explicit orders that no one approach or attempt to enter the aircraft.

Laura and Brad were quietly escorted to a waiting helicopter that flew them directly to the White House, and the meeting with President Dugan. The ride from Andrews was in relative silence, and Brad found himself with his arms around Laura giving comfort and peace of mind. He thought she relaxed somewhat, and was glad she didn't try to push him away.

They were ushered into the White House Blue Room, where most of the cabinet members, along with Colonel Brandt, the 375th Aeromedical Airlift Wing Director of Operations, were waiting, expecting the president to arrive shortly. Colonel Brandt welcomed Brad back, but Brad insisted he could tell him nothing before he talked with the president. On his entry the president focused immediately upon Brad and Laura, greeting them with an outwardly friendly voice, "Major Anderson, finally we meet, I can't help but believe that now we will have some answers to all our questions. Were you treated well today?"

"Yes, Sir, and I'd like to introduce Dr. Laura Ashton."

"Pleased to meet you Miss Ashton." He took her hand for a moment, looked into her eyes, and smiled and then looked back at Brad, "Now let's get down to business. Tell us about your little adventure."

"It's quite impossible until we meet with you privately, Sir!" Brad stated respectfully but firmly.

A swift shadow of anger swept across the president's face, "Mr. Dawson," turning toward the director of the FBI, "Arrest him, and Miss whoever! General Williams, get some men out to Andrews, and search that aircraft!" He abruptly turned on his heel leaving the room.

Art Dawson led them from the room where a couple of FBI agents slapped cuffs on them, and Dawson took Laura's attaché case. They were whisked away directly to the FBI building, where they were searched, and initially separated in order that they could be interrogated simultaneously. It soon became apparent Brad wouldn't talk, and they began to concentrate on Laura. After approximately an hour of no progress, they brought Brad into the same room, where he was forced to watch. If possible he began to love her even more as they began to toss rapid-fire questions at her, while she responded with assurance, expertly defending herself without giving them any real information.

"What did you say your name is?"

"My name is Laura Marie Ashton."

"Is that your real name?"

"The only one I've ever had!"

"And where were you born?"

"I was born in Alexandria, Virginia."

"When?"

"I don't think it's proper for a lady to reveal her age," the beginning of a smile tipped the corners of her mouth.

"Miss, that's not funny! Right now, I wouldn't even call you a lady. Ladies don't lie! We have checked and there is no record of anyone by that name born in Alexandria in the last hundred years. Do you think we were born yesterday?"

"I have no idea when you were born," she replied innocently.

"Miss Ashton, I don't have to tell you that you have a beautiful face. I don't think you want me to mess it up, do you?"

"This is getting us nowhere," he turned to his partner, "I don't want to, but we don't have all day." He slipped his hand inside the neckline of her dress and ripped it off while a couple of other agents held Brad motionless. Turning to Brad he said with a snarl, "If you don't want your girlfriend, or should I say your whore, marked for life, you'll talk." Brad remained motionless, looking particularly for any reaction in Laura's eyes. "Give me your cigarette, Bill!" He slowly took the cigarette from his partner and brought it down close to Laura's exposed skin. His eyes raked boldly over her body as he asked, "How much of this will it take to make you talk, Major Anderson?"

Brad could see her courage didn't waver, as she fearlessly faced the agent, but he had seen enough, and calmly spoke up. "It's time Dr. Ashton, they won't listen to reason." Before he finished speaking, the agents fell to the floor, stunned, and their cuffs disintegrated.

Now that the immediate crisis was over, Laura came to Brad, throwing her arms around him holding on like she needed all the assurance, longing for his protection. He gathered her close, holding her snugly for a moment then remembering her nakedness, reached out taking what remained of her dress and assisted her in covering herself. He removed the smallest agent's coat and helped her put it on.

She put her arms around his neck, "I'm afraid, Brad, what are we going to do now?"

He picked up a lock of her hair and caressed it gently, "Nothing to worry about, but I'm glad your father is able to help. If we can get through to President Dugan, and convince him of the importance of this mission before your father's time is up, we'll be okay. I know now what Dr. Baker meant when he said our job wouldn't be easy." All while he was talking, Laura continued to cling to him with no intention of letting go.

As they turned around to leave the room, the chief, Art Dawson entered, checking on his agent's progress. He stopped, seeing his agents lying on the floor, "What the hell?"

He grabbed for his weapon, but froze as Brad commanded, "Don't," his voice softened, "unless you want to join them. We are going out into the reception area where it's a little more comfortable. Join us there if you would like to talk peacefully."

As they walked out, Art Dawson checked his agents, assuring himself they were alive, and followed Brad and Laura out into the reception area where they sat down on the sofa.

"Okay, I'm listening, what happened in there?"

Brad spoke up, "Maybe you better call the president, and tell him you failed."

"I can't do that," he smiled slightly as he motioned to several additional agents entering the room, "Put the straitjacket on him and we'll get to work."

"Dr. Ashton," Brad again called for assistance, "all but Dawson, please!" The remaining agents fell to the floor. "Dawson, you don't have enough agents to put that thing on me. Now make that call!"

"All right, I guess I have no choice."

"While you are calling, we are going to take over your office. And by the way, you'd better call several ambulances and get these thugs out of here, and yes, we want that attaché case returned."

"It's on my desk," he replied gritting his teeth. "It doesn't matter, we couldn't open it anyway!"

CHAPTER 31

Sir, the latest news broadcasts and commentaries aren't too favorable toward you during the past few days. The media is not satisfied with the statement we made last night after that damn broadcast on all the networks. Most of the editorials in this morning's papers asked a lot of questions, but many are reserving judgment, for a little while anyway." The president's press secretary, Howard Wise, was briefing him on the latest public reaction to the activities of the previous night.

"What about Senator North?" His concern over the events of the last few days was beginning to make him extremely irritable, and he began to snap at everyone within the sound of his voice. "Did he keep his big mouth shut?"

"I don't know, but I think he's getting pressure from other members of Congress. They suspect he knows more than he's saying. I think you should hold a news conference."

"Damn it all! We don't know enough to make even a simple statement. Dawson better get answers from that idiot Anderson. Has he reported in?"

"Not yet! Give him a little time. We have one thing in our favor; we can tell them the aircraft has returned safely."

"It's not enough!"

"Why not meet with Major Anderson as—"

"Never, I'll have him court-martialed!"

Howard fell silent; he had gone on TV the previous evening refuting the previously broadcast as a hoax, and relating to reporters that the president knew nothing before the broadcast, and no United States interceptors had fired on the missing aircraft. There seemed to be no more he could do.

The president broke the silence, "Get with the rest of the staff, and start preparing for a press conference tonight at 9:00 p.m. That will give us a few hours to get some information from that damn traitor."

There was relative calm for a few moments as he thought about the events of the day. The aircraft landed hours ago, yet he knew nothing. A shroud of secrecy had fallen over Andrews, but he didn't know how much longer he could keep the aircraft hidden. The military had cooperated, but now that the rest of the crew and the patients had returned, he didn't know how much longer they could be kept in the hospital under the guise of official observation.

He pushed the lever on his intercom and shouted, venting his anger on his secretary, "Mary, get me Walter Reed!"

"Right away, Sir."

Colonel Billings, the president's chief surgeon, had recently been trying to get him to come in for an evaluation of a lump on his lower back. "Colonel Billings, why haven't you called me with a report on those patients?"

"Sorry, Sir, I've been up to my ass in alligators, and General Williams has ordered me to talk to no one."

The president laughed for the first time in two days. "Well, I guess he's finally obeying orders. What's the condition of those patients?"

"Physically, they're fine. Even General Higgins's daughter is healthy. We haven't found any signs of trauma. I'd like to get with those doctors at Little Rock, and find out why they reported her in critical condition."

The president cut him off, "What? She was supposed to be taking her last breath! What did they have to say?"

"Nothing, I haven't been able to get through. She can't tell us anything and the rest of the crew can add nothing to what we already know. It's a complete mystery. Can you tell me anything?"

"Sorry, Colonel; keep the wraps on this! Forget about contacting Little Rock! We don't want this spread any farther."

"Yes, Sir."

The president's buzzer sounded as soon as he hung up, "Yes."

His secretary warily responded, "Sir, I have calls from General Williams, General Higgins, and Arthur Dawson. They all say it's urgent."

"Put Williams on! Then Dawson, and tell Higgins I can't talk to him."

"Yes, Sir."

"General Williams, what've you got?"

"Sir, our security forces can't get near the aircraft. Several of our men have tried, but they are on the way to the hospital. There's something strange going on; it's as if there is some type of force field around the aircraft, and anyone who attempts getting closer than ten or fifteen feet of the aircraft is knocked down by an invisible barrier. It's the damnedest thing I've ever seen."

"Somehow, that doesn't surprise me! Clamp security even tighter if possible. Leave the aircraft alone until we get answers; I've got Dawson on the line."

"I've got it about secure as we can. There's something very strange going on. I don't know what to make of it; the ground crews reported the aircraft didn't make a sound while taxiing in!"

"Keep everyone away from that hangar!"

"Yes sir, Andrew's security forces have already been doing an excellent job in that area."

"Good, what about those patients and crew? I talked with Colonel Billings at Walter Reed. What can you tell me?"

"Nothing more, none of the crew members remember anything. The copilot says he saw an object in the sky which he couldn't identify, and he can't remember anything else. That story checks with Memphis Center's tapes."

"Have you any idea of the identity of the woman with Major Anderson?"

"No, Sir!"

"What about the Higgins girl? Have you talked with General Higgins?"

"Physically, she is fine, but she recalls nothing since before her accident. I talked with General Higgins briefly, and he is concerned, but doesn't know anything."

"Good, keep it that way. Keep in touch; I need to know what's going on!"

"Yes, Sir."

He pushed the intercom lever, "Put Dawson on!"

"Dawson, what's going on?"

"Sir, I don't know what to say, but—"

"What in hell have you been doing? Have you got anything?"

"No, Sir; we haven't been able to get them to talk, and now it's out of my control."

"What!" He bellowed, "You can't even keep two unarmed people in your custody!"

"Sir, it isn't that. They are here, but eight of my agents are on the way to the hospital, and I have no idea what condition they're in." He continued when the president didn't respond, "I've called for backups, but I don't know what good it will do; those two have control of a force that is way beyond me. They have taken over my office, and at this time all I can do is cooperate. Major Anderson asked me to call you and tell you I failed."

"I don't understand, but see what you can do and keep me informed!"

At this point all he could do was sit and think. All he could think of was calling a cabinet meeting, or the National Security

Council, and see if they could come up with some answers. It didn't make sense, but it seemed he was powerless.

As he sat thinking, he heard Major Anderson speaking plainly as if he were standing next to him. "Mr. President," Brad spoke softly, "don't you think it's about time we had our little talk?"

"Where are you?" He asked in amazement. Involuntarily, he looked around the room.

"In Dawson's office under arrest as you ordered.

"What did you do with those agents?" He asked accusingly.

"Let's say they will never stop us. It's more of a question of what they were attempting to do with us. Sir, do you want to know how barbaric your FBI agents are? No, I guess you aren't interested in that, only in what results they can get for you."

"Major Anderson, you're a traitor! I don't think you know half the problems you've caused. I don't see how one man can create so much havoc in the name of patriotism, and national security."

"Sir, maybe that's because you haven't listened to one word I've said for the last three days. You may wish I would go away, and leave you alone, but that would be too easy, and the mission which I have chosen to endorse would never be accomplished."

"You are making this very difficult for me and digging a hole for yourself so deep—" he knew his threats were falling on deaf ears, but was determined not to back off, "I'll make sure you rot in prison if you don't start talking. Why won't you listen to reason and tell us what's going on?"

"Mr. President, I don't like this any more than you, but the choice is not mine to make! I'm thinking right now, I have no choice except to give you an ultimatum—"

The president interrupted, "You won't give anyone an ultimatum," and began pushing the lever on his intercom.

"Your intercom doesn't work, Sir! Your staff can't get in, and you can't get out until you hear what I have to say. You wanted to know what's going on and I'm giving you a demonstration; it's that simple."

"All right, I'm listening," he said and resigned himself to the fact he had no control over the immediate situation.

"Last night, we took a drastic step and broadcast a message to the nation designed to force you to listen, and allow us to land at Andrews. We thought it was enough to gain an audience with you, but not so. How much more will you suffer before you grant my simple request to see you alone for a few minutes to discuss a matter of national security? I have no intention of giving up until I see you privately." He paused for effect, "Have you ever watched someone tortured? Of course not. Tonight at 7:05, you can join the entire nation watching as your agents tear the clothes off Miss Ashton, and attempt to scar and permanently disfigure her under your orders."

"I never gave such an order!" He vehemently protested. "And even if I did, it was only because you are refusing to cooperate."

"I've heard better excuses from children!" Brad lashed out relentlessly, "You told Mr. Dawson to get the information, and left it entirely up to him how he would do it. It doesn't matter, the nation will judge you and only you on what transpires. I'm not sure how much more we will show, but I don't think your presidency can stand much more. You are likely to be impeached, and ousted from office. That would really be a disaster, considering who would take over the presidency. It occurs to me that you might fear for your safety. I can assure you of one thing for certain. The people I am working with have unlimited power to inflict harm on you directly. If that was their desire, they would have already done it. You can be assured that no physical harm will come from us. We could have used force a long time ago."

"I am aware of that. I'm concerned, but I believe that much."

"Good, because this is my ultimatum: unless you agree to meet alone with us in your office tonight, that message will be broadcast at 7:05. It's up to you."

As soon as Brad stopped talking, the intercom lit up like a Christmas tree, and there was a loud commotion with his staff pounding at the door which continued until the president flipped the intercom switch again and called, "Get me Dawson!"

CHAPTER 32

The president's limousine arrived within the hour to take Laura and Brad directly to the White House. In the meantime, Dawson's secretary found another dress to replace the one Laura had been wearing. The dress wasn't nearly as beautiful as the one needing replacement, but as she modeled it for him, Brad's appreciative eye traveled from head to toe as he spoke in a tone filled with awe and respect, meaning every word, "Laura, you're the most beautiful woman I've ever seen!" He thought to himself, 'With or without clothes.'

They arrived with little fanfare, and were ushered directly to the Oval Office, to meet the president who closed the door behind them. "Welcome to the White House, Major Anderson." The president seemed calm and spoke in an outwardly warm and friendly manner, although Brad knew he was seething inside. "And Miss Ashton, it's a pleasure to see you."

"Thank you Mr. President, it is indeed an honor." Laura spoke sincerely and gave him a slight smile before going about her tasks, opening her case operating the sensors on her computer.

Brad shook his head negatively and motioned with a slight wave of his hand for the president to pay no attention to what she was doing as he greeted him. "Sir, I'm relieved. I'm sorry we had to meet this way, however, I'm glad you agreed to meet with us without further delay."

The president's voice lost some of its friendly tones as he spoke, "I'm tired, so quit playing games, Major, let's get down to business."

Brad stalled, "After, we had our little agreement, Mr. Dawson treated us well. I don't know where he found the dress for Laura so quickly, but it fits her well."

"Brad," Laura interrupted, "I'm finished."

"Good, how many?"

"Seven! Plus the tape recorder he was using."

"Thanks," he turned his attention to the president, who stood astonished, not knowing what to think. "Sir," he went on, "we did a quick scan of your office, and found seven bugs. They are disabled, as well as your tape recorder. Sir that should explain why I could say nothing before."

"But, I—I had the office checked yesterday!" exclaimed the president.

"Laura, why don't you point them out so he will believe us, and we can get on with our work?"

Laura quickly found five of them which were well hidden but not difficult to find. "Sir, the other two are embedded in the wooden paneling of your desk right about here and there." She pointed out the exact places where they could be found. "I wouldn't want to destroy your desk digging them out, but it looks like they've been there a long time."

President Dugan shook his head as Brad pointed out, "I think the FBI can analyze these, and discover who manufactured them. Brad suggested, "Sir, why don't you sit down, and we can get started?" He continued as the president sat down, shaken. "The story we are about to tell may sound unbelievable and far-fetched, but it's true."

The president sighed, "It seems as though you may have an apology coming. Please accept it. You were saying?"

"I'd like to introduce you to Dr. Laura Ashton, who you saw earlier today, but didn't properly recognize as the expert she is, and why she is here."

"I'm sorry Dr. Ashton, Major Anderson is right, I've been a fool. Please go on. I've got many questions, but they can wait."

"Apology accepted, Sir, and please call me Laura."

"All right, Laura."

Brad continued, "Three weeks ago when our aircraft was reported missing—we had an experience with a 'UFO.' No one has yet proven the existence of such phenomena, unless you or the Air Force has purposely kept that information classified. Let me assure you, they exist, or at least one such vehicle exists. Our aircraft was drawn into that vehicle which is comparable in size to our own fictional Enterprise of Star Trek fame." Brad paused to assess President Dugan's reaction.

The president sat back farther in his chair and spoke in a reserved manner, "I don't believe a word of what you're saying, but I'm listening. Go ahead."

"The vehicle was built by the United States government, and completed in 2603, over 600 years in the future. Laura represents the future President who gave the authorization for the craft to be sent back into our time."

"I find that hard to believe, but go on."

"I did too, Sir, and you know how stubborn I can be."

"I do; that's why I'm listening."

"I don't want to disillusion you in any way, but right now you are powerless to leave this room or use your phone, unless those in control of the UFO allow it. They would allow you to conduct any business they deem of a dire nature, but they will be the judge of that. This is not a threat, but I think you will have time to hear us out! You can test the door or the phone if you like."

"I see; that's not necessary. I believe that much."

"If you had been on that ship the last couple of weeks as I have, you would have been convinced, or thought you were dreaming, and in either case, it's not an unpleasant experience." He looked over at Laura and smiled, "See what I mean?"

"I think I do," he said with a twinkle in his eye.

"In any case, the ship christened the Manhattan is orbiting overhead, and providing us with the capability to communicate like we did with you earlier, to broadcast over every satellite network in the country, or to neutralize any force that attempts to stop us, as those thugs you hired as FBI agents found out the hard way. The Manhattan is also providing a force field around the C9 in the hangar at Andrews, protecting it from anyone attempting to enter against my orders. Those military police or maintenance personnel innocently trying to investigate the C9, I suppose under your orders, will be okay in a matter of hours. How many of these occurrences will it take for you to believe us, Sir?"

"We have a common trait. Stubbornness! I don't make up my mind in a hurry, but I'll admit I can't find any other plausible explanation for what has occurred. What about the rest of your crew and the patients?"

"Medical expertise six hundred years in the future is far beyond ours; they simply took care of Dana Higgins, causing her body to speed up the normal process and completely heal itself. The rest of the crew and patients received similar medical help, but were under another type of demobilizing force, sort of a hypnotic state, that prevented them from remembering any of the events they were part of."

"And the interceptors?"

"Unfortunately that shouldn't have happened. Naturally, we were protecting the aircraft with a force field which the missile couldn't penetrate. The missile barely left the first interceptor when it struck the force field, and the ensuing fireball destroyed both fighters. They were far too close, and we didn't expect them to fire at us. We were ready when the second pair fired from far enough away to allow time for us to prevent a recurrence. Can you explain why they fired?"

"No, those were not my orders. I've already ordered a full investigation. I promise you we'll find out why."

President Dugan seemed to warm to the story, and looked much more interested as Brad continued, "Laura has a marvelous little computer with mainframe capacity there in her case which she has programmed to show you more about the Manhattan, and then we will discuss our mission."

Laura began by projecting virtual reality images in the room. "What you see is an image of the Manhattan in orbit over Washington. It's invisible because of a warping of the reflected light and radar frequencies. That technology is an advanced version of the 'stealth' aircraft that fly here in your time." She spent nearly an hour going over details of the ship and some of the technological advances that could be demonstrated on her computer that she was free to divulge. She then activated the medical programs and scanners demonstrating how their physicals were conducted. "I think you'd better have that cyst removed from your lower back; it shows signs of malignancy."

"How did you know about that? Dr. Billings has been trying for weeks to schedule me into surgery to remove it."

"I think that should prove to you we are who we say we are," she replied easily. "Now we will release our hold on your phone system."

Almost before she stopped talking, the buzzer sounded on the president's desk. He pushed the intercom lever answering, "Yes, what is it?"

His secretary heaved a sigh of relief, "Sir, I've been trying to get through to you for over an hour! Howard is ranting and raving about a press conference due to start in fifteen minutes. Almost every staff member is out here demanding I let them break the door down and find out what's going on. The Secret Service agents are beside themselves."

"Get the cabinet together and let them choose a few congressional leaders, and have them ready to meet with me in one hour. I'll call Howard in here in about five minutes." He turned to Brad, "I've got to say something to the American people. I scheduled a press conference for nine, thinking I would have some answers by then." He looked questioningly at Brad and Laura, "I can't imagine where the time has gone!"

"Sir, under the circumstances, we might be able to help you with a prepared statement that your press secretary can release to the public. I'm sorry we had to go to such an extreme as we did in that broadcast, but we are under a deadline which can't be moved forward under any circumstances."

"I guess I deserved that, but now—what do you suggest? Until I know the entire story, I don't know what to release."

Laura spoke up, "Let me suggest this to be read by your press secretary:

'Last night's broadcast was not sanctioned by the president. The president did not order the interceptors to shoot down the C9. As you members of the news media know, that story was unauthorized and broadcast on most networks without approval of this office or any of your networks, but was perpetuated by some unknown persons. Our earlier information was incorrect; the interceptors did fire on the C9, and in the process destroyed two of their own in one case, and were only firing warning shots in front of the C9 in the other. The C9 was intercepted as a matter of national security when it appeared off the east coast of the United States without proper flight authorization. The circumstances of this incident are under full investigation. The C9 landed safely at Andrews Air Force Base this morning at ten o'clock Eastern Standard Time, and all crew and patients are safe under observation at Walter Reed Medical Center. The president will give you more details as soon as more details are known. Thank you.'"

"Thanks Laura, I think that will do fine until we can discuss this further. Do you think you can repeat that for my press secretary when he comes in?"

"No need, I'll have a printout for him in a minute." She grinned, giving him a look which made him laugh out loud.

"I think I met my match in both of you." He flipped the intercom lever, "Send Howard in." Howard came in taking the paper the president handed him. "Howard, just read that, and don't give out any more details. That should be easy, since you don't know any more. Apologize for me for not being able to attend. You can tell them that I will be in session with the cabinet and we are working on the matter." He paused as Howard read the paper, "And by the way, get General Williams to personally take care of notifying the families of those two fighter pilots, and have him give them my sympathy."

"Sir, this is brief and to the point, but I don't think it will satisfy anyone."

"I suppose not, but that's all they will get for now. If they ask for more, tell them you're sorry, but it's the truth and that's all you know. Promise them a more complete news conference tomorrow which should get them off your back. And I want you in the staff meeting if you can get back soon enough."

"Thanks, Sir; I'll do what I can."

As soon as the door was closed and locked, Laura spoke up, "Sir, another bug was activated, but I've taken care of it. It sure looks like somebody wants to know what's going on in here."

"Sir," Brad broke in, "it looks like somebody didn't want us to return. As an Air Force Officer, I don't think those interceptor pilots would have shot at us, on their own, without a heck of a lot more justification than that."

"I agree; now let's continue where we left off."

"Mr. President, everything we have told you so far is yours to do with as you like. I'm sure you will want your staff partially informed. It probably wouldn't be a good idea to inform the rest of the nation about a UFO, but that's up to you. We have some suggestions along that line that might help which we can discuss before tomorrow's press conference. The rest of our information is the heart of our mission. Please treat this as information 'for your eyes only,' as it is vital to the preservation of the world's civilization in the twenty-seventh century."

Laura began her computer show once again, "Essentially, our civilization has depleted the world's supply of oil, and our mission is to bring you enough advanced technology, to allow you to reduce your consumption and waste of petroleum reserves, so we will have enough for our own needs in the twenty-seventh century and beyond. The C9 has been modified by our crew on the Manhattan and is now equipped with electromagnetic propulsion units and systems which will accomplish our goals, if similar equipment is manufactured and installed on all military and civilian aircraft worldwide. Following those installations, we will help with the transition with this type of power for all transportation systems including private automobiles."

"Is that why the C9 was silent while taxiing in?"

Brad grinned, "That's right! They make very little noise."

Laura paused for a moment before continuing, "The second part of our mission is where you come in, and it is the most difficult. If you choose to accept, it is to insure that once our mission is accomplished and our future civilization has enough oil to meet their needs, my president in the twenty-seventh century will fund the 'Manhattan II project' and allow the cycle to take place. This black box pictured here is what we could classify as a 'super-safe' and cannot be opened, even in our time, with any known technology before the time lock expires in the year 2583. As you can see from these demonstrations, it's impervious to all sorts of explosives, acids and any known substance. It can't be opened before its time has expired short of utterly destroying it with a nuclear blast." She went on to explain the contents and the president's part in preserving the secret and providing the needed information to his successors until it would be opened.

"Mr. President," Brad interjected, "You see we are now confronted with the 'chicken or the egg' question. Did their generation—'the chicken'—initiate this exchange of technological data, or did you send this 'egg' that explained the process and convinced them to build the Manhattan? The black box and all the other equipment we have mentioned are on board the C9 and that is why we are protecting it with the shield."

David cut into their conversation, "Laura, it looks like all is well now and we've got to leave. We wish you the best and will be checking on you and your progress in the future. Goodbye."

Laura was sad but comforted, and replied, "Goodbye Dad." That was all she said because she knew he had already signed off.

As far as Brad and Laura were aware, the Manhattan was on its way back to the future as planned, but that wasn't in David's plans. He had more information from the black box that he couldn't share with Laura because of the delicate nature of the balance between the first event and future events. They believed that Laura had to experience the same problems and solve them in the same way if their mission would be guaranteed a success. Other scenarios could be successful, but why change something that worked when further interference could be disastrous. In previous voyages back in time according to the logs and information contained in the black box, the Manhattan did return immediately to the future only to discover they must return to rescue Laura and Brad from sure disaster in terms of mission success. This time they would remain in the twentieth century until all those situations were cleared up.

He knew the date of the next problem that would occur and was no longer in doubt of what was needed to be done to correct the situation. They had several weeks before that date and David decided to make the most of it. He called Roger and the council back in session. He began, "I know you all expect us to begin our journey back home, but that's not what we're going to do. On the 24th of next month, Brad and Laura will be scheduled to meet with the oil producing corporations in Dallas. History records they did that and after their session as they were leaving the building, they were gunned down by assassins waiting in ambush on a rooftop across the street. We are going to be here to insure that doesn't happen."

Roger whistled, "Whew, that's the advantage of recorded history. How can we prevent it?"

"No problem, we'll intercept them before they get to Dallas and let the FBI take care of the assassins. In the meantime, we have another project President Albee asked us to tackle. He asked me to go back and observe the events surrounding the life of Jesus Christ. We aren't to interfere, just observe and record the events for future reference."

Roger interjected, "That's a big undertaking, David. If we project our timeline, compared to our trip here, it would take much longer. That's 2000 years rather than 500 which off the top of my head means we could be as much as 16 years en route one way. We'll definitely be old men before we return."

"Well, it's not as long as we originally thought. According to the black box, the return trip didn't take very long and your calculations were wrong on that end. However, I want you and Warren to study the problem and let me know if it's possible to put everyone in the deep sleep mode for most of the voyage back to the first century. You could even set up an alternating schedule where someone is always on duty monitoring the ship's progress and insuring we don't continue to sleep until we reach prehistoric eras and beyond with no hope of ever returning. I think that you, Roger and Warren, can even participate in the sleep program. I intend to as I want to be alive when we complete our mission."

"But, David, how can we trust the ship to perform that well while we sleep? It's not a comfortable thing to do."

"I understand that and so does President Albee. It's his supposition that the ship will perform as it has in the past, that is flawlessly. We proved that on our voyage here. But even so, if something does happen, you could probably do nothing to prevent it anyway. Just think on it and let me know."

"Okay David, we'll work it out. I'm warming to the idea already. We knew this was a mission to the unknown and it's just going to be more of the same. My only reservation right now is, if we don't get back here safely, we won't be able to prevent Laura's death in Dallas next month."

"You have a valid point. We will prepare for the trip now, but wait until we complete our mission here and then go back to the first century before we go back home."

CHAPTER 33

The days were filled for Laura and Brad as they set up a new organization they called the Solar Magnetics Administration at Wright Patterson AFB. True to his word, President Dugan set them up with all the personnel they needed, and even granted Brad a spot promotion to Lieutenant Colonel. He appointed Charles Bains, an experienced administrator, to assist Brad and Laura in the formal organization which was set up to quickly and efficiently provide the engine technology to all engine manufacturers. Procedures were established to begin the process of modification of all aircraft fleets, beginning in the United States and spread throughout the world. Aircraft were selected first because of the greatest cost and energy savings, but the technology would eventually spread through the automotive and transportation infrastructure.

Arthur Dawson, the FBI chief, while investigating the firing on the C-9 by the interceptors along with the electronic bugs found in the White House, discovered an elaborate scheme to control the destiny of the nation through the control of the supply of oil for centuries to come. He was at a standstill having much of the details, but lacking evidence to arrest the perpetrators. It was a pretty tall order since their chief suspects held chief spots in the current administration, and were difficult to get to. Dana Higgins' accident was no accident, but was part of a plot to take control of ArkTex Oil Company. General Higgins had ordered the murder of his daughter, to allow him to maintain control of ArkTex Oil Company which Dana would have inherited from her mother when she turned 21, and participated in another attempt on her life just days after her release from Walter Reed. Laura and Brad had discovered their treachery and hired Dana Higgins as their receptionist changing her name to Danielle Black to protect her identity. Clifford Burns, director of the CIA, and James Little, the vice president had joined forces with General Higgins several years earlier forming the EMI Corporation which was involved in quasi legal arms sales to third world countries. Control of ArkTex was essential to their plans of controlling the world's oil supply

After their harrowing experiences with the interceptors, the FBI, and the drama of getting through to the president, Brad had asked Laura to marry him several times disregarding David's request, but Laura would have none of it. He tried to convince her he never would have married another woman, but Laura remained resolute turning down his every proposal of marriage. His declarations of love only pushed her farther away as it was the only way she could resist him. He was at wits end not knowing how to proceed as long as Laura remained true to her promise to her president from the future. Brad had taken her home to meet his parents, and Laura had fallen in love with his family, and it broke her heart to tell his mother that there could be no relationship between her and Brad.

The 375th Aeromedical Wing at Scott AFB wanted their airplane back, and Brad couldn't put them off any longer. He planned to spend a couple of days at Scott, flying a couple of local training missions checking out the wing standardization officer before he delivered it to McDonnell Douglas Corporation for the certification process. Laura was providing the technical data that needed to be included in the aircraft manual before the aircrews could be trained.

Alex Newsome, the CEO of the Lear Jet Corporation, agreed to provide them with the latest model 55 for the Solar Magnetics Administration. In turn, Lear would get a couple of engines, install them, and get the Model 55 certified. This provided Lear with a considerable advantage putting them one step ahead of the competition, and providing invaluable free advertising as Brad and Laura flew the Lear from place to place conducting the business of SMA. Lear Corporation would not be able to obtain any additional engines any sooner than their competition, but Brad felt that it was to their advantage. Before returning to Scott for the training, they needed to stop in Dallas for a meeting with the oil producers which President Dugan invited them to attend. Alex Newsome agreed to deliver the Lear to them at Long Beach which they could fly with the conventional engines until Laura could provide the technical support needed for the engines to be installed on the aircraft.

Laura was flying from the left seat as she and Brad departed Wright-Patterson early in the day for their flight to Dallas. He was reluctant to give up any chance of changing Laura's resolve, but he knew, he would be tormented continually, working side by side with her, believing she would never agree to be his wife. He remained silent as the minutes ticked away occasionally glancing over marveling at her beauty, but seething inside knowing he had promised to stay with her, and that wild horses could not take him away. Finally he broke the silence, "Laura, I—I love you, and I always will, but after we deliver the aircraft in Long Beach, I think we'd better go our separate ways. I—"

"No Brad!" Laura was shocked, and fell into an immediate state of depression, "Please—" She pleaded with deep blue yet soft doe-like eyes that tore at Brad's very soul.

"I'm sorry, but I can't continue this way. I would only continue to say those things that would hurt you more each day. I'm sorry I said I would get Dana to marry me; I didn't mean it, but I can't help myself. I think you will get along fine with Bains, and the rest of the organization we've set up. Dana will stay with you, at least until her father is prosecuted, and I'll continue to work with you from the White House or the Pentagon, as long as you and President Dugan want it that way."

Laura sat stunned, tears streaming down her face; she sobbed, "I wish—I wish I'd stayed with my father on the Manhattan."

Brad tried to concentrate on the scenery below, and the puffy white clouds as they drifted by—and suddenly exclaimed, "Look, Laura, look over there!"

"What?"

"It's the Manhattan!" It couldn't be, but there it was, getting bigger by the minute as the familiar black rectangular opening came into view.

"Brad, I'm sorry, I don't really want to go back with my father. I want to stay here with you . . ." She hadn't comprehended what was happening, but she instinctively knew her last words were wrong and out of place.

He glanced at her, seeing the agony there. "Honey, I understand; I don't know what we should do. I want to stay with you but . . ."

"Brad, I do love you!"

"I know." The Manhattan was getting larger and Brad could see Laura was no longer controlling the aircraft as they were drawn into the Manhattan.

CHAPTER 34

Laura's father met them as they climbed out of the aircraft, and threw his arms around Laura and Brad in turn giving them a warm welcome. There was no need for words as Laura clung to her father as he led them inside.

Brad couldn't contain himself any longer, "Why didn't you go back?"

"We did!" David was enjoying their amazement, and savoring every moment of it.

"Well, out with it!" Laura demanded. "Tell us what happened, and why you came back!"

David Ashton became serious as he replied spinning his little white lie, "Laura, we did return, but discovered we had to come back, to prevent someone from murdering you and Brad in Dallas. We discovered that history recorded that you and Brad were assassinated. The only way to prevent it was to come back, and prevent you from going to Dallas. I suppose we could have stopped the attempt by protecting you with the force field, but we have to do it the same way it was done before."

"But, you don't look old enough to have made the return trip!" Laura was disbelieving.

"Well, I took advantage of the deep sleep option. Actually Dr. Dorn made a slight calculation error. Remember how we originally thought that our travel to the twentieth century would only take a few hours? We had it reversed. We actually went forward in time to the twenty-seventh century in just a few hours elapsed time." He briefly told them the whole story, and then turned to Brad, "Your assassins were never found. How about getting hold of your FBI contact, and maybe they can be trapped in Dallas? They should be found on the hospital rooftop across the street from the Dallas Convention Center and will make the attempt as the sun is setting this afternoon. Tell them to be careful, they have high-powered rifles, and have a helicopter for a getaway. And be sure and tell Olson not to take part in that raid. If he does, he will be killed. That's what history recorded.'"

Brad left Laura with her father as he went to the communications room to get in touch with Arthur Olson, the FBI agent who had been working with Brad attempting to uncovered evidence to convict the individuals in the conspiracy. Laura turned to her father, throwing her arms around him sobbing. He tried to comfort her, "It's okay, that's only one of the possible outcomes of your time period; everything will work out fine."

She only sobbed louder, "Dad, I'm sorry; I can't handle it."

He let her cry until she finally ceased sobbing, and looked him in the eyes, "Dad, I love him. What am I going to do?"

"There, there, it can't be that bad." He tried to comfort her, thinking she was upset over the assassination, and then it dawned on him. "It's okay, Laura, it's okay. Does he love you?"

"Yes, he asked me to marry him. He tried to convince me that he wouldn't have married anyone else, but I wouldn't—I couldn't. It broke my heart to tell him that. I—I think he was teasing, but he even threatened to marry Dana. And today, on the way to Dallas, he said he couldn't stay with me, because, well—it's just too difficult. I can't stay here if he leaves."

He couldn't hold back any longer, and laughed deep and long. She protested, "Daddy, it's not funny, I'm going back with you."

He stopped laughing, "Darling, that's exactly what I was tempted to suggest until this moment, but it's your choice. You could educate someone who could carry on in your place if you haven't already got someone up to speed. However, I don't think that's what you want, and maybe I can help." She listened intently as he continued, "I said you and Brad were murdered. That didn't change me, or you, or the future in any way, as far as we can tell. I think you can safely marry him, and be happy."

"Oh, Daddy!" She hugged him even tighter, "That's the best news I've heard all year." And she began crying again, this time overflowing with joy.

"I think you'd better go down to sick bay, and let Dr. Baker check you over. I'll send Brad down after Dr. Baker finishes with you."

"Okay, Dad, anything you say." She winked back at him before going out the door.

Brad tuned into the switchboard at the FBI headquarters and Olson's extension and waited only a minute, "Arthur Olson, may I help you?"

"Arthur, it's Brad.

"Where are you calling from, I thought you were supposed to be in Dallas."

"I was, and as far as the rest of the world is concerned, that's where I will be. I can't explain how I know, but there are assassins on the rooftop of the hospital overlooking the entrance to the Dallas Convention Center with high-powered rifles waiting for us to show so they can gun us down."

"Don't you think you're being a little paranoid? Why do you think someone is trying to kill you?"

"I don't think someone is trying; I know someone will try! This time, we were tipped off and, no, I can't tell you who gave us the tip. Listen carefully, you don't have much time. We are not going to Dallas, but if you could send decoys out to meet the television newsmen after the session, maybe with bulletproof vests, and catch the assassins in the act, you might be able to find out who hired them. They plan on using a medevac helicopter on the rooftop for their escape. And be careful, their timing is critical; they will make the attempt as the sun sets behind the hospital making them invisible in the glare."

"I'm not convinced, but, we'll take care of it from here."

"I'm deadly serious! If you are not a hundred per cent behind me on this, then I will go over your head and call your boss or the president. It's that important to me."

"All right, I understand; I don't know why, but I will make sure we do this right. We will be ready for them.

"And one more thing and this is really important. You are not to be involved personally in that raid. Believe me when I tell you that if you do, you will be killed."

"Now, you're really making me wonder, but my boss has me convinced that I need to take you seriously. I won't be anywhere near that hospital or the Convention Center."

"I'll be back with you soon as I can."

Brad disconnected, and tuned in the Scott Air Force Base telephone switch finding the proper connections to put himself on the DO's intercom on the first try. Colonel Brandt was expecting another call from the command post, and answered immediately, "Colonel Brandt."

"This is Colonel Anderson, how's everything at Scott?"

"Well, better now! I'm glad you called. We just got word from Kansas City Center that our aircraft is missing again. Where are you?"

"Sir, it's a long story, but we're back in Manhattan. I think you will understand without repeating, or asking any more questions. However, we need a cover story! May I suggest that you have the command post call Kansas City Center, and inform them that we had a little electrical difficulty with radio and transponder failure, and have returned safely VFR to Scott?"

"I understand. Maybe you can tell me more next time. Thanks for calling."

Brad left the communications center to talk with Dr. Ashton confident there would be no undue publicity surrounding the missing aircraft. He found David alone, watching a news station on the television monitor.

"Come on in Brad, I've got the news on so we can keep up to date on what's happening."

"Where's Laura, I expected you two to have a lot to talk about?"

"She's with Dr. Baker. I've been a little concerned, and I wanted Dr. Baker to find out how she is holding up under the strain. I'd like you to see him as soon as Laura finishes."

"Sure, Dr. Ashton, but first I need to talk with you. It's about Laura, she—I mean—I—this is more difficult than I thought. She says she loves me, but she can't marry me; what you told me earlier is not—I mean I could never marry another woman." Brad managed to get it all out wondering whether he should have confided in her father. When David didn't say anything right away, Brad continued, "I'm sorry, maybe I'm out of line, but I can't live without her, and I can't live with her under those conditions. Our mission will have to be her mission alone, or you will have to replace me."

David grinned, "Brad, I'm glad you spoke your mind. I didn't know how you felt about Laura until now, and I'm relieved. You see I just spoke with her along similar lines. She's free to marry you if she wants."

Brad was puzzled, but inwardly rejoicing, "What changed your mind?"

"Your death! Even when you died, we weren't changed; in fact I can find no historical event that was changed after your death."

"I see."

"Listen, the newscast we've been waiting for is coming on now." They listened intently after turning up the volume.

"There was another scare in the aviation world this morning as the experimental DC9 flown by Colonel Anderson was reported missing over central Missouri by Kansas City Center. The aircraft had some minor electrical problem losing their radios as well as their transponder, and vanished from the radar screen. They returned safely under visual flight rules to Scott Air Force Base in Illinois. Colonel Anderson and Dr. Ashton were soon back in the air again aboard an Air Force C21 on their way to Dallas to attend a conference with a group of Texas oil executives . . . ."

CHAPTER 35

Laura met Brad as she emerged from sick bay, and ran as fast as she could straight into his arms, and with tears of joy running down her face, she exclaimed, "Oh Brad—" He pulled her into his arms, and kissed her urgently not letting her finish, She could hardly contain herself until he allowed her to speak, "I was so afraid I'd lose you."

"In my heart, I'd never let you go, darling. It was awful, I thought—I don't know what I would do without you. I've been looking for you all my life and I won't ever let you go again."

"I'm sorry, I couldn't help myself. I was so confused—"

"Hush, no more of that. Tell me you will marry me."

"Yes—Oh yes, yes, yes!"

She clung to him, her emotions running wild as she returned his love, kiss for kiss, with a passion she had never before experienced until he broke free. "Darling, you're the most beautiful and desirable woman I've ever met, even when you're crying. But, if we don't stop carrying on like this, I'm warning you, I may not be able to wait for our wedding."

"I don't care. I want to give myself to you; but for now I guess you'd better get on in, and see Dr. Baker."

Dr. Baker gave Brad a hearty welcome as he entered, "Welcome back to the Manhattan, Brad."

"Thanks, Doc, I didn't realize you cared so much."

"Well, you grow on a person. Besides it was really Laura we were concerned about."

"How is she Doc? I mean how is she physically?"

"Fine, she is the picture of perfect health. She has obviously been under quite a strain, but physically she's in great shape."

"I agree with you, Doc." Brad grinned mischievously.

"Okay, enough of that, why don't you get up on that bench and let's take a look at you. Have you been taking those pills I gave you?"

"Sorry, Doc, I haven't had the time. I did take them the first few days."

"Well, let's see how you're doing." He turned on the medical scanner, and monitored the readouts on the computer. He took a small sample of blood this time, and began the test procedure taking his time not saying anything.

"Well, what's it look like Doc? Will I live?"

"Aren't you the anxious one? It takes a little time to complete the examination properly." He waited a couple more minutes until the computer analysis was complete. "Looks like you're physically fit. You have the slight blockage in your arteries—it's a little better than last time, though, I'll have to give you a series of shots." He didn't wait for Brad's reaction, but pushed a needle into Brad's arm and gave him his first shot. "Sorry, Brad, but if you'd taken those pills like I ordered, you wouldn't have needed that."

"Sorry, I guess it's just my life-style."

"Well, see me every day until you get off the Manhattan, and I'll give Laura more to give you later. Now get out of here, Dr. Ashton may have more business with you."

Laura was waiting outside the door, and together, arm in arm, they went to see her father. He was waiting, looking up as they entered, "Well, it looks like all's well with you two; now let's get down to business. We've got some updates for you and we can discuss some strategies."

Laura's curiosity finally got the better of her, asking, "Well, did you find out which came first, the chicken or the egg?"

"Yes, well maybe, at least the egg hatched. That part we know worked well, but your mission was cut far too short, and the organization you left behind couldn't continue without you, Laura. The measurable difference in conservation of petroleum was insignificant."

"We had some luck in uncovering a conspiracy; were they ever prosecuted? What happened with Dana Higgins?"

"As far as we can tell, no. We couldn't find any trace of Dana Higgins in the history books or in newspaper accounts," David remarked sadly.

Brad laughed, "Good, at least that part worked. We were protecting her with a name change; maybe her father didn't find her either."

"What's the name? We'll plug it into the computer, and search newspaper accounts to see if we can find her that way."

"Danielle Black."

David gasped, "You mean Dr. Danielle Black, the noted physicist! She developed the theory behind the Electromagnetic propulsion units. It took 300 years before they were produced, but Dr. Black developed the whole theory in 2013."

Laura beamed, "I knew she was extremely intelligent, and we were wasting her time behind that receptionist desk. If I had taken her back to the lab with me, she probably could have continued the development after we were gone."

"It's too bad we have to change that part of history, but I can see great possibilities for her. Let me tell you the rest of the story, and then you can check the computers for anything else that might help us out." He showed them the articles he found in the newspapers concerning an assassination of President Dugan. "This accident with Air Force One was probably not an accident. No evidence was ever found of sabotage, but no explanation could be given for the simultaneous failure of all four engines either."

Brad was adamant, "We need to warn him. Is it possible we can prevent his death, or is that a part of history we can't change?"

"According to our computer memory banks, he wasn't supposed to die that way; we already changed that part of history! And James Little was not supposed to be President, although he didn't make such a bad president. In the next few days, you can stay here, and communicate with those you need to on the ground. We want to modify the C9 again before you deliver it to McDonnell Douglas. Since the whole world knows about the new engines, we don't have to camouflage them anymore. We want to take the old engine cowlings off and put all the turbine accessories in the tail."

CHAPTER 36

Brad and Laura were oblivious to the outside world when they entered the communications center, and didn't immediately notice one of the crewmembers already at the console connected, and communicating with someone on the ground. They hadn't made a sound, and the operator was so absorbed in his tasks that he didn't see or hear them come in. They stopped frozen in their tracks as they heard him speak into the microphone: ". . . . They know about the snipers on the rooftop of the hospital. Dr. Ashton and Colonel Anderson will not be there!" Brad and Laura couldn't hear the other end of the conversation, and after a moment, he continued. "It doesn't matter who I am; believe me, I know who you are, and they know too. The FBI has evidence linking the three of you to EMI, and the firing on the C9. I'm taking a tremendous chance—" He glanced up at that moment seeing Laura and Brad watching him. He spun off his seat, severed his connection, pulled a weapon from under his shirt, and fired, missing in his haste.

His second shot shouldn't have missed, but it did. Brad reacted instinctively, first throwing Laura to the floor, rolling with her behind another console. The crewman fired again, hitting the console between them touching off an electrical fire that sent alarms throughout the ship. He continued to blast away, panic-stricken as he fled, directly into the grasp of the security forces David sent to intercept him.

Later that night, David sat watching the evening newscast, listening for information concerning the Dallas trap set for the assassins. "Here it is now."

"Good Evening, this is Walt Crane with CBS news. In the headlines today, Colonel Anderson and Dr. Ashton were briefly listed as missing with their experimental DC9, but it was a false alarm as they experienced a minor electrical problem. They were en route to Dallas, where tragedy again struck as three FBI agents were killed while involved in a shoot-out atop the hospital across the street from the Dallas Convention Center where Colonel Anderson and Dr. Ashton were scheduled to meet with the nation's major oil producers. We switch now to Dallas for a live report—"

"Good Evening, I'm standing in front of the wreckage of a Bell Ranger Medevac helicopter which crashed into the street here after a shoot-out on the top of the hospital building involving the five men killed in the helicopter with a score of FBI agents."

David and Laura had a few moments to themselves following the news broadcast. David was indecisive about what to tell her about the traitor in the communications center. Did it matter? In the previous voyage, Brad had died again, but David again had the advantage of recorded history and prevented that crime from being consummated.

Laura raised the question without giving him the chance to decline, "Dad, why weren't we killed in the comm center?

David hesitated but decided to unburden himself, "That was another event that actually happened. It was recorded that Brad was killed then and there. I couldn't tell you ahead of time, I just placed a protective shield around both of you and had the security forces ready. I didn't know who he was and it was probably the easiest way we could find him. However, I did know what was going down so we intercepted his call and the warning was never received."

"I guess you have lots of knowledge you can't share with me and that's okay. I know you won't let anything happen that would jeopardize the mission."

"I don't know, I helped make a decision several years ago that cost your mother's life. Laura, you and I have both paid the price of that decision for too many years. If I had to support that decision all over again knowing what I know, I don't think I would have been able to do it, even though I don't know what else we could have done. Maybe it's fortunate; I didn't have that knowledge then."

"Tell me about her. I have tried, but I can't even remember her face."

His voice broke; tears flowed freely as he held her close. "It's—it's hard, Laura—all you need to do is look in a mirror—you are the spitting image of your mother. I see her every time I look at you. That's another reason why I had to come back to save you and Brad! That's why it was so hard for me to give you up to the twentieth century!"

"What was she like?"

"She was a real lady, like you are. I remember watching her with you in her arms, overflowing with love. Laura, she loved you more than life itself, as I do. Sometimes when I look at you, I think I've gone back in time before that accident. I hope you understand why I sometimes had to walk out of the room with you, especially when you asked about her. That's why I wouldn't talk about her. Can you ever forgive me?"

"Yes, Dad, and I love you even more because of the way you are."

"Thanks, Laura."

"Dad, now you can take the Manhattan back and save her too."

"No, believe me, I've thought about that, but it's not the same. I've come a long way since then. In moments like this, I miss her, but when I get back, I want to try again to get Brenda to marry me."

"Oh, I hope she will. I know you both will be very happy, like Brad and I."

CHAPTER 37

On Monday morning, David brought the crew up to date informing all about the situation with the culprit apprehended in the Communications Center and what actually happened on the previous voyage. One asked, "How did the traitor know about General Higgins? I mean, it doesn't make sense."

"Unfortunately, in our century, EMI, the company founded by General Higgins, still exists; their spy infiltrated our crew, and has been here waiting for his chance since the beginning. Fortunately, time is on our side; we have to smash EMI and their conspiracy here in this century, and then we will have no problem when we return. It's quite possible that they are controlling a large amount of oil, and our civilization isn't in such bad shape as we thought, although we will never know."

"What are we going to do with the traitor?"

Dr. Ashton hesitated, weighing the consequences before replying, "I hesitate because of the possibility of another spy on board; but I will take that chance, and trust each of you. We're going to feed him false information that will help us destroy EMI. Our plans haven't been formalized, so if any of you have any ideas of how to accomplish it, feel free to express yourselves. We haven't been very good in predicting what effect our actions have on the future, but if we destroy EMI, then our 'traitor' may cease to exist."

Laura and Brad left David with his crew and Laura placed a call to their office at SMA where Dana answered with a cheery, "Good morning, Solar Magnetics Administration, may I help you?"

"Hi, Danielle—"

"Where are you?" She exclaimed, "We've been worried sick, nobody knows where you are, or what happened in Dallas. The president's been on the phone, and it's been ringing constantly since Saturday afternoon."

"Whoa, slow down, nothing happened; we are safe here at Scott Air Force Base. Nothing to worry about. Why don't you get Charles on the phone, and I'll only have to give you the news once."

"Sure."

Charles picked up the phone, "If you two scare me one more time—I swear, I should never have joined this outfit."

"Charles, you need a little excitement in your life, I bet you're having a ball. What did the president have to say?"

"He didn't say. I think he wanted to find out first hand why you didn't attend the session in Dallas."

"We'll talk to him. Charles, I think we'd better get a new receptionist. See if you can find another good one, will you?"

Dana broke in, "Wait a cotton picking minute, don't I have anything to say about this?"

"Danielle, you've got the job as long as you want it, but I need you for a more important job. I'll tell you about it when we get back. It'll be your choice."

"I love this job, even if you did leave me out on a limb."

"I know, Charles, make sure the line is secure, and I'll tell you a little more."

Charles turned on the anti-snooper black box Laura had provided, "Okay, it's secure."

"You've heard the news, if Brad and I had gone to Dallas, we would have been killed. Obviously that didn't happen, or at least history has been changed again, because my father came back, and intercepted us before we arrived in Dallas. We are with him now on the Manhattan; Dana, the Manhattan is the UFO we told you about earlier. Make sure no one else hears a word of it. Keep up business as usual. We want to get those manufacturers tooled up for production as quickly as possible."

"We'll take care of this end of it."

"Okay, we'll keep in touch but probably won't be back until sometime next week, or maybe longer."

Brad made the next call to Arthur Olson's office, Arthur was there and immediately came to the phone, "Brad, are you and Laura all right?"

"We weren't, but we're fine now. I'm sorry about those agents; they took the shots that were meant for me."

"I don't understand how you knew they would be there. Don't worry about those agents; they knew the risks. It's only a matter of time before those guys we nabbed will tell us all they know."

"Oh, what kind of tactics are you using to get that information?"

"You wouldn't want to know. Anyway, they have already been traced to ArkTex. One of them had a paycheck stub from one of their subsidiaries."

"Good, I think we're getting somewhere. By the way, there is also a plot to assassinate the president. His helicopter crash was probably not an accident! I received that information at the same time—and, no, I can't tell you my source. Unfortunately, you can't set them up like you did in Dallas. But we are working on a plan to break things wide open."

"Be careful."

Brad put the next call through to Colonel Brandt. "Morning, Sir, Colonel Anderson checking in. How's the airplane we brought back?"

"Very funny! I don't think anyone will ever believe another word I say. Officially, the aircraft is in the hangar. What's going on?"

"I can't guarantee there are no taps on your phone so you'll have to wait for the whole story. With your permission, I'll be back Wednesday evening and fly a couple of locals on Thursday and Friday. I want to check out Jerry Winsome, your wing standardization officer so he can be ready to fly the aircraft if anything happens to us.

"That's approved."

"Good, one more request, I'd like to check out Major Sparks also. He deserves it after all he did for us, and I'd like to use him for another little scheme we've got cooked up. I'll tell you about that Wednesday evening."

"Sounds good to me."

"After our locals, we will fly the aircraft on to McDonnell Douglas.

"Great, does that mean we'll get it back soon? We haven't cancelled any missions, but maintenance complains every day to the Wing Commander. We may lose a local or two this week."

"I suppose that's up to McDonnell Douglas. We may be able to push them, but I'd guess it will take a couple of months. Maybe you can get the depot level maintenance done at the same time?"

"Unfortunately, that aircraft just finished the cycle. We may have to delay putting the next aircraft in until we get this one back though."

"That's probably a good idea anyway. It would make more sense to get it done the same time it's modified. At least the rest of the airplanes won't have to go through the certification process. Sir, I'd like to talk with you more, but it'll have to wait. I've got to call the president."

The president was in his office with his chief of staff, Norm Dressler, when his intercom buzzed. He flipped the switch expecting Mary, his secretary, to be on the line, "Yes."

"Morning, Sir, Colonel Anderson checking in."

"Where the hell have you been?"

"I think you hit the nail of the head, Sir. Are you alone?"

"One moment." He indicated the door, and Dressler left knowing his boss wanted privacy. "Okay, I'm alone."

"Good, Laura and I were killed on Friday afternoon, and you were killed later this week!"

"That's preposterous!"

"Sir, I didn't want to shock you, but it's true. Fortunately for us, the Manhattan is back, and has already insured that it didn't and won't happen."

"But you said we were killed, not that I will be killed."

"That's right. It actually happened. But history is only history until it's changed, and we have another chance."

"That's incredible! Tell me about it."

Brad went on to explain the entire story leaving nothing out, "One event followed the other like a chain reaction. After we were killed, you were on little side trip to Kansas City to attend our memorial service. We appreciate that by the way, but I'm glad it didn't happen this time. On the way back to Washington, your aircraft lost all four engines. There was no way your pilot could land in Saint Louis when he started to lose the engines due to a violent thunderstorm over the airport, so he opted to land at Springfield, Illinois. I think Scott AFB must have been down with the storms also. Anyway, it was too far and when the 4th engine was lost, you crashed short of the runway. The cause of the accident was never discovered, except for some reason, all four engines failed one right after another. We are certain that it was sabotage and someone wants you dead. We have every reason to believe the main conspirators are General Mike Higgins, CIA chief Clifford Burns, and your vice president, James Little."

"That could be, and it agrees with the reports Arthur Olson gave me last week. Jim is a trifle incompetent, but I never really thought he would go that far. Maybe I should confront him, and have it out right now."

"That would only make them go farther underground, and you have no proof; instead we need to flush them out in the open. We are working on a couple of schemes that might work. In the meantime, be inconsistent, I mean never travel the same way twice. Set up transportation and don't use it. Stay off Air Force One and your helicopter."

CHAPTER 38

"How long is your father planning to stay? We haven't even discussed a date!"

"What's the matter? You getting cold feet?" she chided but with a twinkle in her eye.

"'Fraid you can't get out of it that easy. I'd knock you over the head and drag you off to my cave first. Wild horses couldn't drag me away from you, and don't you forget it."

"Dad's in no hurry to leave. He says it's better to stay awhile longer than take another four years to get back to drag us out of hot water again. He thinks he has time travel wired. He is even thinking of giving the crew members a vacation; got any ideas along that line?"

"Oh, there are lots of places that might fit the bill. You or I could shuttle them back and forth. For now, let's go for a walk down to the maintenance hangars. I need to see how they are doing on the C9. Colonel Brandt wants that airplane back in service. We'd better deliver it before we take time out to get married."

"Always business before pleasure. Why can't I ever learn to stay out of someone's life when they're already married to their job?"

"That's a real problem, but as soon as we get the SMA rolling, I'm going to retire and watch our children grow."

"I'll bet! It'll take more than that to get you to retire."

"Right. However, I plan on enjoying every minute of my work right beside you every step of the way."

They didn't take very many of those steps before they arrived in the maintenance area, and checked in with the supervisor. "How's it going? Will you have it finished by Wednesday?"

"Don't you ever slow down? It could be ready, but my men don't want it to end that soon. They enjoy being back on the job."

"Have I got a deal for you. How would you feel if we brought you a different bird to replace it?"

"Well now, that's a challenge I can hardly refuse. It'll be ready by noon Wednesday if we have to work all night today and tomorrow."

"It looks like you've done another beautiful job. Well done—it does look a little strange though, with no engines visible." Brad took a good long look around the airplane, trying to visualize an entire fleet.

"Brad, I think I will stay down here a little longer, and get my hands dirty. I need to have hands-on experience before I start advising the aircraft designers how it should be done." Laura really didn't want to leave Brad by himself, but she knew she should.

"Okay, I can see it all now. I'm going to marry someone who is already married to her job."

"Aw, get out of here before I have you thrown out."

Brad left, going back up to David's office. "Come on in, Brad, let's get together and discuss strategy."

"Okay. I just talked with the maintenance supervisor. I told him we would exchange aircraft, and he could modify another one. I've arranged to pick up a smaller jet which should be ideal for our travel plans. The Air Force wants their airplane back."

"No problem, our guys love to get their hands on antique aircraft. Somehow, I knew you would suggest that. We've decided to stay around a little while until we get this mess straightened out. It'll give them something to do."

Laura decided it would be best for her to stay aboard the Manhattan and spend the time with her father while Brad went to Scott AFB. Brad was happy with that decision, knowing there could be another attempt to kill her and the security wouldn't be as good at Scott as at Wright-Patterson. The security wasn't bad at Scott, but the secret service personnel had been working with the security police at Wright-Patterson for over a month now and they worked well together. The maintenance supervisor was true to his word, and Brad was launched into the sky flying the C9 solo which wasn't a lot different than when he flew local training missions with new pilots assigned to the squadron. He knew it wasn't quite legal since the DC9 was certified for two pilots, but it really wasn't certified anymore with the new engines installed. As long as the FAA didn't give him any hassles, he would live with it.

Brad met with Colonel Brandt, Lt. Colonel Jerry Winsome, and Major Robert Sparks shortly after his arrival. He gave each of them a training manual that Laura had provided asking Jerry and Robert to look it over and be ready for their local in the morning. He emphasized the sections dealing with the new procedures and the cockpit displays. "Don't worry about the rest of the systems. They will be transparent for the most part. The aircraft is easy to fly and will be a real joy for you." The manual was detailed enough to be used by Jerry to prepare the necessary revisions to the Flight Manual for the C9, and prepare for the training of the remainder of the crews. He explained, "We don't have the performance data, but conservatively, the old manual is valid. The new engines far surpass the old in every aspect of aircraft performance."

Brad discussed with Colonel Brandt the events of the past week, telling of the risks they would encounter until the conspiracy plotters were brought to justice.

The next morning Brad spent the usual hour for the preflight briefing going over the systems that were different. He told them not to worry as it would be easier after seeing them in flight. He spoke, tongue in cheek, "Those CRTs aren't really a necessary part of the engine modifications, but since we need a CRT for the engine instruments, then we better do the job right. Since the Air Force won't have to spend as much money on fuel or engine maintenance, they can foot the bill for this part of the modification. We also upgraded the radar which will now be displayed on the moving map display rather than the old scope."

They left the squadron building on schedule, checked the weather, filed their flight plan, and went to breakfast before going to the aircraft. At breakfast, Brad answered more questions his students had from reading the manuals, but most of the time while eating was spent rehashing the events of the last few weeks and the pilot's reactions to the new engine modifications.

Maintenance had gone over the aircraft with a fine tooth comb, changing tires, and servicing all the systems that were not new to them, and stood by as Brad and his crew accomplished their exterior preflight inspection. Jerry and Robert spent a few extra moments looking at the rear of the aircraft where they could find no visible signs of the engines. Brad pointed out the inlet and outlet ports for the compressors and left it at that. He couldn't do much instruction on the exterior since there was quite a bit of noise on the flightline as other aircraft around them were preparing for departure.

Brad would fly from the right seat which was normal while instructing and Jerry would have the honor of flying first. "Whenever you're ready, Jerry, I'll run the checklist."

"Starting engines check," Jerry called.

"Seat belt sign—on. Parking brake!"

"Set."

"Anti-collision light—on. Pitot heat—Captain. Start switches!"

Jerry looked confused, "What about the other checklist items?"

"No longer necessary, just turn the engines on. He pointed to where the fuel control levers were normally located.

Jerry turned the first lever on but looked bewildered. "Nothing happened!"

"The engine is now in standby status, as soon as you push forward on the throttle, you will notice an immediate response."

He turned the other engine lever. "Okay, on, I guess," as he responded to the checklist.

"Engine instruments! The only indication you will get here for the engines themselves is the thrust indicators which should now indicate exactly zero instead of off-scale as they did earlier. The tachs should be at a hundred per cent continuous r.p.m. for the compressors and accessory section, and we need to check the voltage and frequency for the generators."

"Good, I didn't even notice the thrust indicator's movement—checked."

"Engine anti ice—off. This is really not engine anti-ice, it protects the compressor inlet. The engines are not exposed to the elements. Starting engines check complete."

"Before taxi check!"

"External power!"

"Removed."

"Cross tie check!"

Jerry checked both generators and noted they worked exactly the same as before, "Checked."

"Air-conditioning supply switches-auto. Yaw damper-on. Hydraulic supply and pumps-on and checked. Seat belts and shoulder harnesses-fastened. Doors-closed. Lights-Out. Gear pins!"

"Stowed."

"Before taxi check—completed." Brad keyed the mike asking for taxi, and gave the thumbs up signal to the ground handler.

"Taxi to runway three two, altimeter three zero one one," was the immediate reply.

"Roger, three zero one one." Brad turned to Jerry, "Be careful now; nudge those throttles forward slowly and we'll move easily. Just remember how light the aircraft is with no fuel on board."

He slowly moved the throttles forward until the aircraft began to move, and then brought them back to idle. The aircraft began to move, but slowed down coming to a stop. Jerry was bewildered more than ever. "If it's so light, why does it stop when I bring it back to idle?"

"The old engines produce considerable thrust at idle. These at idle mean just that; they are idle. So unless you are taxiing downhill or have a lot of momentum going, you will need to keep a tad of power applied to keep moving."

He applied more power and then backed off a little as the aircraft began a normal taxi, but without the whine of turbojet engines. As they approached the runway, the tower cleared them for takeoff with clearance to Maintain Runway Heading and climb to 3000 feet. Brad confirmed his clearance and spoke to Jerry, "Before-takeoff check complete, it's your baby. Just move the throttles forward to the Take Off detent. Don't worry about spooling the engines up, that is no longer a factor. I've set the detent for the power we want to use today. That is a variable you can set based on your weight and runway conditions. I set them today at 60 percent which will give you approximately the same power as you are used to, but remember with no fuel and very light engines, you are lighter than you have ever been. After you get familiar with the aircraft, we can use more power if you like. If you need more power, you can always override the detent and full power will be immediately available. You can use as much power as you want, but if you do, you would have to raise the nose to a very uncomfortable level immediately after airborne or you would exceed the gear and flap limits before you could raise them, and then you would have trouble leveling at 3,000 feet."

Jerry gradually pushed the throttles forward toward the Take Off detent which pushed him back in the seat, and accelerated the aircraft to liftoff speed at about the same time he reached the Take Off detent. His experience showed as Brad called, GO, V2 and rotate speeds. When airborne, Jerry called for gear and flaps on schedule before he pulled the power back gradually settling down at approximately 250 knots indicated, as they leveled at 3,000 feet.

They came back to the landing pattern and each pilot made several approaches and landings in all configurations. Jerry and Robert were thoroughly impressed and couldn't keep from bubbling over with excitement and were reluctant to quit flying for the day.

After landing, Brad called Robert aside, and he began his pitch, "Bob, I know I told you earlier that I couldn't talk about what happened with the missing aircraft. Well, I need to tell you a little, but the information I am giving you is classified. I'm not going to tell you everything, but I need your help to carry off a scam to trick the perpetrators of a conspiracy to take over the government. Are you interested?"

"You know I am!"

"Good, I know you were checked out in the Lear 35; Colonel Brandt will schedule a couple rides to get you current again. I need you to act like a civilian charter pilot who will do anything for a buck. You will be contracted to transport those conspirators I told you about from Washington National Airport to a UFO that will beam you aboard a short distance from Washington."

"Wow, sounds exciting. What kind of UFO are we talking about?"

"Something beyond your wildest dreams. I'll show you a little more when you come aboard. And yes, that's where the new technology came from."

The next day's flying was much the same, except Brad allowed Jerry and Robert to take control and manage the aircraft throughout most of the flight. He emphasized again the primary difference in flying with the new engines. "The key is power management without the aid of sound effects. Obviously, more power is available than necessary, but that should come in handy in high temperature / high altitude situations, or for short runways, both for takeoff and landing. You should put some restrictions on the crews in the form of optimum power settings for normal takeoffs. In training, it might be to your advantage to go to a runway where max performance takeoffs and climbs can be demonstrated which we will do today."

He requested and received clearance to Whiteman AFB, Missouri where they again made several takeoffs and landings. He simulated engine failures, and allowed each to make single engine landings which were what he emphasized, non-events. "You don't have any adverse yaw, so the use of full rudder until you can trim out the yaw is not necessary. You don't have any fuel crossfeed issues and the generators are not affected since they are not connected to the engines." When they were ready to return to Scott, he requested a max performance climb to 37,000 feet. Brad wanted to show off and took control of the aircraft. When on the runway, he smartly pushed the throttles full forward, lifting off in less than 500 feet and as soon as airborne, simultaneously raised the nose to 45 degrees and raised the landing gear and flaps. He didn't do anything more until they reached 30,000 feet and he gradually brought the throttles back and lowered the nose leveling smoothly at 37,000 feet.

He made his obligatory comment of caution. "Just remember, your liftoff attitude. If you raise that nose rapidly before airborne, you will strike the tail on the runway. Otherwise the performance is like a fighter." He turned the aircraft back to Jerry, "Now, take us back to Scott."

Brad and Laura launched into the clear blue sky shortly after noon on Monday while over the middle of the Mojave Desert. They would have a few minutes to fly under visual flight rules the short distance to the mountains before crossing over into the Los Angeles Basin, and being picked up on radar. Brad wanted an instrument clearance prior to entering the Basin because of the high density of air traffic. He dialed a Los

Angeles Center frequency and checked in, "Los Angeles Center, Solar one one."

"Solar one one, go ahead."

"Solar one one, approaching Palmdale VOR, one two thousand five hundred, request IFR clearance to Long Beach."

"Roger Solar one one, Squawk one two one one and ident. Say type aircraft, requested altitude, true airspeed, pilot's name, home base, and fuel on board."

"DC9 slash alpha, one two thousand, three fifty, Anderson, Wright Patterson Air Force Base, and negative fuel."

"Say again fuel on board!"

"Negative fuel on board."

"Understand, negative fuel?" There was silence for a moment then, "Welcome to Los Angeles, Colonel Anderson, cleared to Long Beach via radar vectors, descend, and maintain one two thousand, and make your heading two three five."

"Roger, descending to one two thousand, and nice recovery."

Laura was flying in the left seat again, and she was soon busy looking for other aircraft, and following the controller's instructions. Within ten minutes, they were on the ground taxiing in toward the McDonnell Douglas hangar at the end of the runway.

Alex Newsome met them, inviting them to lunch. "Colonel Anderson, good to see you again, Miss Ashton, you look as beautiful as ever, welcome to Southern California. I've got a car for you as soon as you finish up here."

"Thanks, it's going to be a couple of hours. I need to fly with their test pilot before we sign the aircraft over to them."

"No problem, I'll spend the time discussing our aircraft modifications with Miss Ashton."

Brad did a double take, but couldn't think of a good reason to refuse. "All right, but remember she is my fiancée."

"Congratulations, you're one lucky man!"

Calvin Branch, president of McDonald Douglas was walking around the aircraft, amazed at how sleek and uncluttered the aircraft looked without the engine pods. Brad and Laura joined him making sure the aircraft had experienced no last-minute problems with FOD, or tire damage during the flight or landing.

"What happened to the engine pods? It looks naked!"

Brad laughed, "Just like a real lady, she looks better that way."

Laura added, "Men are never satisfied."

"What happened?" Calvin was bewildered, "Just last month, all the turbines and accessories were in the engine pods."

"We finished our job getting the first one done properly. We didn't need all that excess drag, so we put it all in the tail compartment. It's a little crowded, but there's still room for the stairwell. Do you have any idea how long the certification process will take? The 375th is anxious to get their bird back."

"I can't say. There are too many unknowns; we will need to repeat the performance tests if we are to provide the Air Force with the charts they require."

"You're not fooling anyone," Brad grinned, "I'd want to keep it as long as I could too. We did keep it until we couldn't put the Air Force off any longer."

"We aren't making any promises, but they should have it back within a couple of months."

"Is your test pilot ready to fly? I don't feel comfortable waiting around here too long without a heck of a lot more security for Dr. Ashton."

"He's ready, and will be here in a few minutes. In the meantime, Dr. Ashton can relax in our office. It's secure."

The pilot arrived before Brad had the flight plan filed; they took off and spent about an hour where Brad demonstrated all the system changes emphasizing the power available. One normal landing sufficed and Brad turned the aircraft over to them. Brad got the required signatures and joined Laura who was the center of attention for a couple of television news reporters as well as several of the workers more interested in her than the C9.

CHAPTER 39

In Washington, Arthur Olson was presenting his case to his boss, Art Dawson. "We have enough evidence on General Higgins, but we lack anything substantial on the other two. We are certain James Little and Clifford Burns are involved, but we have nothing to prove it."

"What makes you so certain they are involved?"

"We finally got a breakthrough on those killers we captured in Dallas; one of them talked. They actually work for EMI, not ArkTex. We had to dig pretty deep, and it took some time, but we also discovered all three of our suspects are partners in the ownership of EMI. That doesn't prove anything except they are involved in a quasi-legal organization that has not been disclosed as required by Federal law. And EMI did manufacture those bugs found in the Oval Office."

"That's enough to make them look bad in the public eye, but not enough to convict them of an attempted assassination of the president."

"All I want is a search warrant for the entire EMI complex." Arthur was certain a surprise raid on EMI would enable them to gather the evidence they needed.

"Sorry, I don't think we have enough to convince the judge. We need to double our efforts, and provide every possible protection for Colonel Anderson and Dr. Ashton."

"I don't even know where they are. I talked with Colonel Anderson, but he wouldn't tell me. Since that raid last Saturday, they are keeping a low profile."

"Everybody else knows where they are! A few minutes ago they were on television delivering the C9 to McDonnell Douglas at Long Beach."

"I hope their secret service escorts were close by."

"I didn't see any, but apparently they carried it off without a hitch. They didn't stay long. Keep up the good work—the pieces will fall into place soon enough."

After lunch, Alex Newsome drove Laura and Brad back to the Long Beach airport, where the blue and white Lear 55B sat on the ramp; "There she is, SMA's first airplane." The Lear looked as beautiful as Brad had pictured in his mind but even he was surprised when he saw the tail number N11SM painted in small letters on the tail.

"Oh Brad, it's beautiful!" Laura exclaimed, "What a surprise! So this is the aircraft you talked about Monday! When did you find enough time to arrange for all this?"

"Nothing too hard to arrange, or too good for you, didn't I manage to send you on enough errands? Remember your trips to the Base Commander's office at Wright-Patterson? It's our getaway vehicle, and I know just the trip to break it in. You fly first, Laura, Alex is going to check us out around the pattern a couple of times until we are comfortable."

Alex was excited; he could never get over the thrill of delivering a new aircraft off the assembly line. During the walk-around, he pointed out the differences between this aircraft and the model 35, which Brad had flown previously. As Laura strapped into the left seat, he kept talking about his product. "It's not difficult to fly, and it's a real hummer. I don't know what size engines you'll want to install, but this bird will climb like a homesick angel to over 50,000 feet at maximum gross weight with stock engines. Its systems are simple and easy to operate. I think you'll enjoy it."

Laura didn't need much instruction as she had spent many hours flying the same model in the simulator. They headed out over the Pacific where they could do a little maneuvering without risking colliding with another aircraft. Alex didn't mind the time, so they spent a couple of hours having a ball putting the aircraft through its paces. Eventually, they wound up back in the pattern where a couple of normal and single engine landings for each were enough to satisfy Alex's high standards.

After the final landing, Alex said, "Let me fill it up with Jet 'A1' for you, and you can be on your way."

"Don't bother, we won't need it." Brad replied."

"But you don't have enough to fly more than a couple hundred miles with any reserve."

"That's okay, we're not going far!"

Alex's curiosity was getting the better of him. "I thought you were going back to some secret base in Tennessee or somewhere like that."

"That's what you get for thinking! I should have let you put the fuel on, and then you wouldn't ask so many questions. Believe me, we don't need much fuel."

"All right, when do you plan on getting it back to us?"

"Maybe a week, maybe a month; I'll give you a call. We'll give you at least a month to complete the certification; of course we want to get it certified as quickly as possible. I hate to rely on the Air Force for our transportation any longer than necessary."

"Where do you want us to pick it up?" Alex was hoping to get some kind of clue as to where they would modify the aircraft.

"Either Andrews or Wright Patterson; I'll let you know. How about a loaner until the certification is complete; a model 35 would be fine."

"No problem, I'll see you soon."

Back on the Manhattan, the Maintenance troops began swarming over the aircraft. The supervisor exclaimed, "It's a beauty, I don't ever remember seeing an aircraft from your century with this much class. I'll say this much, you've sure got an eye for beautiful aircraft."

"They're just like women; I know how to pick them."

CHAPTER 40

Arthur Olson was discouraged at the end of his rope. Nothing was falling into place, except the mounting evidence against General Higgins, but he had nothing that would stand up in court, implicating either Burns or Little. He lost three of his agents, with little to show for it. He racked his brain trying to piece together some plan of action, but came up with zilch. He had been trying for days to make contact with Colonel Anderson, but the message was always the same: "He will be in touch." General Higgins ignored the interceptor investigation report, and unless something broke soon, the trail would be cold. The more he thought about it, the more disgusted he felt, until Brad finally called. He wanted to rant and rave but he managed to control himself, and spoke only a surly, "Good morning, Brad."

"Gee, I thought you would be chomping at the bit. We need to get together, maybe tomorrow afternoon."

"Of course we do. Where the hell are you?"

"Sorry, we didn't want another Dallas, and we've been planning our wedding."

"You gotta be kidding! You are right smack in the middle of somebody's plot to take over the government, and you sit somewhere planning to get married."

"That's right, and since you've already met Laura, you should understand. We've identified the culprits for you, however, apprehending those perpetrators is your job, and I wouldn't want to interfere." He laughed sinisterly, "We do have a few strategies we would like to discuss. Our priority has been getting our new aircraft modified and in the air. We will land at Andrews about two o'clock tomorrow afternoon; why don't you meet us?"

Arthur didn't hesitate, he would adjust his schedule as necessary, "I'll see you at Andrews."

"Good, you can provide transportation to the White House. We'll talk on the way to meet with the president."

"Good morning, Norman, this is Colonel Anderson, checking in. Laura and I, and FBI agent Arthur Olson need an appointment with the president sometime around four or later tomorrow afternoon."

"I'll check; he's in a meeting right now, but it should be no problem."

"Good enough. We'll be standing by in Washington until he can see us."

"Morning, Alex, are you ready?"

Alex Newsome was beginning to like the way Brad operated since he liked to go about business the same way. "I'm ready, just say the word."

"Good, you can pick up N11SM at Andrews tomorrow after two, and keep it until you've got it certified."

Alex was elated, "No problem; I'll be there."

"How about delivering the loaner to Washington National, and leaving it with someone at the FBO? Just leave instructions for it to be serviced, and ready to go for a Mr. Robert Smith to pick up at his convenience. Please don't mention my name, or the Solar Magnetics Administration."

"It'll be there, and mum's the word."

"Good, our aircraft will be at Andrews until you're ready to pick it up."

"Thanks, but I'll be there when you arrive."

Brad made one more call to Colonel Brandt requesting he send Major Sparks TDY to meet him at the Washington National Airport the next day and allow him to spend a week or two working for Brad.

The modified Lear 55 stood silently, slim and trim without its engine pods. Laura wanted to christen it on its maiden voyage. "Fat Man or Little Boy, would have been a good name like the original bomb from the Manhattan Project, but it isn't fat."

"Airplanes are feminine; you can't give it a male name anyway," was Brad's reply.

"How about 'Slim Girl'?"

"Nah, too impersonal, how about 'The Marie'?"

Laura looked at him surprised, "Where'd you get that name? That's my middle name, and my mother's name. I've never mentioned my middle name to you."

"Oh, but you gave it to the interrogators at the FBI. I'm not surprised you forgot that ordeal."

"Okay, 'The Marie' it is." She got ready to crack the bottle of champagne over the nose.

"Careful, that would be an awful expensive christening ceremony. The skin is too thin and delicate for that. Hit it on the tire."

They launched into the midmorning stillness over Kansas at ten thousand feet, since Brad wanted a couple of hours en route to give the bird a good workout before arriving at Andrews. The Manhattan crew, using the tractor beam, would ensure no harm would come to the aircraft during Brad or Alex's flights making unnecessary any test flights like with the C9.

The aircraft was aerodynamically clean, but now it promised spectacular performance; the 3,700-pound thrust engines were replaced with 5,000-pound thrust electromagnetic propulsion units that increased the rate of climb to a phenomenal 10,000 feet per minute plus, all the way to 50,000 feet. The empty weight with the new engines installed was reduced to less than

10,000 pounds and with a maximum landing weight of 17,000 pounds; they could carry a 7,000 pound payload anywhere in the world nonstop.

After an hour of pure enjoyment, they proceeded to Andrews. As they flew along, Brad asked, "How about a September twenty-fifth wedding?"

"Don't think I can wait that long." She reached over, and pulled him toward her.

"You'd better be careful if you don't want to join the mile-high-club," Brad teased.

"What's the 'mile-high club'?"

"That's when you lose your virginity over a mile up in an airplane."

"What makes you think I'm a virgin?" Laura teased.

"A little bird told me. I couldn't imagine you any other way. Besides your father told me you didn't grow up like other girls and that you were innocent."

"Fathers don't know as much as they think they do! Would it matter if I wasn't?"

"Yes, because that's how I see you. I guess I would be disappointed, but I love you more than life itself, and I would continue to love you no matter what. I suppose that would make you a little more human."

Laura was satisfied, but continued to probe, "And what about you? Are you a virgin?"

Brad laughed nervously, "A girl isn't supposed to ask a guy a question like that. She might get an answer she doesn't want to hear." She didn't respond, and he continued, "But honestly, I'm not. I came close to getting married once, and I probably would have, except she couldn't accept the Air Force way of life. I made a mistake, and I've never felt good about it."

"Thanks for being honest with me. I'll have to keep you in suspense until September 25th."

Alex Newsom and Arthur Olson were both on the flight line at Andrews, waiting to meet the aircraft as Brad taxied in.

Laura went over the details of the modifications, while Brad and Arthur stood off to one side watching Alex follow Laura around the aircraft as she opened the tail compartment, indicating the various components. "Alex, she sure is beautiful, isn't she?" Brad commented as he walked up to them.

"She's the most. You're a lucky man, Colonel." Alex stated with obvious admiration.

Brad laughed, and Laura blushed as she handed him the manual she had prepared. She was honored and pleased, but she wouldn't let on. She almost snorted, "Men! They're all alike, you obviously aren't interested in what I'm saying, so read it for yourself. I don't want you to over speed the gear and flaps on your first flight, so I would suggest you limit the power to about 80 per cent for takeoff. After you get it cleaned up, use as much power as you like for the climb. You can't over boost the engines and there is no time limit for maximum thrust."

"Alex, don't forget; we want it back soon."

"I may never get back to Arizona if this thing flies as well as you claim."

"You gotta come down sometime."

They had to wait a few minutes before being ushered into the Oval Office where the president greeted them warmly. "Come on in, it's good to see you again. You gave us a little scare in Dallas. How are things going now?"

"Great, we've been working on a plan to trap Little and Burns; we'd like to get your approval. If you approve, Arthur and I will be meeting with Art Dawson later this afternoon, and make final preparations."

"Well, what do I need to approve?"

"First, your okay to discuss the secret nature of our mission with Arthur, and my friend from the Scott Command Post, Major Robert Sparks. He has the appropriate clearance and will keep his mouth shut."

"Approved!"

Brad went on giving him the details of their plan, and as he concluded, the president remarked, "It's going to take a lot of luck to pull this off, but if anybody can, you will. I think it might work. You've got my approval."

"Great, we'll be ready in about a week."

Brad and Laura met Bob Sparks at Washington National where he allowed Bob to take control of the Lear 35 masquerading as Robert Smith. Brad and Laura didn't want to be seen, and quietly went to the aircraft keeping their faces shielded from view from anyone casually watching. Bob took off with a VFR clearance heading westbound away from Washington, and they were soon on the beam. Brad gave Bob a short tour of the Manhattan and told him what he wanted. "You can stay here aboard the Manhattan for a couple of days and then things are going to get busy. Laura and I will need you to fly us to Andrews where we will pick up a VC9 from the 89th. We need to ferry some VIPs from Washington to the Manhattan without attracting any attention."

Bob was amazed, "How did you get authorization for that. That's the first time I've heard of the 89th allowing someone else to fly one of their airplanes."

"You remember that first day when I talked to you in the Command Post when I told you we had spoken to the President. Since that week he supports us in almost everything we ask of him. He was willing to lean on General Williams who flat out told the wing commander at the 89th to support us. Oh, we also promised him priority in getting new engines for his fleet. When he heard that, he bent over backwards to support us."

CHAPTER 41

Clifford Burns sitting in his office was interrupted by a clear, strong voice that seemed to come from nowhere specific, yet from someone in the room. "Morning, Clifford. Don't get excited, I'm a friend."

Cliff checked behind him guiltily, and demanded of his secretary, "What's going on out there?"

"Nothing, Sir. There's nobody out here, except me. What can I do for you?"

"Nothing, forget it." He released his intercom, "Who in hell are you? What do you want?"

"My name is Bruce Thorpe, commander of the Manhattan."

"Commander of what?"

"The time machine that Dr. Ashton used to travel to your time."

"What do you want from me?"

"I came back to help you, and to insure our interests are met. Unless we work together, it will only be a matter of time before you are convicted of conspiracy to assassinate President Dugan, the murders of his helicopter crew and the murder of Dana Higgins. The president knows the full extent of your treason, Cliff; he just doesn't have all the proof he needs. He's planning on giving you just enough rope to hang yourself."

"Nonsense! Go and leave me alone, or I'll call security."

"Sorry, Can't do that. It wouldn't do you any good; they wouldn't find me. Are you ready to talk?"

"Damn you, where are you?"

"I'm on the Manhattan; I don't need to get more specific than that."

"You've got my attention, what do you want?"

"I want to help you, and take care of some common problems that are of vital concern to me."

"I'm listening!"

"You remember Dr. Ashton said she came from the twenty-seventh century. I represent another group from the twenty-seventh century, and we have no intention of allowing her to alter the past. Dr. Ashton's father was forced to return because the time machine has a limited window of opportunity. He made another voyage which prevented you from killing his daughter and Colonel Anderson. When he returned, we gained the advantage, and took over his ship."

"Why should I believe you? Why should I help you?"

"You've got it all wrong; I came to help you. If you don't want to work with me, you'll probably face execution, or at the very least, a life term in prison. It's only a matter of time before the president and the FBI get enough evidence to convict you, James Little, and Mike Higgins."

"Convict us! Of what?"

"Don't play games with me. I have access to your EMI files, and I know how you three took over control of ArkTex after the murder of Dana Higgins."

"That's ridiculous, we don't control ArkTex!"

"Maybe so, but in time you will! Your plans worked, and the combination of ArkTex and EMI has been a powerful force for us in the United States for over six hundred years. I noticed you didn't deny killing General Higgins' daughter, but that doesn't concern me. I could go on, and tell you all about how EMI was formed, but you know all that. We are losing control of ArkTex in the twenty-seventh century because of Ashton's interference, and your fiasco in Dallas. I control EMI, but it's vital that you regain control before it's too late. If Dr. Ashton is allowed to continue, I will lose that too."

"What do you want from me?"

"I want to meet with the three of you tonight. I will send an agent to bring you aboard the Manhattan where we can meet privately."

"Do I have any choice?" he asked disdainfully.

"Of course, I told you I came to help! If you don't want my help, I'll help the FBI gather enough evidence against you to make the convictions stick and then replace you. I can't let you blow it, and threaten my position any longer."

"It wouldn't do you any good! There is no evidence!"

"Oh there's evidence all right. It's just a matter of how much we want to release without damaging EMI. Consider EMI's role in the Middle East for starters and your part in illegal arms trafficking. If we can't find enough evidence, framing you could be a barrel of laughs. We have videos of your henchmen tinkering with Dana Higgins' car before her accident. With those, I'm sure the FBI can link you to that murder attempt. We have video of the murder of Dana in her dormitory. We have plenty and a little professional tinkering with the recordings could make it hot for you. I might even enjoy making sure the right people get their hands on it! I have another idea. The next time the three of you meet, your conversations will be recorded and I could transmit the recording directly to the FBI. I will be monitoring and recording every conversation you, Mike, or James has from now on, no matter where you hide. You should know by now that we have the power to do that. I'm telling you, every move you make will be monitored. I bet you will be looking over your shoulder so much your neck will ache. Dr. Ashton's father wouldn't do that; I believe he said it was unethical. I don't have his scruples and you can take that to the bank. Make no mistake, we will prevail!"

Cliff wasted no time sending their secret signal informing the other two that they must meet together that evening. James and Mike had been expecting the call for several days, and Mike had already devised an excuse for his trip to Washington.

Brad found Bob in the entertainment center participating in an interactive movie where he took on the role of the main character. He abruptly turned the entertainment module off, and grinned at Bob's reaction, "Sorry, Bob, you were probably getting involved with the main female character, but it's time."

Bob was willing, although disappointed, "It's okay, are you ready to go to Andrews?"

"Yes, things are rapidly falling into place. First you need to ferry Karl Hampton to Washington. As soon as you drop him off, you can come back for us. We don't want Karl to see me or Laura, and we don't want you to talk with him. Just answer questions with minimal non-committal words. He thinks you are just a pilot hired to do a job."

It didn't take long for Bob to make the round trip, and Brad and Laura were on their way to Andrews when Brad gave Bob his final instructions, "After you drop us off, fly on over to Washington National, service the aircraft and wait. Karl will come to you and you can bring them on up to the Manhattan."

The VC9s used by the 89th Military Airlift Wing were modified versions of the same DC9-30 that were in use by the 375th at Scott. They were set up in a VIP configuration primarily used to transport the Vice President and members of Congress on routine trips throughout the United States. Their aircraft was ready and preflighted by one of the 89th aircrews and the passengers were already on board, hosted by Dana Higgins, who would act as flight attendant on the short trip to the Manhattan. The aircraft had a few additional features that Brad was unfamiliar with, although the basics were the same, but Laura had never flown a DC9 equipped with turbojet engines even though she had flown many in the simulator. Laura and Brad spent a couple of enjoyable hours in the simulator during the past week, and were comfortable flying the aircraft. Dana spent a few hours before the passengers were loaded with a crew from the 89th who had prepared her for minimal tasks.

As soon as they were in the air heading west, they were brought aboard the Manhattan on the beam. The maintenance crew moved the aircraft to another area of the ship and sealed it off from view of visitors that would come later.

James Little, Mike Higgins and Clifford Burns arrived at the EMI complex separately, but within minutes of each other. Clifford waited until they had been seated around the conference table before he related the strange discussion he had that morning.

"Sounds like a trap to me." James Little responded immediately.

Mike thought about it for a minute, "It could be, and then again, he might be for real. I wonder how this agent will show up. Maybe we can force the real truth out of him."

Cliff continued, "I don't know what to think, but whoever I talked with earlier had the power to control our conversation. I couldn't hang up on him since we weren't using the telephone. He knows all about our illegal activities and he is either who he says he is, or someone with just as much power. He could do a lot of damage to our organization. If they can control our conversation and hear our responses, they certainly can record them."

"What are the odds it's Ashton's father? Couldn't he try to trap us with this phony setup?" James was unconvinced.

"Whoever he is, we have problems." Cliff said, "The president talked with me again today, and wants that report on you, Mike. He says he's waited long enough; I can't stall him any longer."

"What's in the report?" James wondered if it hadn't already leaked to the president.

"It's been completed by my investigations unit, and I'm afraid it's pretty damaging. They discovered Mike has control of

EMI, and an advisory role with ArkTex; they know that it leaves him in a conflict of interest position."

"How many people know about the report?"

"Difficult to say, but several know about his link to EMI. I don't think any of them know the full extent and scope of EMI's operation. As far as the report goes, it doesn't mention any link between EMI and you or me."

James corrected him, "Somebody knows the scope of EMI's activities in Iran, or that Thorpe is a magician of some kind. However, I don't think he knows anything about my brother or our links to terrorism."

"The OSI has a report on the interceptor investigation that points to the Tactical Air Command headquarters. The investigator said copies of the report have been sent to the White House. There is no way they can pin it on me, but it would be better if it hadn't been released. I was pretty cagy when I sent those messages; they point more toward the OSI than the Tactical Air Command. The testimonies of those interceptor pilots are quite damaging, however, I think we're overreacting. I can't take over ArkTex and hold my military position in the Air Force; maybe the report can't do that much damage if I retire and you whitewash it."

James asked, "Mike, what was in those messages that would convince the interceptor pilots to fire at the C9?"

Mike laughed, "An intel report that warned of a terrorist group armed with a nuclear weapon that could be using a hijacked aircraft to deliver the bomb to Washington."

"That would certainly be convincing. I don't know how that will help us though. This Thorpe fellow threatened to release information on our Iranian operations! If that happens, we are ruined."

The intercom came alive as the guard at the main entrance interrupted, "We've got someone out here who insists on seeing the boss. He claims it's important."

"Bring him in!" James ordered.

The guards brought him in, shackled him to a chair, and handed a locked briefcase to General Higgins, "He brought this with him, but refuses to open it."

James ordered the guards out, waiting until they left, "Now tell us what you're doing here!"

"Bruce Thorpe sent me. My name is Karl Hampton, and I have come to escort you to the Manhattan."

Cliff reacted, "Do you think we're stupid? You're with the FBI, who sent you?"

"No, not the FBI, but I certainly am a spy, and can prove it. I've been hiding aboard the Manhattan for several years waiting for the right time to act! I worked for EMI in the year 2615 for Mr. Thorpe, and he arranged to have me hired as a crew member aboard the Manhattan to prepare for his takeover. I know your organization from top to bottom, since I've worked here for over twenty years. I know you've made a couple of attempts to get Ashton, and I can tell you why they failed. For instance, the force field generated by the Manhattan prevented your interceptors from downing the C9."

"What's to stop them from using it again?"

"They lost it! We took control of the Manhattan."

"Can you prove it?"

"Yes, that should be obvious since this morning. We can't show you any fancy force fields inside this room, but if you'll go outside, we can give you another demonstration."

"Oh, so now you admit you can't record our conversations while in this room. Maybe you're not as all powerful as you claim."

"We do have our limits, but you can't hide behind your shields forever. We'll catch you when you least suspect it. Don't get too cocky about this room, you do have intercom and telephone wires to the outside. We can use those to record your conversations. Commander Thorpe is probably listening in on what we are saying right now."

"Ashton's father could do that!"

"Maybe, but I know everything about your organization, and can answer any questions you can throw at me concerning EMI. He couldn't; he didn't even know we existed until we took over his ship!"

"Why tonight? What's the big rush?"

"The time machine has a serious limitation; it has a small window of just a few days before it has to return, or we would be lost in time for all eternity. It takes several years to make the voyage, so the original crew members were too old to make more than two trips. That's what made it possible for us to infiltrate the new crew, and take over the ship."

"Assuming we believe all that, why come here?"

"We want to stop Ashton, and help you make this organization stronger."

"And how do we do that?"

"If we provide you with enough information and equipment you can. If you release me, I'll show you how."

They didn't trust him, but they released him, and allowed him to open his briefcase. He pulled out a laser pistol, and yelled as James tried to alert the guards, "Don't! Please." He fired the pistol at a chair across the room, and watched it smolder and disintegrate. He handed the gun over to Higgins, and gloated, "I could have used it on you. That weapon is just a sample of what we can do for you, or against you."

"I don't understand why you want to help us." James was trying to understand the logic but couldn't quite see it.

"Suppose Ashton is successful with the engines. Oil will be so plentiful that ArkTex will be bankrupt. When you are convicted, EMI will not survive, and therefore our present organization in the twenty-seventh century wouldn't exist either. Dr. Ashton has convinced President Dugan we ran out of oil in our century. That's utterly ridiculous, we had them all fooled. ArkTex has been controlling the supply, and keeping the price where we want it. Now do you see why we want to help?"

"Yes, but we'll get rid of her on our own. We don't need your help."

"That's where you're wrong. I just returned from the future. History records the opposite—that is, Ashton lived, and you failed. Since the Manhattan's first trip, ArkTex was dissolved, and EMI barely exists."

"Incredible."

"The gun you have in your hands is lethal no matter whether you hit a human target accurately or not. It has such shocking power that a wound on the arm is enough to kill. We have several other similar items you could use."

"Like what for instance?" Mike demanded.

"We need something to wipe out the Communists." James was on his favorite soapbox.

"Forget the Communists. In a few years, they will be out of the picture. Remember the interceptors;" Karl reminded him, "they were no match for a C9 because of a simple force field. You could use that force in a number of beneficial ways. Your imagination is the limit! Think of the electromagnetic propulsion units; we want to stamp them out in your time, but that doesn't mean that EMI shouldn't have them for your own use. How would you like to be able to communicate like we did with you this afternoon? You can do that, and have a captive audience as well. How about devices that could find rich mineral deposits accurately? How about inexpensive desalinization equipment; or equipment to remove valuable minerals from sea water? We can provide a number of devices in every conceivable field that would give your organization superiority over any competition."

"What if they just build another time machine?"

"Give us a little credit. If you take care of your end, we will be much stronger in the future. It's too expensive and takes too long

"Why don't you use your power to wipe out Ashton and the president for us?"

"We'd like to, and we considered that, but it might cause a lot of panic, and the resulting disruption would not be in our best interests. We want to insure our power structure in the future, not change history drastically. We like things the way they were before Ashton interfered. If we can gain a little advantage, why not?"

"All right, how do we proceed?"

"We are limited in what we can ship. We might be able to get a few guns or simple devices through the time warp, but the real value is in providing basic technical knowledge. That way, you can take credit for developing the weapon systems yourselves. We can only stay a few days before our time is up, but we'd like you to spend that time aboard the Manhattan where we will discuss strategy and give you all the technical information you can use. We haven't planned much beyond that, but it would be conceivable for us to make another trip back to your time if that option becomes desirable."

"Sounds like a trap to me." James only felt secure in the familiar surroundings of the EMI complex.

"I can't do any more to convince you, but I'm sure my boss can. If he doesn't, then you were just along for the ride. If we are setting a trap for you, then it certainly won't hurt to see it. If we wanted you dead, we wouldn't bother. Please come with me, unless you're afraid to go aboard!"

That was all the challenge Clifford needed as he replied, "All right, when do we go?"

CHAPTER 42

Major Bob Sparks in civilian clothes was sitting on the steps of the Lear 35 at Washington National Airport waiting. He had been alternately pacing the ramp, sitting on the steps and looking the aircraft over for almost two hours before Karl Hampton arrived, and got out of a limousine that stopped near the left wingtip. He walked toward Bob challenging, "We need you to get us back on the Manhattan as soon as possible."

"Yes, Sir. As soon as you're aboard."

Karl motioned to the others who all wore dark glasses with their collars pulled up high to prevent anyone from recognizing them, even though Bob had no desire to learn their identities. They took off heading in a westerly direction, climbing to forty-five hundred feet.

The aircraft flew on a few more minutes until the stillness of the night was broken by the voice Clifford recognized from earlier in the day, and all aboard realized it didn't come through the radio speakers, "Welcome to the Manhattan! You can lower the landing gear, and cut the engines. We have you on the beam."

Bob did as requested, and they touched down smoothly, while the huge doors were already closing behind them. A distinguished looking man met them at the steps of the Lear,

"Welcome aboard, I'm Bruce Thorpe, I trust your short trip was pleasant."

"Thanks, commander." Karl introduced those present.

"Come let me give you a tour of the Manhattan before we get down to business."

After a leisurely tour of the ship, Bruce led the party into the conference room where he could brief them on the various systems using the large video screen on the opposite side of the room. He asked Karl to stay with them in the hope they had developed some sort of rapport, and pave the way to gain their confidence.

Bruce began, "We've got approximately three days before we need to return to make our window. You've seen the ship, have you any doubt about who we are?"

James began, "Somehow, this seems too good to be true. I'm just not convinced."

Bruce laughed sinisterly, "I don't like to do things like this, but you don't give me much choice. Mike, do you know where your daughter is?"

"Certainly. She died in a brutal attack shortly after her ordeal on the missing C9."

"And I suppose you know who hired those who did the deed?"

"No."

"We know! Clifford hired the thugs, and James paid for it from EMI funds. Those records were in your safe in 2615. Here's a copy of the memo."

Mike took it, examining it closely, recognizing the stationery they used, and noting the age of the paper. He looked accusingly at them and began to yell, "You killed my daughter, you rotten good-for-nothing—"

Bruce interrupted, "Wait a minute, you knew it all along, so don't play the distressed father for us. You may find it distasteful at the moment, but it served your purpose. We know all the details concerning the Iran oil and arms deals, the electronic snooping at the White House and more. I could go on all night revealing the details that you think are secret. Karl, why don't you tell them about EMI, and ArkTex of the future?"

That was all he needed, and Karl began to talk about how EMI and ArkTex were interrelated talking for over an hour giving details that only members of EMI knew. He spoke of the secret codes that were used, praising them highly, and the three of them realized that they were the same as they had been using for years.

James finally admitted, "You certainly know about our organization."

Bruce was beginning to feel confident for the first time, "We certainly know enough to put you behind bars if we wanted." He went on to enumerate the various crimes that were committed by them during the last few years. "I may have added a few that history has blamed on you, but I think my sources are pretty accurate. I certainly hope all of that hasn't been for naught. You have made arrangements to stay on board three days, haven't you?"

"No," Mike said, "I've been away from Tactical Air Command headquarters too much already during the past few months."

Bruce glared, "What about that interceptor investigation, can't you think of a reason for that to take you away?"

"I suppose so."

"All right, we'll take you to the comm center and show you how to use the equipment. You can call anyone you see fit, and then relax for the evening. I want you to enjoy the comforts of the ship before we get down to business tomorrow."

The three of them were wined and dined throughout the evening, and basically, but not completely, given the run of the ship. They wandered about discussing the twenty-seventh century culture with several of the crew members, as well as several ingenious devices which were demonstrated as possible weapons for their use in the twentieth century.

Sleep came easily for them, unaware of the drug they were given, and they slept soundly before beginning the next day's business in the conference room, starting where they left off the previous evening.

Clifford was totally convinced, "What do you want from us? We wasted a beautiful opportunity to take care of Dugan in Dallas, trying to get Anderson and Ashton."

Bruce handed them the newspaper clippings concerning Dr. Ashton and Colonel Anderson's death as well as President Dugan's accident. "You didn't do too bad. It happened until someone from the future changed all that! How do you suppose they knew your assassins were on that hospital rooftop?"

"I saw that site several years ago and was waiting for the ideal time. I really had Dugan in mind when I saw it, though. It's too bad, but there will be lots more opportunities," James added.

"Not if Ashton keeps feeding Dugan information that will help him get to your organization first," Bruce cautioned.

Mike broke in, "They never discovered how or why Air Force One crashed, did they? We can get Dugan the next time he flies on Air Force One. We put an oil additive in the engines that gets extremely abrasive when hot. A little of that in each engine, and a little flight over water, and that will be it." Mike was bragging now, "The beauty of it is; it can't be detected unless the oil is hot. They won't find the cause the second time around either."

Bruce acted innocent. "That's incredible, how will you get it in the engines?"

"Easy; ArkTex has the contract for supplying oil and other fuels for the 89th Military Airlift Wing."

"Is that what happened to Dugan's helicopter?"

Clifford laughed, "Naw, that was just a little plastic explosive! It didn't take very much, not enough to leave a trace. We've got an inside track with the maintenance at Andrews. It was just too bad he wasn't on board."

Bruce couldn't believe his ears, but continued, "We were never able to piece together exactly how you got control of ArkTex from the records you left—how'd you do that?"

James volunteered, "Mike's daughter would have had controlling interest, but we made sure she didn't live to collect on it."

They continued to discuss options on how to successfully terminate Dr. Ashton and Colonel Anderson, and finally decided to plant a bomb in their offices at Wright-Patterson, and place the blame on various oil producers. James Little offered, "The president is going to meet with Middle East heads of state in Athens in a couple of weeks, and it would be an excellent time for that oil additive on a long trip over the Atlantic."

Bruce pushed a button under the table, and watched the expressions on the three men as the glass screen opened and the three conspirators stood looking at their judge and jury. Mike grabbed the laser from Karl, killing him, and turned on Bruce.

CHAPTER 43

Dr. David Ashton smiled grimly as he watched Mike Higgins repeatedly pull the trigger in vain as the laser ray couldn't penetrate the force field barrier protecting him as he impersonated Bruce Thorpe. He reached out his hand, "Please, it's over, hand me the weapon."

General Higgins looked at the men and women standing behind the glass, and began to comply, until he recognized his daughter, Dana, with tears streaming down her face, watching his every move. He reversed the gun, and once more pulled the trigger. Dana screamed, but it was too late, her father crumpled before her eyes.

Laura comforted her as best she could while Arthur Olson read the rights to Vice President James Little and Clifford Burns. The remains of General Higgins and Karl Hampton were covered and carried out while the others prepared to return to Washington.

Brad went to the communications room and connected himself directly to the president. "Mr. President, it looks like it's over. We have Little and Burns in custody, and General Higgins killed himself."

"Good, I'm glad that's over, now I can get back to business as usual, and get on with my life."

"Well, not so fast. We got the head, but there is a lot of their organization still at large. Until we can develop a test for the presence of that additive, you are at extreme risk. I thought our plan worked better than expected, except for Higgins' suicide. We hypnotized Karl Hampton, the spy we caught on board and convinced him we were backing EMI and ArkTex from the twenty-seventh century, and he gave them all the truth they needed. He brought them aboard the Manhattan, and they plotted to assassinate you and kill us, with the chief justice, attorney general, and several congressmen watching. That's about the whole story, Sir."

CHAPTER 44

A month later, Brad walked into the SMA office a little later than usual, and couldn't help frowning, seeing Dana, knowing he couldn't talk her into looking after her own business interests. She wanted nothing to do with ArkTex, although she had the controlling interest. Charles Bains had been guiding her in finding the right person to manage her interests, and provide her with frequent updates until such time as she was ready to take over, if she ever had the desire to do so. She was having too much fun; she was excited about the projects the Solar Magnetics Administration was involved in, and she wanted to be a part of it. Her inheritance made her one of the most fabulously wealthy women in the United States, with no need to work, but it didn't change her outlook.

"Morning, Sunshine!" Brad removed the frown almost as quickly as it had formed.

"Hi Brad, isn't Laura with you?" She had a worried look on her face.

"No, hasn't she been here?"

"I haven't seen her since she left here with you last evening. She always lets me know when she isn't coming home."

"She left to go home before nine last night. Are you sure she didn't come in?" Brad was beginning to feel a knot of fear well up in the pit of his stomach.

"Yes, I'm sure. Do you think something happened to her?"

"Stay by the phone! If she calls, let me know as soon as you hear. I don't know what happened, but we have too many enemies, particularly with many of EMI's hired killers on the loose." As he walked into his office, he yelled back, "Get me Olson!"

Arthur answered immediately, "Morning Brad, Dana sounded scared this morning, what's wrong?"

"Arthur, I'm—I may be crying wolf, but Laura is missing. I don't know—"

"Brad, don't give up on her before you give her a chance! She's intelligent enough to take care of herself. Don't panic, we'll find her. Give me the particulars."

"There's not much to go on. She left to go to her apartment where she is staying with Dana before nine last night, and according to Dana, she never arrived."

"What about her bodyguards?"

"I don't know, nobody has seen them today, and they didn't report anything abnormal last night."

"Have you found her car?"

"No, just what I told you. I thought I'd better get your advice before we did anything."

"Okay, I'll take it from here. Just be where I can reach you. We have some good men in Dayton, and I'll get them on it. When those Secret Service agents show up, I'd like to talk with them!"

"Okay, Arthur, I'll be here."

He pushed the intercom, "Dana, get me the president!"

A few minutes later the president came on the line, "Morning, Brad, what's the matter? My secretary said Dana was unusually upset. What's going on?"

"I hope nothing, Sir, but Laura is missing. We suspect she has been kidnapped."

"Oh no . . . What can I do?"

"The FBI is already on the case, and we don't know anything. I wanted to clue you in before the news hits the street."

"Thanks for calling; I'll do what I can." The president did call Art Dawson to make sure the case had the FBI's top priority, which it had already been given.

Brad wanted to make one more call—this time to the Manhattan, but Laura had the communications gear. He would have to wait until either Laura called, or her father called him.

Each passing moment seemed like an hour, but they received no calls from Laura, or her abductors. Finally, Olson called back; they found her car in a parking lot near the apartment with the left front window broken. The lifeless bodies of her secret service agents were found nearby.

Brad tried to catch up on paperwork he had been putting aside for the past couple of weeks, but his heart wasn't in it. Dana buzzed him on the intercom, "Alex Newsome is on the line; would you like to talk to him?"

"Thanks, I'll take it." He picked up the receiver, and gave Alex his usual cheery, "Morning, Alex, how's everything in the sunny south?"

"Great! We have your bird certified. It came through with flying colors. Whoever designed the additional systems to match the aircraft did an excellent job."

"Laura did the lion's share of it."

"Great, she must be as intelligent as she is beautiful. When do you want it delivered? I don't have any excuse to keep it longer, but I'll fly it to you, if you like."

"Thanks. I'm sorry I don't sound too enthused about the aircraft right now, but you can bring it to Wright-Patterson Air Force Base, and we'll exchange whenever you get a chance."

Alex was perplexed, "What's wrong? Are you hiding something?"

"Keep it under your hat, but Laura has been kidnapped."

"Sorry to hear that. I shouldn't have bothered you."

"No, that's okay, she may turn up soon, and we'll have worried for nothing. Anyway, bring the airplane at your convenience. If we want it before then, I'll come and get it."

"That would take away my opportunity to fly it once more. I'll deliver it tomorrow morning."

"Fine. How about calling first? We may be tied up; on the other hand, we may need the bird. See you in the morning."

The FBI agent chief of the Dayton district brought all the articles found in Laura's car into the office just after noon, gave Brad an update and tried to discover any leads Brad might be able to give.

Laura's briefcase was with her belongings, which enabled Brad to call David who answered immediately, "Hi Laura how's my beautiful daughter?"

"It's Brad, has Laura been in touch with you today? Do you know where she is?"

"No, I haven't talked with her in the last couple of days. What's wrong?"

"She's missing, probably kidnapped. You were our last hope; is there any way you can locate her?"

"It sounds like you have her computer, so I'd say no. We could have traced her communications equipment if it was turned on, but we can't make contact unless we know where to look."

"Have you any suggestions?"

"No, not offhand. Do you have any suspects other than EMI?"

"No. The FBI is on the case, and trying to track it down, but no trace."

"Brad, don't give up! We'll monitor any communications to and from EMI. Call us if you discover any additional clues."

"Okay."

CHAPTER 45

They had been waiting over twenty-four hours when a plain white envelope bearing a single line address of the Solar Magnetics Administration postmarked in Dayton arrived with the morning mail run. Brad forced himself to be patient as the FBI agents carefully opened it, reading the short note inside:

Colonel Anderson! Dr. Laura Ashton will die!!! Her head will be mailed to you in a plain brown wrapper unless Clifford Burns and James Little are released within 48 hours. The time clock starts now! There will be no negotiations concerning their release; it must be unconditional. If there are any tricks, SHE IS DEAD!!!

No fingerprints or other clues could be found on the letter. The characters appeared to have been typed on an IBM Selectric III typewriter such as might be found in any government office. Arthur Olson arrived at Wright-Patterson earlier that morning to personally handle the investigation, and tried to make them see the brighter side, "The letter appears untraceable, but we have plenty of time to find her. We'll start with the car and backtrack along the route she took; we'll find something."

Brad surprisingly calm, replied, "Go ahead, I'm going to check out another theory of mine. I'll be out of touch, leave a message with Dana and I'll be checking with her often. If I find what I'm looking for, I'll call you."

Brad took Laura's briefcase and left to go to the flight line where Alex would be delivering the Marie to him within the hour. While he waited for Alex, he put through another call to the Manhattan, "Morning David, we received a note from the kidnappers this morning giving us forty-eight hours to release Clifford Burns and James Little or she will be killed."

"Well, Brad, that gives us a little time. Come on up and we'll see if we can find a solution."

Alex was excited as he climbed out of the aircraft. "Brad, that's one helleva airplane. We'll sell a million of them, I'll guarantee it!"

"Well, you won't sell any unless we can get you some more engines. Laura is the only one who can deliver on that."

"You mean to tell me she alone has the ability to manufacture those engines! I can't believe one person alone knows the secret."

"She's the brains behind it, and her loss would set the program back a long time. That's one of the reasons why it's vital to find her before it's too late. Oh, your aircraft has full fuel tanks ready to go. I've got to be on my way. Thanks much for your cooperation."

Alex watched Brad take off, and begin his climb. He took his eye off him for a moment, but when he looked back the aircraft was gone. He turned away scowling, thinking he needed to get his eyes checked.

Brad went right to David's office to discuss the problem. "David, is there any way we can go back in time, and discover where she is?"

"No need; we have her location. It took time, but the signal is coming in strong."

"Great, where is she?"

"In a warehouse on a pier in Bayonne, New Jersey. It's a military port used for shipping autos to overseas locations which I suspect is the port used by EMI for their illegal shipping."

"Is she okay?"

"As near as we can tell, she's fine. We will protect her with the force fields so you can direct the FBI in without worrying about endangering her. They should get quite a haul."

CHAPTER 46

Inside the warehouse, nearly fifty men loyal to EMI waited, led by Samuel Burns. Samuel was Clifford's younger brother, and acted as his field general performing much of the day-to-day undercover operation of EMI, and was their contact man with most of the terrorist organizations worldwide. He held Laura hostage, but Samuel and his men were there to prepare for a widespread terrorist campaign in the event the government would not accede to their demands. They had large quantities of plastic explosives, automatic weapons, and surface-to-air missiles, holding all of American hostage to their fear of terrorists. They believed one or two Boeing 747 jumbo jets downed while on final approach to JFK would spread terror into the heart of every American.

Arthur Olson wasted little time setting up a siege surrounding the area. As soon as he was aware of their presence, Samuel left Laura, locked in a small closet area securely bound with her mouth taped shut. She was his ace in the hole, and he would not hesitate to use her as a hostage in making their escape. He had no inkling that he could not enter the room where she was locked, or that he had no control over her any longer.

The nation woke the next morning with every network broadcasting the same story:

". . . . live from Bayonne, New Jersey. I'm standing in the street a block away from a military warehouse most recently used to ship private autos overseas for military personnel. An unknown number of men armed with automatic weapons are holed up inside, surrounded by the FBI and several police units from surrounding communities. The first action occurred late last night when two agents were killed attempting to surround the warehouse. They have one known hostage, kidnapped late Wednesday night in Dayton, Ohio. The kidnap victim is Dr. Laura Ashton, who is the head of the newly created Solar Magnetics Administration. We are told she is being held as a hostage in an attempt to free Vice President James Little and Clifford Burns. We need to confirm this story, but our latest information source indicates this warehouse was being used to ship illegal weapons to terrorist units around the world by the EMI Corporation, which has been controlled by those officials indicted last month. The FBI has been unable to establish communications with the kidnappers inside, and we have no word on how they intend to proceed. They have several military units standing by with helicopter gunships capable of striking through the roof of the warehouse. We will be standing by to report the news as it breaks."

Arthur used his bullhorn in an attempt to reach those inside the warehouse: "Attention! Attention inside the warehouse! We want to talk. Call 911 and we will discuss your demands. We are prepared to begin an assault on the building! You have ten minutes." Even as he spoke, Army helicopters overhead were lowering SWAT teams, and military assault personnel onto the roof of the warehouse.

Samuel Burns' reaction to Arthur's warning was predictable: he sent several men to the roof with orders to block that entrance. His orders were issued too late, but several of his men opened up with automatic weapons fire on the helicopter about to land with its full load of assault troops. Before the pilot could change course, a missile entered the right engine exhaust pipe; the helicopter disintegrated sending showers of burning debris, and bodies onto the street below. Vietnam veteran pilots in the backup helicopter gunship instinctively returned cannon and rocket fire, sending Samuel's men scurrying below, leaving their weapons on the roof, which exploded, engulfing the rooftop in flames.

Brad was on Laura's communicator, "Dad, the roof is engulfed in flame; can you protect her from the heat and fire?"

"Don't worry, Brad, she is located in a small room in the middle of the building. We've prevented the terrorists from entering the room, and our force field will protect her from the fire!"

"Thank God you're here. I'd better get back with Arthur and see if I can help."

Arthur saw him coming, "I'm sorry, Brad, if she's in that inferno—we should have waited them out a little longer."

"Don't worry, as you said, she can take care of herself. Just get the situation under control."

Firefighters began arriving, coming as close as they dared, protecting nearby buildings as the flames engulfed weapons caches inside, exploding, blasting away much of one wall, exposing the interior of the building. The terrorists not killed in the blasts came pouring out trying to escape the flames, and attacked police and FBI personnel behind the barricades erected in the street. Most were killed by a lethal dose of cannon fire from the gunship hovering overhead, and the rest threw down their weapons and surrendered.

Firefighters waited until the dangers of the exploding weapons subsided, and entered the burning warehouse in search of Laura. They found her exhausted but unharmed, huddled in the corner of the untouched closet used as her prison cell. They wrapped her in fire retardant blankets, fastened a portable oxygen mask to her face, and carried her through the burning debris as the firefighters kept a steady stream of flame retardant foam on them until they exited the burning warehouse. They left none too soon, as the entire warehouse became engulfed in flame and was completely destroyed.

Laura was placed in a waiting ambulance where Brad assisted in removing the tape binding her arms and legs. She was unconscious, overcome with fatigue and exposure to the smoke and fumes. The paramedics administered oxygen, and Laura quickly responded to their treatment.

Brad was unsure of her condition, but was certain that Dr. Baker aboard the Manhattan would be able to give her the best treatment, and insisted, "Take us to Teterboro Airport!"

The paramedics resisted, "We can't do that, Sir; we have our orders, and are taking her to New York General Hospital."

Brad didn't hestitate, "Dad, take care of the paramedics for me, please."

"Sure, no problem."

The paramedics fell into a deep sleep of their own, and Brad ordered the driver, "Take us to Teterboro!"

They spent a couple of days together aboard the Manhattan until Laura recovered, then she delivered Brad to Wright-Patterson and returned to the Manhattan by herself. She wanted to spend more time with her father but knew Brad needed to get back to work. She was sure her father was getting anxious although he had promised to be there for her wedding. She asked, "Dad, it's going to be a couple of months before the wedding. Are you sure you can stay around that long?"

"Don't worry. I need to confess a few little white lies I've been telling. I told you we went back home. We didn't. We have been here all along making sure everything went okay."

Laura was shocked, "I don't believe it. You never lied to me before. I didn't think you could!"

"Well, it wasn't easy. I had to turn my head away more than once. Please forgive me. You remember the instruction package you were given by the president?"

"Sure, that was the beginning of this adventure for me."

"My instruction package was different. Besides having the plans for the time machine which Roger had already perfected, I was given a detailed account of the first voyages. We knew well in advance of the recorded event of your deaths in Dallas. We knew that Brad died in the Comm Center; we knew of your kidnapping ordeal, and had a locator planted in one of your teeth. That's why we found you so quickly. The original Manhattan had to return to prevent those deaths. We didn't, so rather than spend the years going and coming, we stayed. I couldn't tell you because you might have reacted differently and who knows how successful the mission would have been. I knew you would marry Brad from the beginning, but I told you different. Will you forgive me?"

"I shouldn't, but I will."

"You should know that our return trip will be a matter of hours rather than years, so that should relieve your mind on that score."

"You bet it does. I won't worry about your trip home anymore."

"I've got another job I need to do for President Albee. Some of that will be pushing the limit of the Manhattan, but we will have quite an adventure. We are going back to the first century where we can observe and record the events surrounding the life of Jesus."

"Wow, are you really going to jeopardize the primary mission for that?"

David laughed, "Not in the least. Our part in the mission is complete. You have the ball now and, we don't expect any more problems. Oh, you will have difficulties, but nothing you can't take care of on your own. History has already recorded your success. If we are lost in time, it doesn't matter. It will solve another problem and that is the difficult dilemma concerning the disposition of the Manhattan. We have been talking about what if someone gained control of the Manhattan and used it for personal use."

"Well, you could destroy it!"

"Yes, that's an option, but it may be needed again. President Albee will have to make those kinds of decisions. We don't know all the answers, but you can be assured that your mission was and will be successful. I'm proud of all you have done and all you will accomplish."

"Thanks, Dad." She hugged him, "How will I know how successful your new mission will be?"

"We will leave within a couple of days, but I plan on returning for your wedding. If I'm not here, you will know we were unsuccessful. Don't worry; I'm confident we'll be back. We plan on being back within a few days of leaving although the journey may take 15 to 20 years. What will you do in the meantime?"

"I've got to meet with a couple of manufacturers while Brad is in Washington testifying before Congress. We are hoping he will be through in Washington so we can meet with the automakers on August thirteenth in Detroit, so we'll be busy but my heart will be with you."

CHAPTER 47

After Laura launched, David ordered Roger to move the Manhattan in orbit over Israel and begin the countdown setting their arrival time as close to the year one as they could calculate. It didn't take long as the countdown had been practiced many times during the last few weeks when they had waited to rescue Laura. The ship vibrated slightly and began its spiraling journey back to the meridian of time where they hoped they could be witnesses to the greatest miracles of all time when Jesus walked the earth.

Roger Dorn resisted David's pleas to submit to the deep sleep process. "I have no life except aboard this ship. No family left at home and my wife and I have no desire to go back to the University. I have completed my dream and when or if the Manhattan is destroyed, there will be nothing left for us. Nothing else matters and I think it is vital for human control at all times. I am probably the only one aboard this ship that can do anything in the event something does go wrong en route. I don't expect any problems, but you know Murphy's Law. Besides, Warren will tell you that the aging process has been slowed dramatically in the sterile environment aboard this ship, particularly if I use the Drug treatment Warren has developed to retard the aging process. Don't worry, I won't be alone, my wife will remain with me."

David could not persuade him to change his mind and finally gave up. "All right Roger, I can't force you and if it makes you feel better. Go ahead. You are now in command of the ship until our arrival. Your sacrifice is noted and appreciated."

Roger worked hard during the first couple of years tweaking the performance of the time machine. He was finally satisfied with the results which nearly doubled the speed in which the Manhattan hurtled through time. It was quite transparent and there were no adverse effects. In the close orbit above the earth, there was little chance of hitting space debris or space junk as occurred after the advent of orbital flights of the space age begun in the latter half of the twentieth century.

After six years with less than one year to go, Roger revived Warren first to be in charge of the revival process and then David who after a short period of adjustment with recuperative therapy took over again in command of the Manhattan. He felt refreshed and renewed, fully recovered from his long years of stress and strain that were a part of heading up the Manhattan Project. They had a couple of months before their arrival which David and most of the crew members used to exercise rigorously to restore their muscles and body tone.

His moments of relaxation were spent in reading the bible and all historical data available from that period. He read the gospels of Matthew, Mark, Luke and John several times, and most of the crew members participated in discussions concerning the events of the time. Much of the rest of his time was spent with memories of Marie, Brenda, and Laura. It was difficult for him to separate them in his mind. Laura looked almost identical to what Marie looked like those many years ago, and Brenda somehow blended in, particularly in personality and actions. Each one had a special place in his heart, and he hoped it would not be long before he could once again be with Brenda. Laura was and would be okay with Brad and her life in the twentieth century, but the more he thought about her, the more he missed Brenda. Throughout their mission, he had been preoccupied, but now his mind was free and he hoped that Brenda would relent and become his wife when he returned.

CHAPTER 48

They recorded most of the important events in the life of Jesus along with the role of Roman occupation forces which would definitely be of interest to historians specializing in the Roman Empire. As they placed their greatest emphasis on the events of the holy week, David could not watch as the urgings to interfere were strong, especially as Jesus was hung on the cross. He would watch the videos later when he couldn't do anything but watch.

Following Pentecost, when they were ready to travel back to the twentieth century, the council met to discuss the trip. Roger pointed out that there would be no need for deep sleep as the earlier voyages had proven that traveling forward was relatively fast, a matter of hours rather than years. Roger avowed, "I have one request."

Roger waited for a response, so David added, "Go ahead, I'm listening."

"After we stop for Laura's wedding, I think we should stop en route and save the lives of Marie and Commander White before returning to our time."

"No way!" David was abrupt and without hesitation. "That is not going to happen. I will forget you ever mentioned it, but I don't want to hear any more about it."

Roger grinned sheepishly, "Okay David, have it your way. I had to try so I hope you won't hold it against me."

"Don't worry about that, I've forgotten already. Let's get ready to go back."

The initial hearings requiring Brad's presence were completed, with trial dates set for late October, but probably delayed longer. The Attorney General was unwilling to drop any charges for plea bargaining and both James Little and Clifford Burns were held without bond. EMI was shut down, and investigations continued on several illegal arms deals dating back to the Iran-Contra scandals and earlier. A new board of directors was appointed to operate ArkTex, until Dana was ready to accept her responsibilities.

Brad wasn't the least bit sad to leave Washington, and get back to work as Laura picked him up at Andrews. He greeted her with a warm hug and kiss, but it wasn't until they went back into the airplane and the door was closed behind them that he took her in his arms, and kissed her like there was no tomorrow. She didn't want him to let her go, but she finally broke free, "Brad, we've got to get going, or the ground crew will think we're doing something we shouldn't be doing."

"Well, if I was in their position, I'd wonder about me if we didn't do something. After all, it's been over two weeks, and I haven't been able to think of anything except you."

"That's nice, but now it's time we were on our way. We've got a busy schedule ahead of us."

They were in the air climbing through 20,000 feet before Brad sensed something was wrong. Laura just seemed to clam up, "What's the matter Laura? You're far too quiet."

"I'm worried about Dad. He isn't back yet."

"I thought he was going to stay until after our wedding."

"He went back to the first century and promised to return within days. I'm afraid something has happened to them. He left right after my ordeal with the kidnapping." She told him all about the planned trip.

"It's only been two weeks. Give him a little time."

"I know, I'm not ready to throw in the towel, but I'm troubled. He said it would be no big deal if they didn't make it back as their primary mission has already been accomplished."

"How long has it been since you tried to contact him?"

"At least an hour." She grinned.

"Let me have the controls and try again."

She relinquished the controls, pulled out her computer and tried to contact the Manhattan again. This time, David responded immediately, He answered with a joyful shout! "Laura, how's everything with my favorite daughter?"

"You mean your only daughter. How do you think? I've been on pins and needles for over two weeks."

"Well I guess we missed our target by a few days. Not bad though for traveling almost two thousand years."

"How was the trip?"

"We just got back and it's going to take us a little time to evaluate, but it seems like everything went fine. You don't have a thing to worry about. We'll be ready to come down for your wedding."

CHAPTER 49

Brad was called back to Washington for more testimony and that left Laura by herself. Laura left with the Marie, stopping at Wright-Patterson to pick up Dana, and then headed directly to Independence. "Why Independence? I thought we were going to Kansas." Dana was puzzled but not surprised, as Laura often did strange things with or without Brad.

"I've been waiting for the opportunity to meet with Brad's parents alone. I fabricated a story on most of those other trips for an excuse to get the use of the airplane. I'll probably have to go to those plants, but they aren't ready. They really need to have the assembly line up and running first. I'll probably go to Pratt and Whitney's plant next week, and General Electric's in the near future." She changed the subject, "Have you ever had the chance to fly?"

"No, I've been too busy. You know basketball and all those other sports."

"Well, take the controls and try it for a while. It's easy, but be real gentle on the controls. This aircraft is pretty responsive, but it'll get away from you in a hurry if you let it."

Dana sat concentrating for some time trying to get enough of the feel to keep the aircraft generally within plus or minus

1,000 feet. She gradually settled down, and tried again to question Laura, "Why do you want to see Brad's parents?"

"Gee, Dana, I thought flying the aircraft would keep you from asking so many questions." Laura laughed, "I think I'll wait, and let you see for yourself. I do have another reason though; to make plans for our wedding."

They flew along in silence while Laura showed her how to connect the autopilot, and control the aircraft the easy way. Dana soon became totally engrossed in the navigation procedures and programming of the autopilot. Laura commented, "You learn fast. I think you like the technical aspects of your job, don't you?"

"Sure, and I'm eager to learn all I can."

"Do you have any idea what you would have been doing this fall, if Brad and I were no longer around?" Laura probed.

"I suppose I would continue to work with Charles. I find this work challenging."

"All right, I'll quit beating around the bush. When we were killed, the secret of the new engine technology died with us. Charles Bains couldn't recover, and Solar Magnetics Administration no longer existed. Charles helped you enroll in the Massachusetts Institute of Technology; you got your doctorate in Physics and you went on to become the leading expert in the Solar Magnetics field. What I'm saying is that you have the potential to do whatever you want in life. I'm not sure you're doing yourself a favor by continuing to work as our receptionist."

"Wow! You mean I actually got a doctorate in Physics? That's hard to believe! Laura, you're the world's leading expert in that field; I couldn't do the same thing, but I'd like to continue to work with you, and learn as much as I can from you."

"You're too bright to waste your time that way! Yes, you would learn the mechanics of it, but probably never learn the theory or create anything on your own. This field opens thousands of new opportunities, especially in the synthetic material fields. Your company needs to expand out of the fuels technology into the leading edge of synthetic engineering, or face bankruptcy. You see, these new units could never be produced without materials created from your oil products."

"I don't know what to say—it's overwhelming."

"Well, you don't have to make any hasty decisions. You can go to school, and work with me in the laboratory. But, I think you need to consider your inheritance, and what it might mean to you."

"I'll think about it."

They landed at the downtown Kansas City airport, and rented a car to go to Brad's home. Laura said, "You know Dana, I didn't even bother calling Brad's folks. I felt so comfortable and at home with them last time; I don't feel any pressing need to call first. I hope they're home and they welcome us without Brad."

"You're as silly and impulsive as I am. Crazy is more like it, but I don't care. I'm having a good time whatever way it turns out."

"Isn't this country beautiful?"

"It's kind of flat. I loved the mountains in Arkansas. I loved to drive through those hills. But I suppose they will always remind me of my accident."

They were at the driveway now as Laura turned in toward the house. "I hope you don't let that stop you from enjoying the beauty of the Ozarks."

"Oh no, I want to go back to Arkansas, and I want to see the rest of the basketball team. I'm not sure I want to go back to play ball again though."

Marty Anderson was out in the front yard, and it only took him a minute to recognize Laura. "You must be Laura Ashton. What a welcome surprise. I'm Marty, Brad's brother, come on in."

"Sorry to barge in on you like this. Are your parents home?"

"No, sorry; Dad took Mom to see the doctor. Her condition isn't improving, and she's in constant pain."

She indicated her companion. "This is Dana Higgins."

"Hi, Dana, welcome to Missouri. Come on in. Mary, my wife, is trying to take over a little of the housecleaning burden from Dad."

Mary threw her arms around them, welcoming Laura into the family. "It's good to meet you both. Dana, I've heard a lot about you. I'm sorry about your father!"

"Where are your kids, Mary, I thought you had some little ones?"

"Oh no, all of mine are grown. I have two, and they are both in college. Brian may be here later this afternoon."

"It seems I never meet any of Brad's brothers and sisters when I come. I'm probably mixing you up with another of Brad's brothers or sisters."

"Oh, don't worry about that, you'll see so much of us that you'll probably want to stay in Ohio."

"Dana and I both were an only child, and I definitely want to get to know all the family."

"Here comes Brian now." They watched as a young man with definite Anderson features got out of his car, and walked toward the house. Mary introduced them, "Brian, this is Laura Ashton, and her friend, Dana Higgins."

"Nice to meet you. Saw you on TV this morning, but you look even more beautiful in person." Brian turned toward Dana, "The house is full of pretty girls today."

Dana smiled, "Mary said you're in college; what school?"

"University of Missouri in Columbia," he proudly replied, "you know where that is?"

"Yup, trounced them in basketball twice last winter. You interested in basketball?"

"I am if you are. Would you like to shoot some baskets?"

"I'd love to; I've been just too busy to stay in practice!"

"You better look out, Brian," Laura challenged, "I've seen her play!" He led Dana off to the back of the house leaving Laura alone with Mary and Marty. Laura began tentatively, "Marty, what's your mother's prognosis?"

"Not good, I'm afraid she seems to be in more pain every day. The doctors can't do anything for her except give her something to reduce the pain. She has faith in God, and hopes she might be healed in some way, but she's beginning to give up."

"I know where she can be helped. Would she be willing to go with me to see my doctor?"

Marty bristled, "Laura, I respect you for who you are, and because Brad cares for you, but I don't want you, or anybody else coming around here, raising her hopes, then letting her down with a big disappointment. Do I make myself perfectly clear?"

Laura was momentarily at a loss, but recovered quickly, "Marty, you sound just like Brad! I bet you're as stubborn too. I wouldn't do that to your mom. I fell in love with her the first time we met, and I sensed an awful lot of love behind all her pain and suffering. You misunderstand me, I may not have been positive enough. I know my doctor can help Mom."

Marty was furious, "You aren't listening! Mom has seen enough doctors to last a lifetime, and has been disappointed too many times. Why did you come around here without Brad? Did you already ask him?"

Mary interrupted, "Marty, please, just listen to her for a minute! Laura, you sound so positive, how can you know such a thing? Do you know any others who have been healed?"

"Yes, you just saw one. Dana wasn't much more than a vegetable when she was taken to my doctor. You can see she is perfectly healthy!"

"That's not what President Dugan said!"

"I know, and I shouldn't tell you more, but Mom and Dad already are aware of our story. Can you keep this confidential?"

Marty answered for both of them, "It doesn't matter what I think of you, if you want to confide something in us, we will honor those wishes."

"Okay, remember the story President Dugan told about the missing C9?"

"Sure, that was all we talked about for a while; it didn't make sense then, and it still doesn't."

"It wasn't true. The UFO stories that were circulating were closer to the truth. Dana was in critical condition, but when the story came out, it was altered because Dana's smashed and mutilated body was mended by a doctor who he couldn't reveal. That same doctor can treat your mom."

"I wish I could believe you, but I can't," Marty said as he walked away.

"Wait, Marty please give me a chance," she begged.

He slowly turned back taking her by the shoulders, "It's only because of Brad, but I'll listen."

"Thank you, I could go, and find the other patients that were aboard the C9 that day. Two of them had serious cases of arthritis, and they were cured. They don't know how, but they are living proof."

"Just stand still for a minute." She began to scan Marty from head to toe. "Remember President Dugan's surgery a couple weeks ago?"

"Sure, he had some type of tumor on his back, didn't he?"

"Yes, I suggested he go to his doctor after doing this procedure on him!" She began interpreting the printout from her computer, "Well, let's see, your blood type is A positive, your sugar level is slightly elevated, you had a triple bypass, and you better keep your eye on your cholesterol level; it's slightly higher than normal. Blood pressure: normal, pulse: high, probably due to your excited emotional condition. You have a metal peg in your left knee probably due to some injury sustained several years ago. You had all the normal childhood diseases and an exceptionally hard case of the measles probably later in life than usual. Health is overall excellent." She waited a minute, "Did I miss anything?"

"No, unless you count my moles. How did you do that?" Marty was impressed, but skeptical, "I'll bet Brad told you all my medical history."

"Brad doesn't speak much about his family; he never confided anything about you. I didn't know Brad had any brothers or sisters until your mom told me."

Marty replied, "I'm sorry, Brad doesn't know most of that, and wouldn't have told you; so, how did you do it?"

"I have some medical knowledge and equipment, and can make limited diagnoses, but the doctor of whom I speak can do much more. The medical knowledge comes from the same advanced civilization that produced the engines that Brad and I are working on. The president's explanation of that wasn't quite true either."

"Are you trying to tell me you're an alien, and there really was a UFO?"

Laura grinned, "I don't like to be called an alien because I have always been an American citizen. But I did come here on what you would call a UFO. Until their business is finished, my doctor on board is available and willing to help Mom!"

"That's incredible! If Mom wants to try again, I'll support you. But, why don't you wait and let Brad convince Mom and Dad? I'm afraid you don't know them very well. Dad will be your biggest obstacle!"

"I should wait, and let Brad do it as you say; but I want so much to give this gift of health, this gift of love to your Mom, and to Brad. If we waited, we'd have to postpone our wedding. It would also delay my father on his return journey. I can't wait. Somehow, Brad feels he's to blame for his mother's health, maybe I can help him. Anyway, it's the way he does things, and I work the same way!"

She waited until later that evening after dinner, as they were all sitting around the table, and began to plant the seed, "Mom, how did your doctor's appointment go today?"

"Nothing new! That old quack keeps taking our money, but I'm afraid nothing changes,"

"I suppose he won't let you go anywhere, or do anything except stay around the house."

"That old goat couldn't stop me if he tried. I get along fine in my chair, and if I want to go somewhere, I'll go. Won't we, Dad?" She needed Dad to assist her wherever she went.

"How would you like to go see the airplane Brad and I just acquired? It's a model 55 Learjet we just finished modifying, a great little airplane! Maybe I could take you for a ride over

Independence tomorrow; that is, if you think the doctor will let you."

"Let him try to stop me! I'd like that! I haven't been in an airplane in years. Now if you can convince Dad to go along."

Dad hesitated, "I don't know, I like to keep my feet on the ground."

Laura tried to put the icing on, "I bet you're afraid to go up with me." She was treading on thin ice and knew it, looking toward Marty for help.

Marty added, "Dad, it would do Mom a world of good to get off the farm for a while."

"All right, we'll go with you, Laura."

Dad insisted on driving the next morning since it was so much easier to carry the wheelchair in his station wagon. Laura was satisfied, hoping Marty and Mary would understand when they weren't invited along for the ride. She knew Brian wanted to see the airplane, but it didn't take long for Dana to convince him to take her to see the Kansas City Royals instead.

Laura showed them the Lear with pride; she supposed Dad knew a little about airplanes from Brad's life as a pilot, and could appreciate the clean lines, especially with the engine pods missing from their usual places. He looked at Laura with appreciation in his eyes as he spoke, "It's a beauty; I can see how Brad feels about it. Where are we going?"

"The sky's the limit! Where would you like to go?"

"We don't care about going that far; maybe we should wait until Brad comes home."

"It's kind of late to back down unless you want to disappoint Mom. Besides we're not going very far, just up over Independence to see what you can see."

Laura requested a little help from the linesman, and Mom was seated in a comfortable VIP seat near the cockpit while Dad followed Laura around inspecting the aircraft. She spoke to the linesman, "There won't be any noise from the engines so watch for my signal. I'll flip the nose light on and off when ready to taxi."

He looked as excited as a small boy with candy, "I wish I had my camera, you don't mind if we take pictures, do you?"

"Not at all, we want the public to be excited about this airplane. We'll be back here often; I'm sure you will have your chance."

Dad sat in back with Mom for the takeoff and departure, but came up front when Laura called for him after their initial climb. He sat down in the copilot's seat, enthusiastically looking around the cockpit. Laura decided it was time to break the news to him. "Dad." He was so engrossed in his excitement he didn't hear her the first time and she repeated, "Dad!"

"Yes, Laura."

"Dad, I've got a confession to make . . . I didn't invite you on this flight to show off the aircraft."

He looked back at Mom, "Why then?"

Laura bravely continued, "I want to take you and Mom aboard the Manhattan, I think it's time you met my father."

"I don't know about that; I'm beginning to think we should have stayed on the ground. You said he would be at your wedding; that's soon enough considering."

Laura ignored the implied meaning, "That's only part of it." Neither of them spoke for a moment, "I want Mom to see my doctor."

Dad looked at her with disgust, "Laura, now I'm really disappointed, I thought you understood. She's been through enough."

She sensed his disappointment and rejection. "I'm sorry, Dad, I . . . We knew you would look at it this way; that's why Marty and I decided this was the only way we could . . ."

He interrupted in a loud voice, "Marty! He had something to do with this?"

Mom hearing him raise his voice, cried out, "What's the matter?"

He looked back seeing the alarm on her face, "Nothing, nothing at all, I'll be back with you in a minute."

Laura devoted a few minutes to her flying, guiding the aircraft away from the populated areas before she spoke, "Marty wasn't easy to convince, but he agreed to let me try after I told him the full story. You already know our story; maybe you don't believe us."

He didn't know how she did it, but he was now on the defensive, "Absolutely not! Your story was preposterous."

"Brad told me you have a strong faith in God, and believe Mom will be healed. Don't you think God can work through many different and mysterious ways?"

"Yes, but I think your magic must come directly from Satan. You're trying to play God!"

"I'm sorry; I thought you understood. You don't even believe your son! Right now, I don't even want to sit next to you. Why don't you go back, and sit with Mom?" We're going aboard the Manhattan, and I'm taking Mom to see my doctor, whether you approve or not."

Dad felt keenly disappointed with her, and had misgivings for coming along, but he didn't argue any longer since he couldn't force her to return to the airport. He went back with Mom, who was concerned, especially when she saw the angry look on his face, "What's wrong, Dad? What were you and Laura arguing about?"

"We weren't exactly arguing. We came to an understanding. You know I didn't believe a word of the story she and Brad told us, and now she knows it. I don't think she is the Miss Right for Brad after all. I'm sorry we agreed to come along on this flight. At least I now know her for who she is!"

Mom was shocked, "I knew no such thing! You mean you have been pretending to believe them? How can you say such things?"

"I don't believe it's possible to travel through time. What's been done is done, and that's all there is to it."

"Well, I think you're wrong! Are we going to land now?"

"She says she is going to take us aboard that UFO, and take you to see her doctor. Bah! I think she's a lunatic!"

She sensed his disgust, but she remembered the first time she met Laura, and couldn't deny the overwhelming feelings of love that emanated from her and Brad when they were together. She remembered the pain and suffering that Laura felt when she told of her refusal of Brad's marriage proposal. Those feelings weren't easy to forget. "Dad! I think you owe her an apology. I believe she is right, and this may be the answer to my prayers."

"That's what I was afraid of."

"I can take it for myself; I resigned myself to live the rest of my life in this condition a long time ago. Sure I had hopes each time I went to a new doctor, but I left my life in God's hands. If Laura is not who she says she is, then that will hurt. I'd be so sorry for Brad, and very disappointed in Laura. It's best that we find out now rather than wait until after they're married. You've told me many times that God works in mysterious ways. Who am I to question him in how he wants to do it?"

When the Marie was on the beam, she began confiding with her father, "Dad, I blew it. I brought Brad's folks with me today under false pretenses; I don't think his father will ever forgive me. Brad probably won't either."

"Dear, you now see how painful loving someone can be. Keep loving them, and we'll see. How does Brad's mother feel?"

"I don't know. I thought they both believed our story, but Brad's father informed me he just went along for Brad's sake."

"It's not so bad; he'll have to believe once he's aboard, and sees the ship. His mother will have her choice whether or not she wants to be treated."

"I wanted so much to help Brad's mother without confiding in Brad. I wanted his Mom to really surprise him when she walks up to him without pain for the first time in years. Brad blames himself for his mother's condition. He thinks she would be healthy today if she hadn't had her last child, him."

David came out to meet them, "Welcome aboard the Manhattan. I'm Laura's father. She's told me so much about you already; I feel like I know you."

Dad couldn't bring himself to dislike David since he radiated the same kind of love and respect that Laura showed them, unless he was a very good actor. He helped Mom out of the Lear into her wheelchair and they were ushered into the main part of the ship. He finally spoke up, "Where are we, and what is this thing?"

"I think Laura already explained," David said in a matter of fact tone, "but you'll have to see for yourself."

Mom spoke up, "Laura I'm ready, take me to your doctor! Leave these men to discuss whether or not this is real." Dad began to object, but she would have no part of it. "Stay out of it, Dad! You stay with Laura's father, and maybe he can convince you. I believe Laura, and if she says I can be healed, then I will be healed!"

Laura was beaming, she knew she won with Mom, and her father could handle Dad. She took charge of the wheelchair, and went on down toward the hospital ward. She stopped, around the corner, out of Dad's sight, threw her arms around Mom, and wept, "Thanks, Mom, I only want to help you. I couldn't stand to see you suffer when I knew we could help you. Thanks for understanding!"

"It doesn't matter whether your doctor can help or not, Laura, I believe in what you're trying to do, and you can't hurt me by doing what you have to do. The only possible way you could hurt me is to hurt Brad, and somehow I don't think you will do that. Laura, I love you as much as my own sons and daughters."

"Oh, Mom, I love you, and Dr. Baker can help you!

"Good, let's go see him!"

Dr. Baker met them at the door, and escorted Mom toward the examining scanner helping her get as comfortable as possible on the soft table top. "Mrs. Anderson, relax and let this little machine get a good look at you. We want to be sure you have no other problems along with your arthritis."

"Doctor, do you know what causes arthritis?"

"Honestly, no! We have discovered that some agent stimulates the nuclei of cells surrounding the bones, particularly in the joints, causing them to destroy themselves. We can't isolate the agent, we don't know what it is, and we don't know how it invades the body, but we can neutralize it. Do you understand what I'm trying to say?"

"You mean you don't know why, but some drugs you have developed stop it?"

"That's precisely it. We developed the drug in relation to some genetic research, and discovered quite by accident it works against arthritis. It's not really a drug, but you can think of it in those terms."

"But, if the cells are destroyed, how can you help me?"

"It's a three-step process: first we stop the spread, then we stop the pain, and then we induce your body to repair itself. That's the secret to modern medicine; we first take away the cause, and then get the body to do the rest."

"What about my plastic hip?"

"That's a good question; we may leave that in, but in any case you should never know the difference."

"How long will it take?"

"It's hard to say, we can stop the spread in a few hours. The rest depends on how fast your body reacts. You should get rid of the pain soon after, although it may take a couple of days, and maybe you can be walking again in a couple of weeks."

"I already feel better!"

"Okay, now we've got some results from the computer. Let me get a blood sample, and then we can begin."

He took the blood sample, and let the computer analyze the blood as he discussed her diagnosis. "Other than your arthritis, you seem to be in pretty good health. The arthritis agent is very active, which means your condition could only get worse, unless treated. Are you ready?"

"I've been ready for twenty years."

"Good, I'm going to hook you up to that machine over there which will give you a 90 percent blood transfusion. The other

10 percent will be the drug to neutralize the agent and cleanse the parts of your blood we want you to keep. That will help your immune system stay on track." He brought the machine over to her, and began to connect the tubes to her arms. "This will take a couple of hours, so relax, and it will soon be over."

In less than five minutes, she was sleeping peacefully as the restoring process began to permeate every part of her body.

Laura picked Brad up at Andrews Air Force Base the day before their wedding and they flew to Independence where he spent the night with friends. Laura stayed with his folks making final preparations for the wedding set for 2:00 P.M. the following day, while Brad would make one more trip to the Manhattan to deliver Laura's father along with a few of Laura's friends to the wedding. He wouldn't see his family until the wedding.

The president was true to his word keeping his activities a secret from the press, as he arrived with his wife and a very small group of Secret Service personnel. The Secret Service checked out the church hours before, and would be mostly inconspicuous in their surveillance during the ceremonies, and Brad assured the president that the crew aboard the Manhattan would protect him. Word was certain to leak to the press, but Brad and Laura hoped it would be too late to disrupt the serenity of the ceremonies.

Brad's brothers and sisters were buzzing over the cure their mother received, and finally in desperation, she sent them all on their way, leaving the house to Laura, Dana, and her other bridesmaids, preparing for the wedding. They were having all sorts of girl talk as Laura's father arrived, bearing a large box, explaining he brought it back to Laura on his last trip, as he knew she would be married before she would ever consent to return. She was in seventh heaven as she unpacked her mother's wedding dress, and tried it on with the girls watching and helping. It fit perfectly, and would have transformed any young girl into Cinderella, but on Laura it was absolutely stunning with each strand of material glistening in the light as it sparkled like diamonds reflecting the light, yet one could not detect the invisible threads which gave it its glamorous, otherworldly glow.

Brad followed Bob Sparks, his best man, to the front of the church, and froze in awe as he turned and faced those in attendance. He saw the president and first lady, sitting in the front row, and his mother and family on the other side. He noticed his mother sitting on the front pew beside his father, without her wheelchair, with such happiness beaming from her face that he wondered how many pain pills she had to take that morning. His mind was so filled with the events surrounding him, that the absence of the wheelchair did not sink in, nor the fact that she looked almost as if he were seeing her twenty years earlier. It did look strange, but he supposed that it was the absence of pain, and the joy she was sharing with him and Laura.

The organist played the traditional wedding march as Laura's party made their way to the front. As the tempo increased, everyone stood, and he beheld Laura entering the aisle on her father's arm in the most breathtaking wedding gown he could ever imagine. He didn't even notice how easily his mother stood on her feet. He had eyes only for Laura as she made her way down the aisle.

She was radiant, the happiest she had ever been in her life, yet a bit nervous as she felt her father's steady pressure on her arm. She could hardly take her eyes off Brad, but managed to smile up at her father, as he smiled back, giving her the assurance she needed.

The ceremony was brief, and they were soon man and wife. Laura's last ceremonial act was to give Brad's mother a bouquet of roses. He could hardly believe his eyes as his mother accepted with hands that were no longer misshapen as they grasped the roses, and tenderly touched Laura's cheek as they briefly kissed each other before Laura rejoined Brad, and they made their way down the aisle.

As Brad's mother and father were ushered down the aisle, there was not a dry eye in the church as Laura whispered to Brad, "One of my wedding gifts to you."

Aboard the Manhattan, Laura bid her father farewell as they prepared to be released from the Manhattan for the last time. The Marie eased away from the Manhattan and they watched as the Manhattan was there one moment and gone the next.

CHAPTER 50

For the first time in many years, Roger Dorn left the ship after convincing David he needed a few hours by himself. He had no family left except for his wife and those aboard the Manhattan, but he manufactured an excuse to give him time and the opportunity to prepare for the trip he and Warren Baker had been planning for some time. He took the shuttle to the station on the outskirts of Washington DC going directly to the White House where he had no difficulty getting in to see the President.

President Alan Talmage kept his curiosity in check, inviting him in and waiting for him to get comfortable before asking, "Roger, it's good to see you, but I'm beginning to wonder what's going on. What can I do for you?"

Roger didn't waste time with formalities, "I want you to invite David Ashton here on some pretense, anything to get him off the ship. I want him to be away long enough for me to take command of the Manhattan and accomplish a task he would not otherwise do or approve because of personal involvement."

"I don't understand . . ."

"Most of this happened almost thirty years ago when Commander White and Marie Ashton lost their lives during the pirate raid at Space Station Juliet?"

"Of course, that was a small, but significant historical event for all time. It was tragic for your mission, but it signaled the end of the space pirates. We have you and your crew to thank for that!"

"Then you would agree that David has accomplished all that has been asked of him."

"Yes, I agree. I don't know how the nation can ever repay the debt we owe him and the entire crew of the Manhattan."

"I do." He paused, "If you will grant my request, I will go back and take his wife Marie off that shuttle before it explodes and prevent her death. David has never fully recovered from that loss and now he has given up his daughter for the good of his country. You, by authorizing this mission, can make his life whole again."

The president shook his head sadly, "I can't do that, even a change that small in time could affect the outcome of your entire mission. It's too risky."

"I thought you would say that . . . David said the same thing. But I've thought it through and I know my plan would not compromise the mission. If we go back now, rescue her and Commander White, we could place her in a protective new identity status where David will not know she is here. If none of the crew aboard the Excalibur or the Manhattan is aware of her existence until thirty years later, what possible effect could that have to jeopardize the mission? Then a couple of days from now, when David comes to Washington he can be reunited with his wife. Your request will then not be under false pretenses. You and former President Albee alone will know who she is all those years. We can also save Commander White and his wife. Their presence, unknown to any of us on the mission will not change history either."

David remained aboard the Manhattan expecting Brenda to show up at any time. He was disappointed that she hadn't already been there to welcome them back. He was a little bit on the stubborn side resisting the urging of his heart to call her or get to her as quickly as possible. A few hours later, David received a priority message calling for his immediate presence at the White House. Roger was out so that left Dr. Baker in command. He realized it didn't matter as the ground crew had already taken over and would be checking out the Manhattan.

Warren saw him to the shuttle and waited until lift-off before hurrying back to the control room where he welcomed Kevin Haugen aboard. Kevin had been absent all these years without much contact, but Roger thought it would be fitting that he should return to participate in the rescue of his commander. All they had to do now was wait for Roger's return and they would be off.

As soon as his shuttle landed, Roger joined Warren in the control room and took the PA, "Attention, all crewmembers! This is what we have been waiting for. Prepare for immediate departure. We are going back to change history once again and save the lives of Marie Ashton, Tom and Annette White." He gave the orders and the massive doors were opened as the Manhattan launched into orbit and vanished.

The entire crew radiated the excitement which seemed to pulse throughout the ship as they began their journey. This was something worthwhile they could do for their beloved commander. Many were part of the original crew and had vivid memories of Marie and the Whites, and were keenly aware of that loss. It took longer for the trip to Space Station Juliet than to travel back the twenty six years but they arrived perfectly timed to watch history being made as the Excalibur approached Space Station Juliet.

Kevin coordinated their movements insuring no interference with the starfighters surrounding the Excalibur. The mission would be relatively easy, but tricky as the shuttle had to be taken aboard the Manhattan and the occupants removed, and then the shuttle had to be placed back on its original course within a split second of the time it was removed.

In the shuttle, Marie Ashton heard the warning from the approach controller and abruptly applied full right turn and descent, and that was the last she remembered as the shuttle was taken aboard the Manhattan on the beam. The shuttle lurched abruptly to one side causing Marie's head to come in contact with a window post knocking her unconscious.

She opened her eyes slowly blinking against the bright white light while looking up into a kindly, benevolent face peering down at her. He looked vaguely familiar, but she couldn't quite place him. She suddenly remembered being on the shuttle and the controller's warning. She sat up quickly, instinctively, but futilely, reaching for the controls to alter her flight path. As the gentleman calmed her, she sat still and blinked, asking, "Who are you?"

The older man calmly replied, "Relax, everything is going to be fine."

Marie's mind was racing as she attempted to remain calm, relying on her training to evaluate the situation. She demanded, "Where am I? Where are Commander and Mrs. White?"

"They're resting comfortably. Something you should do for a couple more hours."

"Where are we? And what happened to the shuttle?

"You're aboard the Manhattan, a starship from your future. I know you don't recall, but the space pirates attacked your shuttle about half a second after you were warned. It was too late for Kevin and his starfighters to protect you and your shuttle was destroyed."

"Then why am I alive, or am I?"

"History has recorded your deaths and the Excalibur went on without you and the Whites. Now, twenty six years later, we have the necessary technology and we came back and plucked you off the shuttle to save your lives."

"This can't be! Where's David?"

"In our time, he's with the president waiting for you. In your time, he's aboard the Excalibur."

"You mean the president is aboard the Excalibur! How did he get here?"

"Marie, please just relax and it will all make sense. You were aware of Roger's time travel experiments. Just think of the consequences."

She could hardly believe her ears, and looked on in amazement as another vaguely familiar man entered accompanied by Commander White and greeted her warmly. "Marie, it's good to see you alive and well after all these years."

Marie felt bewildered looking from one man to the next. She turned to her commander, "Tom, what is going on here? Where are we and who are these gentlemen?"

Tom hesitated a moment before responding, "Marie, I'm afraid our part in the mission was terminated early. As I understand it, we are still in our time but they will not allow us to go back aboard the Excalibur."

She demanded, "Why not? And you haven't answered my question! Who are these men?"

Tom blurted out, "Roger Dorn and Warren Baker. It hasn't been that long for you since you've seen them."

Recognition dawned slowly on Marie as she pondered her predicament. "What happened to them?"

Roger laughed, "Nothing except thirty plus years of aging. We have come back from twenty six years in your future. We're thirty years older, that's all.

Warren added, "We've had a slight scare with you. We had a slight malfunction in the controller for our power beam and according to Tom's description; it must have been like you experiencing severe turbulence in the atmosphere. As far as I can tell, you're okay, but you've been out for several minutes. Nothing to worry about."

Marie pleaded, "I'm okay. I feel fine. Please put me back on the Excalibur."

Roger sighed and sadly shook his head, "Sorry, Marie. We can't do that. For all practical purposes, you are dead in your time and cannot reappear until our time twenty six years later.

If you will remember, we were on a critical mission, vital to the survival of our world. If we have learned anything in the last twenty six years, we know we cannot go back and change even a small part of history without endangering the entire mission. The president authorized us to rescue you, as a reward for David, but he would not consider risking everything to put you back on that mission."

Marie was close to tears, "But, why did you come back and rescue me if you will not allow me to be with the man I love or ever again be with my daughter?"

Roger continued, "Marie, we can't tell you all of what has happened in the intervening years, but we can tell you David has not remarried and he loves you. If you can accept the president's offer and not reveal your identity, you will have the opportunity to help him from a distance and have a big impact on the life of your daughter. In time, you can reveal your identity to him and be with him again."

"But, I'll be an old woman by then!"

Warren laughed, "And we are dirty old men, I suppose. Even in the last few years, life expectancy has increased and the aging process has been reduced dramatically. You will have many good years together."

Roger pointed to an exterior viewing port, "Take a last good look out there. The battle is over, but the Excalibur is still in orbit around Juliet. They haven't launched the backup shuttle for their passengers, but they will soon. We're getting ready to launch on a high sub warp speed trip back to Earth so I'll leave you while I go to the control center. We'll have you back in Washington in a few months."

The Excalibur and Space Station Juliet were already fading into the distance as she cried softly, "Goodbye David, Goodbye Laura."

A few months later or nearly eight years later depending on the frame of reference, the Manhattan arrived entering an orbit over Washington DC, and docked at the space station where they left months earlier. The Manhattan was just another cruiser belonging to the Space Command and didn't raise any suspicions as long as they didn't remain for an extended period. Roger escorted Marie and the Whites to the launch area where they climbed aboard a shuttle that would take them to Washington. They settled into their seats and Roger began, "Time may be a bit mixed up, but I think you will adjust rapidly. If you recall, it was several months after your departure when the accident occurred. Now it's almost eight years later on Earth. We are helping you out a little, not making you wait the extra eight years. You'll have about three months to get accustomed to your new status before the Excalibur returns safely and I might add, successfully. Of course that will make you considerably younger than David and by the time your daughter discovers who you really are, she could be almost as old as you are now. Tom, you and Annette will have to maintain separate identities so I don't think which time you re-enter should be important to you. It may be easier for you to appear eight years later so your old friends will probably not recognize you if you make contact by chance."

Tom and Annette left under separate escort and Roger continued to escort Marie to the White House. Marie asked, "Roger, do you mean I won't be able to see Laura grow up?"

"No, all is not lost. You will become her foster mom and meet the most important needs in her life. She will be eleven years old and will not recognize you so you can have as much contact as we can arrange as long as you don't reveal your identity. David will be spending a lot of time working on the Manhattan and will need someone to care for Laura. You can be that someone. In time, you will be able to reveal yourself to them."

"Well, I guess that's better than nothing."

"We are taking you to see President Albee. I have contacted former President Gardiner and he arranged for this flight to be semi legitimate and he will escort you to see President Albee. I really had to do some swift talking to convince Gardiner. You or President Gardiner will have to convince President Albee."

"Aren't you going to be there?"

"No, I won't leave the shuttle." He handed her a large envelope. "This package contains the wishes of our future president who respectfully requests that President Albee carries them out. It's up to you and Bill Gardiner to convince him he should."

Former President Gardiner met them at the shuttle port wrapping his arms around her, welcoming her back to Washington. "It's sure good to see you. My wife and I were shocked when we heard of your deaths, and elated to learn of your return. Since Roger and you returned in this time machine, I know the Excalibur's mission was successful. That takes a big load off my mind. Let's go see the president."

As a former president, Bill had the White House transportation access codes and escorted her directly to the Oval Office. As President Albee rose to greet them, Bill Gardiner made the introductions, "President Albee, this is Marie Ashton. I don't want to shock you, but yes she is the same astronaut who was reported killed on the Excalibur mission eight years ago."

President Alan Albee held out his hand and guided Marie to a seat in front of his desk. "Please sit down and fill me in with the details. How is this possible?"

"Well," Marie began, "I don't know where to begin. It's a mind boggling experience for me. And my dear friend Bill Gardiner has just heard it himself." Marie sat and gathered her thoughts

"Take your time. I sense that history is being made today."

"All right. First the Excalibur is about to slow to sub warp speed and should be entering the solar system shortly. They should arrive here in less than three months."

"Are you sure?" Alan Albee turned to Bill, "Is she on the level?"

"Yup, she sure is. The mission was highly successful and the ship is loaded to the gills with crude oil."

"Wow, and not a moment too soon. But we really didn't expect them back for several more years. But, please go on with your story Miss Ashton. Why are you here?"

"It's Mrs., but please call me Marie. I was killed as history records, but a future time traveler rescued me twenty six years later. I know it sounds crazy, but if you stop and think, with time travel, stranger things are possible." She changed tactics abruptly, "Anyway, you will soon have the honor of opening the last box under that desk." She pointed to a desk on the side of the room."

Alan gasped, "How . . . How did you know about that? Bill did you tell her? As I recall, you told me that was a sacred traditional trust known only to presidents over the last five hundred years."

Bill slowly shook his head in the negative, "No Alan, I said nothing."

Marie sighed, "The man who put that box here in your office told me about it. He traveled through time and placed the box here in your office hundreds of years ago. It contains plans for constructing the time machine I told you about." She handed him the envelope Roger gave her, "I wish I didn't have to give you this, but I'm convinced it's the only way I can see my daughter again."

"I don't understand; where is your daughter?"

"Go ahead and open the envelope, it'll help explain and I know it's up to you, but I've committed myself to the success of this mission and I will not in any way try to change the plans our future president made. I will not tell my daughter or David, but with your permission I would like to have contact with my mother. She will keep my presence secret."

President Albee opened the envelope and sat reading silently with an occasional raised eyebrow. He finally set it aside and turned to the former president, "Bill, I apologize to you. I blamed you in part for the fake stories you told about a critical oil shortage. There is no oil shortage! You've been in on it all from the beginning. We have been convinced of the shortage so that we would fund the Excalibur and this next mission which has been dubbed 'The Manhattan Project'."

Bill was confused, "Thanks for your vote of confidence; may I see the letters?"

"Sure go ahead and read a little of history in the remaking." He turned to Marie, "I thank you for the great sacrifice you and the whole crew of the Excalibur has already made. Today, we as a nation have an abundance of crude oil because of what your husband and Roger Dorn have accomplished. We will have a welcome home celebration for the Excalibur but the nation will probably never know the full implications of the mission. Even the crew cannot be told the whole truth. That will be a secret the three of us must keep." Bill handed the letters to Marie, "I suppose you should read these too, as long as you are so deeply involved."

After Marie finished reading the letters, she responded sadly, "I will be Brenda Kay Brockway, if that is your wish."

The Manhattan with Roger in command returned to its launch pad within seconds of its departure without David, en route to the White House, being aware of its absence. David stewed and fretted, trying to guess the reason for his summons to the White House, but he finally gave up and went to sleep and didn't awaken until his shuttle arrived in Washington.

He waited outside the Oval Office a few minutes before the president's private secretary ushered him in. President Talmage greeted him cheerfully. "Hi David, I'm sure you know the rest of these gentlemen."

David was surprised to see the two former presidents he had worked with over the years, and greeted them warmly.

Alan Talmage waited until David was comfortable, "David, I suppose you are wondering why we brought you here." He paused, but David said nothing, "We heard that you have proposed marriage to Brenda Brockway."

David, startled, nodded, "But, she refused . . . Did she tell you?"

"Yes, she told me a few days ago, but even if she hadn't refused, we couldn't allow it!"

David was totally confused and looked toward the former presidents, but they offered no explanation. He stammered, "Why . . . Why not?"

President Talmage grinned, "Because you're already married!"

He pushed his buzzer and Marie walked in. Her hair was relatively short but it was already mostly back to her original red color. As she walked toward David, she took off her dark framed glasses revealing for David's view her full facial features the first time in almost thirty years. She took another couple of steps toward him and pulled the retainer and crowns from her mouth revealing perfectly straight teeth. Her voice changed and there was no longer any doubt in David's mind as Marie covered the remaining distance throwing herself into his arms.

After several minutes, David and Marie became aware that the president and the two former presidents were patiently waiting. David stammered, "Sorry . . . Sorry sir. You have no idea what this means to me. I don't know how it all happened; I'm overwhelmed."

President Talmage threw his arms around both of them, "David and Marie, it's our pleasure. The three of us have been planning this session for a long time. In terms you would understand, Roger Dorn visited me a few hours ago and asked me to bring you here. While you were en route, he took the Manhattan on a rescue mission and brought Marie back several years ago. You can thank him and please forgive us for keeping Marie's identity from you all these years. Marie can explain everything."

David turned to his wife, "I'm sorry Marie; I encouraged Laura to remain in the twentieth century. You will never see her again."

Marie responded lovingly, "It's all right David. I knew she would stay long before you did. We made the most of it for the last fourteen years. I was her mother in every sense of the word.

She didn't know who I was, but she called and treated me like her own Mom. I'm glad I was able to be there for her."

President Albee chuckled, "Don't be so hard on yourself David. I'm sorry we couldn't let you in on the secret. It was a good secret around here and watching you and Brenda tiptoe around was more fun than a barrel of monkeys."

"But what about Commander White? Did he come back too?"

"Yes, who do you think we sent on the return mission?"

David could only shake his head.

"David, I think we can help. Remember your mission back to the time of Christ?"

"Sure, I really enjoyed that and I hope those videos and images helped someone learn more about Jesus Christ. He certainly became real for us!"

"You are about to embark on another mission back to the twentieth century. This time Marie can go and spend as much time as she likes with her daughter. You can delay that trip until the birth of your first grandchild if you like, but you'd better get back to the Manhattan and prepare for a couple of visitors from the past."

CHAPTER 51

David called the executive council together to plan for the arrival of their visitors. Marie took her place back on the council and Thomas and Annette White were invited to join them as honorary members. David began, "The President didn't say who they are, only that they would arrive from the twentieth century sometime this week and we would have to take them back with the Manhattan. He said they will inadvertently come through one of our warps you've been monitoring."

A few days later, Roger called on the intercom, "David, it's happening. Someone is in the warp!"

"Who is it?"

"Hard to say, it's a small craft similar in size to the Marie. It appears to be solar powered; either that or the engines have been shut down. There are two small heat sources, probably two souls onboard."

"I'll be right there."

David joined Roger along with most of the council in the control room and waited anxiously until Roger finally confirmed, "They're on the beam, David. You can communicate with them now."

David's voice was projected across space into the cockpit of the small aircraft, "Unidentified aircraft, Identify yourselves!"

Startled, the pilot pressed the transmit switch, "We are Solar Two Four One en route to Tel Aviv. Who are you?"

David's voice came back warmly, "This is Manhattan Control. There is no need for alarm nor is there a need to use the radio. We will have you on the ground in a few moments. You have no need to fear us."

The pilot came back almost immediately, "Doctor Ashton, I presume?"

David stammered back, "You . . . You know who we are?"

"If you are Doctor David Ashton, Commander of the Manhattan, we do."

"Who are you?"

"I'm Paul Barnes with my wife Sara. We work for Colonel Anderson and your daughter Laura."

"That partially explains it, but why . . . I mean why . . . Did they tell you all about us?"

"They didn't tell us everything. What year is this?"

"Twenty six Oh Five. Lower your landing gear and we'll bring you aboard the Manhattan on our beam." The aircraft was gently lowered and pulled inside the Manhattan. Paul helped Sara out of the aircraft as they stepped out onto the deck. The hangar structure loomed ominously above them as they walked toward the entrance, escorted to Dr. Ashton's office by Sandra Davis, one of the young ladies from the Manhattan's crew.

David, greeting them warmly, "Sorry we didn't recognize your names immediately. Laura did mention you in her diary and we have found you in our computer data base. How are you feeling?"

Paul let Sara speak for them both, "We're fine. A little dizzy, but okay. We were spinning like crazy in the time warp, but it must not have been that long."

"Good, how did you know you were in a time warp?"

Paul laughed, "This wasn't our first trip! There must be a lot of those warps in that part of the world."

David was thoughtful, "Unfortunately, you're probably right. We know and keep track of only a few of them. You're the first humans we can say for sure who came through one, although we suspect others have encountered them before. It might explain some of those unsolved mysteries we hear so much about. The Burmuda Triangle mysteries may finally be solved."

"How many are there? Where do they come from?"

"They might be a natural occurrence, but the one you traveled through today is man-made. It's a passageway between your time and ours created by the Manhattan on one of our trips returning back from the twentieth century. We've been constantly on alert watching for travelers like you who may have accidentally fallen into one of them."

Paul was slightly puzzled, "But we traveled both ways from our time to the time of Christ and back. Is there some connection?"

"Possibly, we made one round trip back from the twentieth century to that time period. Tell us about it!"

"I was a twentieth century fighter pilot, shot down over Israel when I fell through the first time warp. I found myself in a completely different world, two thousand years earlier, during the time of Christ. I met Sara and we became disciples of Jesus. After His crucifixion, we built a balloon, re-entered the time warp and arrived back in the twentieth century. We made the mistake of telling our story to the wrong people. Of course the Israeli government didn't believe our story and the Mossad, their secret police, began harassing us. Brad and Laura heard about our tale of time travel and pulled us out of trouble when they came to investigate. We were on our way back to Israel working for the Solar Magnetics Administration when one of the Israeli fighters attacked us. We would have gotten away except for my concern about Sara's advanced stage of pregnancy. I know a missile was launched at us and the next thing we knew, we were in another of your time warps."

Sara winced in pain, "Paul . . . ." She grabbed his arm gripping hard for a moment, "It's time. He's not going to wait any longer."

CHAPTER 52

Christopher Allen Barnes was born July 21, 2605 in the infirmary aboard the Manhattan. He was a product of the first, twentieth and twenty seventh centuries. Dr. Baker assured Paul that everything was fine before he left Sara's bedside. Paul went in search of Dr. Ashton and tried to make up new words to the old Johnny Cash song that kept running through his head, "I've got a nineteen fifty, fifty one, fifty two, fifty three, fifty four, fifty five, fifty six, fifty seven, fifty eight, fifty nine automobile."

After a couple of wrong turns in the corridors, he was finally directed back to David's office. David stood, "Paul, come on in and let me be the first to congratulate you. Dr. Baker tells me everything's going just fine."

"It would be if Christopher can ever reconcile his birthdate. I think this future shock may be too much for me let alone Sara, or Christopher. Sara was just getting used to the twentieth century."

"I understand how you feel, but I know you both have enough faith in God to carry you through. Up until a few minutes ago, I didn't have any idea why we needed to take you back. But President Talmage said we would have that opportunity, and my wife and I are both excited about the possibilities. It may take us up to four years to make the trip, but we're ready.

"But if you make one of these warps whenever you traveled through time, couldn't we get back in one, going the other way?"

"That's a definite possibility. Dr. Dorn is checking out your theory right now. A time warp in which we could travel as often as we like might come in handy. We could even see our grandchildren once in a while."

"That must be hard on you and Laura too. But if you could go as often as you like, it would be like traveling crosstown. Like normal grandparents, except you wouldn't have to be sitting on pins and needles waiting for the grandchildren to be born."

David laughed, "It hasn't been easy, but at least we have Laura's diary. Gee, if those warps would stay open . . . . Right now neither Sara nor your son should be subjected to any such trip. Let's wait and see how things go."

Two years later, Roger announced that the time warp was open and as far as he could tell the warp they planned to use would deposit them in close proximity to the time Brad and Laura's first child was born. If not the exact time, they could do a short leap to arrive when they wanted. David wasted no time in preparation for their voyage not wanting to risk the closure of the warp before they had a chance to use it. Paul, Sara and Christopher had been on standby waiting and were on the Manhattan within a couple of hours ready to return home. As soon as they were aboard and safely strapped in, David gave the launch order and Roger began the countdown placing the Manhattan into position to enter the warp.

Paul and Sara had experienced the warp earlier, but nobody knew whether the warp was large enough to handle the Manhattan or how the Manhattan would ride it out. Roger deftly moved the Manhattan closer until entry was confirmed by the spinning motion which was strong enough to encompass the entire ship. Roger felt helpless as control was lost, and the

Manhattan spun slowly and all concepts of time and space vanished. Even though disoriented, Roger kept a constant vigil waiting until that moment they would be expelled at the other end of the warp. At that moment he hoped the ship would be in a stable orbit over the earth, but he would need to restore power to the cloaking devices to prevent someone in the past from getting a glimpse of the Manhattan.

"Brad, I wonder what really happened to Paul and Sara. Her baby would have been about two now." Laura mused.

"I don't know dear. They never found a trace of them or the aircraft." It was two days after Laura had given birth to a baby girl they named Gail Marie. Brad brought them home from the hospital and Laura was nursing Gail prior to laying her in her crib. "Laura, you might as well put them out of your mind. You've got your own daughter to take care of now."

"I know, but it's hard and there's no way I can forget them so easily. Sara and I had so very much in common. We were both time travelers even if we were from the opposite extremes. I can't find anyone else like her anywhere. I wonder if she ever felt as out of place as I often do. The world is so unfair . . ." She clenched her fist and raised her voice, "I'll bet Paul's old commander, Colonel Kabron, was the culprit." Gail let out an annoyed squawk and Laura instantly relaxed.

Brad watched her settle back before responding, "President Dugan said as much, but he had no proof and the Israelis weren't interested in pursuing it any further. You know you are missing your father and feeling your loss more acutely, which is only natural at a time like this. How about taking a trip to see Mom and Dad as soon as you feel up to it. They'll want to see Gail."

"I don't know. Maybe, but your family can never take Dad's place no matter how hard they try. All of your family has been so good to me. I don't want to be dramatic yet I feel something important is missing in my life. I feel fine, but I'm not sure I feel up to taking Gail anywhere soon. I had a relatively easy time, but I sure missed Doctor Baker's expertise."

"Maybe Mom and Dad will come here for a visit?"

"Let's wait a week or so and then we can take a few days and visit the whole family. Of course they are welcome to come anytime, but it would be much easier for us to do the traveling."

Three weeks later, they were in the 'Marie' winging their way across mid America heading for Independence. Laura felt better after spending a few days at the office, getting adjusted to the world in which she lived.

Laura's face lit up like a lamp as she spoke up excitedly, "Brad, Look over there!" She pointed ahead and slightly above them. "It's the Manhattan?"

Brad watched the small object grow larger in the windscreen, "Well, I'll be darned!" He cancelled his flight plan.

Brad turned the transponder off as David's booming voice filled the cockpit, "Solar One One, you're on the beam. Welcome home!"

Laura could hardly speak, "Dad, what are you doing here?"

"Had to come back to visit my favorite daughter and my first grandchild, didn't I?"

"How did you know? I mean, that's silly, of course you know. But . . ."

Laura was out of her seat before the aircraft could be secured. She unstrapped Gail and hurried out as soon as the hangar crew opened the door. She stepped down gingerly as her father reached up to help her down, enfolding them both in his arms as she stepped off the last step. She passed Gail to her father almost dropping her as she caught a glimpse of Sara and Paul standing off to one side with Christopher at their side. Leaving Gail with her father, she threw herself into Sara's arms babbling excitedly and getting no answers to her almost incoherent questions.

David laughed at their confused expressions, "All in good time. But first, it's way past time for you to say hello to someone very special to you." He drew forward a beautiful lady, who looked like a slightly older carbon copy of Laura.

Laura screamed with delight and threw herself into her mother's arms, "Mom, oh Mom . . . . It's so good to see you again." After a moment, she broke the embrace taking a closer look at her mother, "What did you do with your hair? It's beautiful." Marie smiled broadly and Laura exclaimed with glee, "Your teeth, you've gone all out." She looked over at her dad, "You two got married didn't you?"

David grinned sheepishly, "Yup, we certainly did. A long time ago."

Marie was smiling brightly and clinging to Laura and finally spoke, "My Laura, my daughter. My baby and now with a baby of your own."

Laura was puzzled, she blinked, "Brenda, you sound different. What happened to your lisp?"

"I don't need the disguise anymore, and I'm not Brenda, I'm Marie. Didn't you say I would always be your Mom?"

"You look just like the pictures of my real mom."

"That's right, I am your mother; and always have been. Now can I see my granddaughter? She took Gail from David's arms and promptly took on the grandmotherly role.